SEE YO
THE ICE

M.D. RANDALL

SLOW HOUND
MEDIA

ISBN: 9798836610487

Cover design by: M. D. RANDALL
Cover photograph: Alex (Adobe Stock)

1.

Saturday 12th January

7:40pm Jack messages Chloe

Dear Chloe,

I've left the keys to my flat in your mailbox. Please don't forget to pass them to the agent on Monday (first thing).

Jack

PS We both know you'll forget, but I feel better for having put it in writing.

7:42pm Chloe messages Jack

'Dear Chloe'?

Who are you, and what have you done with my friend Jack?

Chloe

PS No one starts a message with *'Dear'*. You're not in the trenches and I'm not your sweetheart.

7:44pm Jack messages Chloe

Dear Miss Walker,

To enhance the chances of my flat keys finding their way to the agent, I felt a degree of formality was called for, to raise the status of the message in question to *important* and thus distinguishing it from our usual exchanges which are best described as banal.

Jack

PS Also 'hey' is for when you're twelve or live just around the corner, which I won't be anymore.

7:45pm Chloe messages Jack

Hey! Where are you anyway? Have you managed to get past the Siegfried Line?

Chloe

7:46pm Jack messages Chloe

I've arrived, just!

Jack

7:47pm Chloe messages Jack

'Just', as in just arrived?

Or 'just', as in you've arrived, but only *just* because someone/something tried to kill you?

Chloe

7:48pm Jack messages Chloe

Both.

I'm waiting for the agent who has the keys to my new place. Bursting for a pee! I thought you were going out with the gang tonight.

7:50pm Chloe messages Jack

I am. Rainbows. 80's night.

I'm waiting for Katie to tell me what time I'm to be 'clicked and collected.'

What's it looking like there?

Chloe

PS My hair's too short to back-comb so I've gone for double lip gloss. Trashy over classy.

7:51pm Jack messages Chloe

It's not looking much like the photos you showed me on their Facebook page.

Jack

7:52pm Chloe messages Jack

Are you sure you're in the right place? Your sense of direction isn't up to much. Remember Bloxwich?

C

7:54pm Jack messages Chloe

I know I'm in the right place because Attic Priory welcomed me (but only if I was a careful driver). Being welcomed didn't appear to be a priority for my lunatic taxi driver Craig – (the someone/something which contrived to try and kill me, *just*) - he gave me three near death experiences, but to his credit, did pass on his knowledge of fishing bait free of charge (despite me consistently showing no interest in the subject).

J

7:56pm Chloe messages Jack

Was he dressed entirely in green? Fishermen do that. I've never understood why. If it's for reasons of camouflage, they'd be better off disguising themselves as a shopping trolley/bike/syringe/cadaver (delete as appropriate). That's what the fish are used to seeing round here.

Chloe

7:59pm Jack messages Chloe

Craig wasn't wearing green. He was wearing beige, which as a colour, was a happy partner for his personality. He was ramping up the fishing anecdotes, so I decided an interjection was called for - a puerile one - so I risked prolonging my fishing lesson further and asked him if it had been a while since he'd had a bite on his scrub worm. He seemed pleased with my interest and replied with 'I tend to hook-up with red wigglers these days'. After that, he lost his thread and switched to his other pastime of trying to kill us both.

8:00pm Chloe messages Jack

Craig sounds like a good advert for walking. The NHS should use him in an ad campaign.

Has he dropped you in the village centre?

8:02pm Jack messages Chloe

Yeah, I can see the canoe on the village green; the one the 'Britain in Bloom' judges got excited about. There aren't any Busy Lizzies stuffed into it now though.

8:02pm Chloe messages Jack

Well, there wouldn't be, it's January.

8:03pm Jack messages Chloe

Talking of which, on Attic Priory's site, they missed out the bit about how cold it is up here. No matter how careful a driver you are, you're still welcomed with hypothermia the second you open the car door.

J

8:05pm Chloe messages Jack

Don't worry. It warms up around late June. Barry, one of the 'Britain in Bloom' judges said, in 1994 'There can be no better place to find yourself on the summer solstice'. Come to think of it, the accompanying photo is of Barry raising a pint glass, so that could be more of a comment on the pub rather than the village itself.

8:06pm Jack messages Chloe

It's nice that Barry found himself.

8:07pm Chloe messages Jack

Looking at Barry, if I were him, finding *myself* would rank at least five places below finding an alligator in my bath and finding an axe murderer in my wardrobe.

What was the journey like?

8:09pm Jack messages Chloe

Great. I spent most of it looking at an obese man who breathed too loudly while grinning at his phone. I was too angry to sleep so I distracted myself for three hours with a scratch on the window that looked like Gary Lineker (the D'Artagnon years). So, I'm knackered. Not as knackered as that time I piggy-backed you back to your flat after that vodka promotion at 'The Courtyard'. But still knackered.

8:10pm Chloe messages Jack

First things first, have you found the pub?

8:14pm Jack messages Chloe

The Hunter's Arms? Yeah, I'm standing pretty much opposite it. Looks OK from the outside although the hanging baskets carrying last summer's dead petunias look a touch tragic (you should probably let Barry know). I'm going to dash in to use their toilet. Say hi to the gang.

Jack

PS I seem to have an email thanking me for my interest in a group called The Attic Priory Players and extending an invitation to meet the Chairman, a Mr Michael Brains. Ironic surname given he's spelled 'committee' with one T. Anyway, as emails go, it was overly formal. If I had any intention of turning up, I'd feel under pressure to present myself to Mr Brains wearing a tie and maybe even my trousers and pants. Weird email. Know anything about it????!

PPS Where's this bloody agent? Christ, I really am knackered.

8:18pm Chloe messages Jack

God you're such a drama queen. You've relocated to Northumberland for work - you haven't done the Inca trail bare foot. Grow a pair. Will you go down The Hunter's later? You could regale the locals with tales of your arduous expedition up North.

They'd really love that - how you survived the perilous trip against all the odds despite having to negotiate two trains, a bus, and a taxi. The barmaid will be swooning. I'm assuming there'll be a barmaid. Sexist of me really. Let me know if I was gender accurate. I won't sleep until I know.

Chloe

PS Did you mean to leave your fridge magnet behind? Y'know, the one that reads 'I survived the rapids at Drayton Manor'? I mean, it looks a bit pedestrian now compared to your journey of death to The North.

PPS Theatre? Invitation? Michael Brains? Nope. Don't know why you'd think I might know something about it. Having said that, don't be late and don't turn up wearing that bloody awful anorak.

11:45pm Chloe messages Jack

I'mt walkkng lik an Egyyptian. Tqwatted.

Chloeee xxxcxcx

2.

10:12am. Chloe messages Jack

One of my ears is one and a half centimetres lower than the other. I've just measured it.

C

10:14am. Jack messages Chloe

Right. This is a new revelation. When did you notice this? (by which I mean, you've lived for 29 years without stressing about your ears, so I doubt it's as much as 1.5cm)

J

10:16am. Chloe messages Jack

I can't believe I hadn't noticed it before, but if I'm honest, I've always had an inkling something wasn't right.

10:17am. Jack messages Chloe

Talk me through your measuring approach.

10:20am. Chloe messages Jack

That's easy. I rested my chin on the kitchen worktop and held a ruler by the side of my head, then with my spare hand took a photo of the ruler/ear which gave me the distance from worktop to underside of lobe (repeat for other ear). Then I took one measurement away from the other to get 1.5cm. Ingenious really.

C

PS On my first attempt, I was relieved to find the difference was only 0.6, but as bad luck would have it, I'd been using the inches side of the ruler.

10:22am. Jack messages Chloe

As measurement approaches go, it couldn't be described as one undertaken under laboratory conditions. I mean, how can you be certain your head was vertical?

That said, you must be excited to receive your Nobel prize for physics for your invention of a new SI unit for length: the 'ear'.

'Give me some more slack on that rope will you Terry? Another few ears should do it.'

10:24am. Chloe messages Jack

What if I ever have to wear glasses? I'll be all on the piss.

10:25am. Jack messages Chloe

By the time your eyesight has failed you, chances are you won't care. I mean, look at Mike, he gave up years ago.

PS Talking of being on the piss, how was the 80s night?

10:26am. Chloe messages Jack

Messy. Katie stacked it during 'Come on Eileen' and Connor claimed to have pulled a hamstring during 'Oops Upside Your Head'.

I'm off to find a new gym.

Chloe

10:27am. Jack messages Chloe

I think the action of finding a new gym rather relies on you having membership of an existing gym.

J

PS Just on the tiniest off-chance you grow tired of your new gym by this time next week, it might be best to find one you can pay as you go.

PPS Don't attempt the running machine – not with your lop-sided head.

7:20pm. Jack messages Chloe

I need to be quick. I'm messaging from The Brains' bathroom. The whole committee are here. They lined up like a bloody wedding party and Brains felt the need to introduce me to them one by one! It took 10 minutes and twelve limp handshakes to get to the end of the line.

Unless there's a delegation from the UN still to arrive, I think Mrs Brains may have over-catered. She's laid on a spread that looks capable of sustaining Connor (pre gastric band) for an entire year.

Gotta go.

J

7:42pm. Jack messages Chloe

Buffet update. The treasurer sneezed over the pork pie platter just as I was about to take a piece. He takes snuff apparently. I mean who the hell still does that?! I really wanted a piece of that pork pie. It was the sort with an egg in the middle. Mrs Brains was furious. It's tense.

8:52pm. Chloe messages Jack

Sorry. I'm out with Katie, Mike and Connor. Mike's trying (and failing) to be funny. Hope you're being nice to everyone. Probably best if you don't trot out your usual sarcastic stuff. Your humour's an acquired taste.

So... Have they accepted you into the fold? What happens next?

Chloe

PS Mike has taken your fridge magnet. Reckons he can flog it on eBay. Hope that's OK.

10:14pm. Jack messages Chloe

Only just 'home'. Got halfway back and realised I'd left my anorak. After the buffet, the group's musical director, a James Starling, sat down at The Brains' upright piano and asked what audition piece I'd brought along to sing! *Audition? Sing?* I badly wanted to point out that joining their poxy group wasn't even my idea, but the brainchild of a girl who I used to be friends with.

Anyway, long story short, James didn't know 'Murders in the Rue Morgue' by Iron Maiden, so one gutsy verse of Happy Birthday later, Brains clapped me on the back and said I was in. Not only that, but I'm also to play a part in their upcoming show. I'm replacing a Dom O'Connor who's had some sort of farming accident.

J

10:16pm. Jack messages Chloe

Oh, and my new house wasn't ready as it turned out. The agent got his dates mixed up. I've taken a room at The Hunter's. On the plus side, I get breakfast. On the downside, just being here is a health hazard. I don't think it's been cleaned since the Britain in Bloom judges stayed here. The landlady introduced herself as being called 'Tiny'. She didn't specify if that was a nickname or her real name. She's neither a big woman which would make it ironic, nor small which would lend her name an accuracy. Totally baffling. I told her that my friend Connor back in London owns a stick insect called Tiny. I mean, I know he doesn't, but I felt under pressure to make conversation.

J

PS Tiny the landlady is to be our prompt for the play. Strange choice given she has one of the worst stammers I've ever heard.

PPS Mike's always had his eye on my fridge magnet. Tell him I want it back.

10:17pm. Chloe messages Jack

What's the play? I might have done it. What part are you playing? When's the first rehearsal? When's opening night? Right... I'm gonna finish my pickled onions (silverskin) before getting my stuff together for work. I need an early night.

Chloe

PS Jen messaged me for your new address. Said she might pay you a visit. Bit weird. Did you two have a thing? Come to think of it she didn't sound so happy. I hope you haven't upset Jen; you know how fragile she's been since her tortoise died.

3.

Monday 14th January

14 days 'til curtain up

1:30pm. Connor messages Jack

Alright mate. You get there OK?

Just checking you haven't forgotten it's Chloe's birthday next month. We're thinking of chipping in for a decent sized present given it's her 30th. Any ideas?

Connor

Btw, Chloe says you've seen my "stick insect" and have branded it as tiny. I've added speech marks to "stick insect" since we both know I've never purchased any creature defined as a phasmid. I must therefore conclude you were using "stick insect" as part of an infantile gag.

(I'd still like to know when you saw it and whether it was one of the more impressive phasmids you've clapped eyes on).

1:33pm. Jack messages Connor

Dear Connor,

No, I didn't get here OK. Unfortunately, my train derailed just North of Darlington. Hundreds of people dead. It won't have made the news because London had 2mm of rain fall within a 72-hour period which flooded a grocery store in Wandsworth.

They're still trying to resuscitate me but it's not looking good. It isn't all bad, there are currently no less than five women weeping over my broken, (yet still handsome) body. If the worst happens, my luggage will find its way to you. You'll find a secret compartment in my suitcase, within which you'll discover a small key. This key opens a safety deposit box held by Credit Suisse (Zurich). It contains €3m. You'll need my security details.

My memorable information is 'CONNORISATWAT'

My passcode is 12 digits long. Write it down. It's 492... [flatline]

Warmest regards,

Nurse Hazel

(on behalf of Jack White)

PS Shortly before Jack's demise, he mentioned that he'd seen a rather 'pitiful stick insect' whose owner was swaying at the urinal adjacent to his. It was during a dreary stag weekend in Stevenage.

Jack's last words were accompanied by a death rattle and a lot of wheezing, so it's possible I misheard.

(but I didn't)

1:43pm. Connor messages Jack

Thanks Nurse Hazel.

What a pity. I've just won big on The Lottery and was going to buy all my friends (and Jack) a house. Oh well, Chloe, Mike and Katie will get bigger pads now, I guess.

6:48pm. Katie messages Jack

Hi Jack.

I won't ask you if you got there OK. Only an idiot (or a Mother) would do that. What do you think to the following ideas for Chloe's birthday?

1. *Telescopic coffee mug that extends into a Bong*

2. *A drone in the shape of Snoopy sat on his doghouse*

3. *Skeleton butler side table*

4. *Pooping dogs Calendar*

5. *Bedside butt light (slap activated)*

6. *Foot activated toilet piano (lets you make music while you poo)*

7. *Back massaging robot.*

Katie x

Btw, if Mike gets in touch with any suggestions, just ignore him, they'll be stupid.

6:57pm. Jack messages Katie

Hi Katie.

I'm struggling to work out if you're aiming for a whimsical gift or a left-it-a-bit-late gift. I'm leaning towards the latter.

I was just going to give her money. I'm fully aware, she'll probably waste it on some of the things on your list but at least I'll have a clear conscience.

Jack

PS Mike won't message me because he knows he's done a bad thing and stolen my property. He's probably meeting with his fence as I type.

PPS Chloe's met Connor so she won't want another drone.

PPPS Given Chloe's body dysmorphia (do you think my elbows are fat? I'm sure my right ankle has a bigger circumference than my left; stop looking at my lazy eye, you're making it/me paranoid etc. etc.), I'd probably steer clear of anything skeleton-themed.

Jack

9:02pm. Jack messages Chloe

Dear Chloe

KEYS?

9:02pm. Chloe messages Jack

Shit!

9:03pm. Jack messages Chloe

You have one chance to redeem yourself: tell me you didn't actually pass my details to Jen? (The correct answer to this question is 'No').

9:13pm. Mike messages Jack

Hi mate.

Have you taken all your stuff with you? Could do with borrowing your socket spanner set.

Cheers

Mike

9:22pm. Jack messages Mike

Your girlfriend has told me to ignore you.

Jack

4.

13 days 'til curtain up

12:02pm. Chloe messages Jack

Completely forgot to say, Connor has engineered himself a date. With Ravi.

12:04pm. Jack messages Chloe

Is that the guy who works at 'The Courtyard'? The one with no chin?

12:05pm. Chloe messages Jack

Yup. That's him!

12:06pm. Jack messages Chloe

Thank fuck for that. Those two have been tip-toeing round each other for weeks. As mating dances go, it was getting wearisome. Connor was risking a glassing if he asked me one more time *'is he looking at me?'*

Anyway, that's great news.

12:08pm. Chloe messages Jack

What? No it isn't! That means I'm left with two smug couples. It used to be one smug couple, two social misfits and moi. This is turning into a bad day.

C

12:09pm. Jack messages Chloe

Mike and Katie - smug? I'm not sure Mike has even sussed he's in a relationship. He could go for days without even realising he's co-habiting. It's like when you own a cat. It'll wander into a room, stop, and look at you as if it's the first time it's ever noticed you; this despite you having shared your house with the bloody thing for ten years, feeding it and taking it to the vet. Mike's like that cat. There are many words I could draw upon to describe Mike and Katie's relationship; smug would not be one of them. *Non-existent* would make the cut, however.

J

PS I don't think Connor and Ravi hooking up for a date affords them couple-status.

12:11pm. Chloe messages Jack

Connor has already asked if Ravi can be added to our group chats. I played that one with a straight bat and gave a resounding NO.

I told him that Ravi's on group probation, and that more importantly I needed time to come to terms with the fact that now you've left, I'm the only single person.

12:13pm. Jack messages Chloe

Katie and me had one of those pacts where, if we hadn't found a partner, we'd marry each other when we reached fifty. We were laughing (sobbing) about it the other week, but she said she's settled now (actually I think she might have said she's had to settle). Whatever. You can jump in at 49 if you like.

I did ask you before Katie but you'd just started seeing Neil from Kwik Fit and told me to fuck off.

12:15pm. Chloe messages Jack

Great. What a generous offer. Thanks. I've got 19 years. Even I reckon I can find someone that isn't a complete wanker in that time.

PS

Do you remember Connor's old cat, Alan? He looked the spitting image of Neil from Kwik Fit.

12:17pm. Jack messages Chloe

I thought it was Katie's gerbil 'Phil' who looked like Neil from Kwik Fit.

12:18pm. Chloe messages Jack

No. Connor's cat was definitely Neil from Kwik Fit. Katie's gerbil was Lionel Richie.

8:30pm. Jack messages Chloe

I'm at our first rehearsal. It's a fairly large cast. The Director's a bloke called Donald MacMary. Short guy. Terrified of his wife. Anyway, we're using the theatre itself for rehearsals- well a room within it which smells. It's hard to describe the smell. If you pressed me, I'd say it's a cross between the residents' lounge of a nursing home and a pair of Mike's socks.

8:33pm. Jack messages Chloe

So... we're having a tea break. And it's literally just tea. We've left the nursing home lounge to sit by the bar in the foyer. The bar isn't open. Why isn't the bar open? What's the point having a bar and not opening it? Is this normal? I thought there'd be alcohol. Was banking on it.

8:35pm. Jack messages Chloe

I'm starting to think this whole thing is a bad idea. Scratch that - I thought that at Michael Brains' house and I definitely thought it earlier when the Director had us doing breathing exercises while shaking our arms to 'get loose', as he put it. Why bother? All we did when we'd finished all that malarky was sit down in a circle and read the play. I don't know about the others, but I didn't need to wave my arms about like a jumper in a washing machine while humming up and down a scale in order to achieve that. Pretty sure Donald MacMary must have read somewhere that this is how any Director worth their salt should kick off a rehearsal. He definitely picked up the wrong book at the library - the one entitled 'interpretive dance for arseholes'.

8:42pm. Jack messages Chloe

I'm not sure I can put myself through this bollocks. I might pack it in.

PS I was told to arrive early for a tour of the theatre. I'm not a fire prevention officer but I'm fairly sure it can't be best practice to have your only means of escape through a wood and scenery store. If there's a fire and I die, tell Mike I begrudgingly bequeath him my fridge magnet. Have you got that back off him yet by the way?

PPS Opening night is 28th January. It's just under 2 weeks away. The rest of the cast have been rehearsing from just before Christmas. They'd normally rehearse for 6 weeks but the first couple of weeks were a write-off after the theatre roof sprung a leak; the village hall was booked-out so they couldn't find a room big enough for them to rehearse in. When I asked if there wasn't a school hall they could have used, glances were exchanged, and a chap called Howard Cobham moved the conversation along. Weird.

8:44pm. Jack messages Chloe

Anyway, long and short of it is we're being asked to rehearse most nights. Sounds like a lot. I'm sure that's not necessary. Wait... being called back in.

8:47pm. Chloe messages Jack

The lack of alcohol, the warmups and perilous working environment are all perfectly normal. Just get on with it.

Chloe

PS I can't believe you typed all that but didn't see fit to tell me the title of the play you've been reading. I won't ask again!

10:30pm. Jack messages Chloe

In The Hunter's along with half the cast. Tiny came across and barked something at us. Blank faces all round. After several uncomfortable seconds of silence, Tim Waddle said 'Thanks Tiny, I'll have a bitter shandy'. Then we all named a drink.

It seems Tim is the only one who can understand Tiny. He hears words, I just hear a pretty good impression of a Kalashnikov.

Oh, and the female pub regulars are hanging on Christian Schmidt's every word. He's one of the actors. I overheard him boring them with how his share portfolio was currently mirroring his acting career, given they're both on an upward trajectory. He has the women all wide-eyed and cooing over him. No idea why. Anyone can tell the bloke's gay.

10:33pm. Jack messages Chloe

By the way, as you know, I'm not a fan of people staring at their phones while in a pub, but right now I'm not messaging you, I'm messaging my sister who's ill in hospital. This fabrication is out of necessity. I've ended up perched next to a man called Trevor. At least I think that's his name. It's so long since he introduced himself, and for the last God knows how many minutes he's been boring me with tales of all the theatre sets he's designed and constructed.

He claims to be the first set designer in the UK to construct his sets from scaffolding. In fact, every set of his, no matter what the play, appear to have been made primarily from scaffolding. I suggested he might want to hold back the scaffolding vibe for when a play about a construction site lands in his in-tray.

I'm assuming this is why the others do their best to avoid Trevor. Well, that and the indescribable body odour.

It also explains the tactical jockeying for position around this table when we arrived. I couldn't swear to it, but it looked for all the world like one of the cast members deliberately remained standing and conducted an entire conversation across the pub with someone who didn't exist, just to avoid committing to a chair before Trevor had chosen his. The rest of the group circled the table, slowly at first but then gathered pace, worried the music might stop at any second. At its peak, the whole thing resembled the finale of River Dance.

Trevor's just gone to the toilet. I'd better be sociable.

Jack

10:37pm. Chloe messages Jack

Ooh I've just been on The Attic Priory Players' Facebook Page. They have an actors' archive which has headshots of everyone who's ever graced their stage. Some photos of past shows too. Trevor sounds fascinating. It's lovely that you've made a friend.

Chloe

PS Christian Schmidt's headshot - is that his own hair?

10:39pm. Jack messages Chloe

No.

10:40pm. Chloe messages Jack

I don't want to point out the obvious, but you still haven't told me the thing I said I wouldn't ask you again about. And infuriatingly there's no clue on the group's Facebook page.

C

PS Your director Donald MacMary really is short, isn't he? Did you know he's acted before too? Touring production of Lord of the Rings. Understudied Bilbo Baggins.

10:52pm. Jack messages Chloe

Yes. At the last count he'd told me five times. He also told me that his wife Mary was a tour-de-force when she played a two-hander with Donald Sinden in Peterborough.

She herself told me in no uncertain terms that she's the leading actress in the area. I didn't know quite how to respond so I just said 'That's nice. Well done'.

She was also at pains to tell me that her critically acclaimed Lady Macbeth is much talked about to this day. I've been here four days now and haven't heard a peep about it.

Jack

PS I have to go into the office tomorrow to say hello and all that. They have my car ready too. I worked out that I haven't driven a car for over seven years.

PPS I know I've had a couple of drinks but there's really nothing to this acting lark. You always made out it was this great skill. I was always suspicious about that. When it comes down to it, it's just reading aloud. Anyone could do it. Well, maybe not Tiny the landlady, but pretty much anyone else.

11:57pm. Jo-Ann Pinchley-Cooke messages Jack

Hey Jack. Tiny gave me your number. I'm to play opposite you. Sorry I didn't make it to rehearsal. Traffic was murder getting back from Dunstanburgh. The girl who does my nails had a cancellation and squeezed me in last minute.

Anyway, I'll be there tomorrow. How was everyone? Did you guys go to the pub? Have you met Trevor yet?

Did Donald MacMary make everyone get naked? He usually gets everyone naked first rehearsal. Please tell me he didn't do the naked thing?

Jo-Ann xxxxxxxxx

11:59pm. Jack messages Chloe

Chloe. This is important. My next message to you will be a copy of a message I just received from the woman I'm to act against. She's my character's love interest if you will. I want you to take particular note of the last paragraph. You can't miss it... it contains the word 'naked' no fewer than three times.

What the hell have you got me into?

Jack

PS The play requires that I must kiss this Jo-Ann Pinchley-Cooke. The script actually says, 'he kisses her with vigour'. Vigour? Have you ever kissed anyone with vigour before? I snogged Mary Jenkins with herpes once. Hers not mine. Vigour? What does that involve? Oh and £10 and a jar of your favourite peanut butter says she's ugly. No. Not ugly. Plain. She'll be plain. Plain and naked.

PPS On my way up the stairs to my room, I heard a noise reminiscent of a cat hacking up a fur ball. I looked back and it was Tiny. By the intonation in her voice, I concluded she was asking me a question. All I caught was the word 'pillows'. I replied with a tentative 'yes please' which in hindsight could have been a mistake.

12:03am. Jack messages Chloe

I've spared you the whole of Jo-Ann's message. Below is the important bit:

'Did Donald MacMary make everyone get naked? He usually gets everyone naked first rehearsal. Please tell me he didn't do the naked thing?

Jo-Ann xxxxxxxxx'

12:05am. Chloe messages Jack

If a poll was conducted (with a decent sample size and a varied demographic), I'm convinced the results of the study would conclude that the 'important' part of that message was the number of kisses blown your way, by a woman you haven't even met yet.

Chloe

12:07am. Jack messages Chloe

If we assume for the moment that Ipsos MORI haven't been commissioned and focus on the part which is 'important' (critical) TO ME.

Jack

PS For the avoidance of doubt, the important part is the act of getting naked ((in front of strangers) (for no apparent reason) (for no monetary reward))

12:12am. Jack messages Chloe

Where'd you go? I'm not sure you've grasped the seriousness or indeed urgency of this potential predicament.

12:15am. Chloe messages Jack

I have.

I'm asleep.

(xxxxxxxxx)

5.

Wednesday 16th January

12 days 'til curtain up

7:10am. Chloe messages Jack

I've looked up Jo-Ann Pinchley-Cooke in the actors' directory. You were right, she's plain. She looks to be about 25 but there's so much soft focus going on with her headshot, she could be anything between 20 and 45. Either way I'm not sure you'd take pleasure in kissing her with vigour - naked or not.

Definitely not your type.

Chloe

PS I'm curious as to what you decided to wear to rehearsal?

7:11am. Jack messages Chloe

Why the hell are you asking me what I was wearing? This isn't a sex chat line. If you must know, (and I'm saying this in my best husky voice while curling a lock of hair around my finger) I wore a T-shirt and jeans.

Jack

7:12am. Chloe messages Jack

Which T-shirt? Not the one that says 'I shaved my balls for this?'

C

7:13am. Jack messages Chloe

Nope. The Kellogg's Cornflakes one.

Seriously, I won't be making the mistake of wearing just a t-shirt again. It was bloody bitter in there. It's freezing up here. I joked that they should rename the place 'Arctic Priory'. No one laughed. I don't think they got it.

J.

7:15am. Chloe messages Jack

Oh, they got it.

C.

7:18am. Jack messages Chloe

Oh, I got a message from Jen. It was a bit confusing if I'm honest.

Jack

7:21am. Chloe messages Jack

What did it say?

7:23am. Jack messages Chloe

It didn't say anything. She'd just typed a colon.

J

7:25am. Chloe messages Jack

That's it? Just a colon? As in ':'? What do you think it means?

C

7:27am. Jack messages Chloe

Buggered if I know. She was probably in the middle of typing out a smiley face but got distracted.

J

7:29am. Chloe messages Jack

Christ Jack. No one types out a smiley face anymore. It won't be that. Anyway, how do you know it wasn't the start of a sad face? What did you reply?

7:31am. Jack messages Chloe

I didn't. What idiot would reply to a colon? What would you reply?

I'm not keen on getting into a message thread with Jen. She's unstable.

Got to go for this meet and greet at work. You'd better get off your arse too. Those houses won't sell themselves.

Jack.

PS We've been told by Donald MacMary to bring a roll of wallpaper to rehearsal tonight. I waited for an explanation, but none was forthcoming. Any idea what that's all about?

7:33am. Chloe messages Jack

Yes.

PS I'd avoid anaglypta.

PPS... :

11:38am. Jack messages Chloe

Kill me now! At the office. I'm to work alongside a chap called Colin Inglis. He was wearing a comedy tie with one of those Minion things on it. Y'know that yellow thing with one big eye. Worse still, Colin helps out with lighting or something at the theatre. I'm starting to see the pitfalls of living in a small place.

I zoned out while he was talking to me and focused on the cup he was holding. It had a picture of a small glass and the caption 'MUG SHOT!' Surely a picture of a shot glass holding its arrest number card would have worked better? And why the exclamation mark? That doesn't miraculously turn a weak gag into a good one.

11:44am. Jack messages Chloe

Colin and me are to sit opposite each other. At least my monitor is a decent size, although I have a feeling just hearing him will be irritating. Reminds me of Dave Holding back in the Hammersmith office. Remember him? You met him once at 'The Courtyard'. That fella who was rage-inducing just to look at? The one with the annoying shaped head. The sort of bloke who, despite your leanings towards pacifism, you wouldn't feel guilty about punching. You also know your colleagues would thank you for it but when push comes to shove you can't quite bring yourself to do it. A bit like sex with Claire from reception.

Anyway, I'm off to buy a jumper and wallpaper. What are the chances of me being able to get both of those from the same store? Minimal I reckon.

Jack

1:23pm. Chloe messages Jack

When did you nearly have sex with Claire? I think I met her once. Was she the tall one with the overbite? Again... not your type at all. Enjoy your rehearsal.

C

PS I'm out with the gang at 'The Courtyard' later. Quiz night in case you've forgotten - so my phone will be off in case you're dying to message me. There's an air of optimism cos Mike reckons we'll have a better chance now you're not going to be there.

5:59pm. Jack messages Chloe

Bloody hell. I fell asleep. Just woken up. Still haven't been shopping yet. Not going to have time to eat anything before rehearsal. Gotta fly.

J

PS Yeah that's her. Red Rum. Messy office party. I aborted after kissing. Injury risk.

6:15pm. Chloe messages Jack

Good luck at rehearsal. Enjoy getting naked with Miss Plain Pinchley-Cooke

Chloe

8:30pm. Jack messages Chloe

On a tea break. The bar's shuttered grille is taunting me again.

The wallpaper thing was very odd. Donald told us to write a history of our character on the back of the roll. He said to start at the top with your character's early years and work down the roll to create a timeline until you reach the date our play is set. We were told to include things like where we've come from, past relationships, job successes/failures, aspirations, character traits etc. etc.

The rest were scribbling furiously. I thought I'd start by writing the year of my character's birth. It took me five minutes of leafing through the script to find that my character's age wasn't mentioned, but luckily on page 3 I spotted a character breakdown which listed my role as having a playing age of 'thirties'. That established, I set about looking for the year the play is set in. This wasn't mentioned anywhere either, but it seemed to have a pre-war vibe about it. All this took me bloody yonks. When we were asked to read out what we'd come up with, all of the others unravelled miles of lengthy scrolls. It was touch and go whether Christian Schmidt would run out of wallpaper.

When it came to my turn all I had was *Frederick: Born circa 1895*. I read it out slowly and added that my character was somewhat of a mystery. Donald liked that. He said it showed I'd really given it some thought and proved that I'd already immersed myself in the role.

Jack

PS Do you need any wallpaper. I've got tonnes of it. It's pelican themed.

10:13pm. Chloe messages Jack

Nice going. I can see you've got the hang of it. So... what was Jo-Ann Pinchley-Cooke like? Done any heavy petting yet?

Chloe

PS Waiting for quiz scores to be read out. I think we got more right answers than normal.

PPS Did you manage to buy a jumper? You need to keep your chest warm at your age.

10:18pm. Jack messages Chloe

Your interest in Miss P-C is heart-warming. She rang Donald to say she'd be late. Something about a fund raiser.

As it turned out she didn't show up at all, but Donald's just said she's going to meet us at the pub. He seemed very happy about that.

Let me know your quiz placing. I'm keen that you don't do well.

Jack

PS I excelled myself and managed to buy both the wallpaper and a jumper type thing from the same store.

10:20pm. Chloe messages Jack

Jumper 'type thing'?

I must say I have a bad feeling about this. Please describe.

C

10:22pm. Jack messages Chloe

It's great. It's hard to describe the colour. Wet sand maybe? Or pumice.

Anyway, it's sleeveless (I asked the assistant if they did one with sleeves, but she sort of sniggered and said that they didn't). But the best thing is it has loads of pockets and loops you can hook stuff onto. If the look the designer was going for was 'Commando' then they nailed it. Warm and rugged looking, yet stylish.

I wore it tonight. I've already filled the pockets. It's a game changer.

Jack

10:29pm. Chloe messages Jack

You've bought a workman's gilet you dickhead.

C

PS Never ever wear that in my company.

PPS We came 2nd. Missed out on top spot by 1/2 point. Still, it was a podium finish. We haven't had one of those since 'Quiz on my Face' were disqualified for colluding with 'The Shiraz Sisters'.

11:49pm. Jo-Ann Pinchley-Cooke messages Jack

Hey babe. Lovely to meet you finally! Thanks for saving me from Trevor. Lol! And then from Mary MacMary. God she's awful. She told me earlier that she could see a lot of herself in me and that one day, if I was lucky, I might be as good as she is!

Anyway, that short arse Donald told me we're going to do our kiss on Friday. Me and you! 'To get any awkwardness out of the way' as he put it. He's the one making a thing of it by turning it into a big deal.

Your impression of Tiny was bang on by the way! Hahahaha. Please say you'll come to the skittles night?? It's on Saturday.

God, I need sleep. Oh, I never asked you what you did for a living. We were having too much of a giggle. I think I was a bit drunk. Did you come straight from work earlier? Are you a carpenter? I need my loft boarding. Do you do that sort of thing?

Jo-Ann xxxxxx

11:53pm. Jo-Ann Pinchley-Cooke messages Jack

Oh, I hear they did the wallpaper thing. I never know what to put on that. I mean it's basically doing the writer's job for them. *My backstory?* You're the bloody author, you tell me! Lol.

Right. I'll stop jabbering on. Sleep awaits.

Night

Jo-Ann

Xxxxxxxx

11:59pm. Jack messages Jo-Ann Pinchley-Cooke

Yeah, great to see you too.

This is my first foray into theatre so I'm kinda finding my feet!

Night.

Jack

PS No, I'm not a carpenter.

6.

Thursday 17th January

11 days 'til curtain up

11:43am. Jack messages Chloe

Why half a point?

Which questions did you screw up on?

Jack

PS I think Jo-Ann likes me. Must be my boyish good looks, sparkling personality, and rapier-like wit. Throw my new jumper into the mix and it's not hard to see why she'd be interested.

PPS She's FAR from plain. But then you knew that.

11:53am. Chloe messages Jack

IT'S NOT A JUMPER!!!

There were a couple of questions we could have done better with. Our main downfall was Science and Nature. We had an almighty row over a question about whales.

Chloe

PS If you were on any form of social media, you'd know that as well as being extremely attractive, J-A P-C is 'in a relationship'.

2:25pm. Jack messages Chloe

It'll have been hump-backed or sperm or pilot or minke or blue. Doubt if it would be blue. Too obvious.

J

PS Not 'killer' either. That's not a whale.

2:28pm. Chloe messages Jack

I didn't even tell you the question. You've just named some whales. You always do this, the scatter gun approach. While the rest of us apply logic and quietly think of what the answer might be, you reel off a list of possible answers.

Then… if we end up getting the question wrong but the right answer was among the 900 that you suggested, you always shout out 'I SAID THAT!'.

C

PS … and it's annoying

6:20pm. Jack messages Chloe

What was the answer?

J

6:22pm. Chloe messages Jack

Sperm.

6:23pm. Jack messages Chloe

What answer did you put?

6:25pm. Chloe messages Jack

Blue.

6:26pm. Jack messages Chloe

No way! I told you that was too obvious.

6:32pm. Chloe messages Jack

God, I nearly forgot. You slipped up and told me the name of your character. FREDERICK! You're bloody well doing The Sound of Music. Oh brilliant! Hahahahaha.

Crikey, you're a bit old though. He's the eldest kid, isn't he? Or was that Kurt? I can never remember. Is the whole cast way too old for their parts? Who's playing Maria Von Trapp? Mary MacMary? I've seen her photo. She's 65 if she's a day. Oh, this is priceless!

Mind you, casting people who are way too old is par for the course in am-dram. Our group once cast a fifty-year-old with a muffin top as Eliza Doolittle. The miscasting wasn't lost on the critic in our local rag. He was three lines into his review when he penned *'Liz Jordan playing cockney flower girl Eliza Doolittle, could have 'danced all night' but only with the aid of a walking stick'*

The Sound of Music hahahaha. You've made my day!

Chloe

PS Here are a few of my favourite things:

Raindrops on roses

Pot Noodle

Merlot

PPS Who's playing Liesl? Is it Jo-Ann with her thigh gap? I actually don't know that she has a thigh gap. I bet she has a thigh gap. Does she have a thigh gap?

7:03pm. Jack messages Chloe

What are you on about? Thigh gap? I don't even know what that is. If it means that much to you, I'll ask her if she has one.

Glad you've cheered up though. You were grouchy earlier. Have the BBC been messing about with the start time of Gardeners' World again? That always makes you crazy (which I always thought was odd, seeing as you don't have a garden).

J

PS It's not The Sound of Music, but there is singing involved. The Musical Director is taking part of tomorrow's rehearsal.

PPS Does every amateur theatre show get reviewed? No one warned me about this. I didn't sign up for potential character assassination!

7:24pm. Chloe messages Jack

Review? Yeah, pretty much. If you're lucky the newspaper sends the guy who writes the motoring section who'll just copy and paste the synopsis and state the running dates. That way they can leave at the interval.

I'll see if The Attic Priory Players post their reviews online.

Chloe

7:32pm. Jack messages Chloe

What? No! Don't. I'd rather not know!

J

7:40pm. Chloe messages Jack

Attic Priory Gazette: 28th July 2013 on Brian Dill's portrayal of Richard III:

'... Watching Brian Dill limp about the stage, dragging one leg behind him, reminded me of wounded roadkill that for everyone's sake needed to be put out of its misery. I would gladly have given Mr Dill a kingdom AND a horse if he'd done the honourable thing and removed himself from the stage...'

7:45pm. Jack messages Chloe

What?!!! And they post this on their own Web thingy?? Why would they do that?!!

Jack

7:47pm. Chloe messages Jack

It seems they have a bizarre arrangement with a local theatre critic. They ask this Gary McPeter guy to review all their shows and then according to Chairman Brains, the theatre group agree to publish his reviews 'for good or ill'.

I'm assuming the committee are so far up their own arses they expected to receive only glowing critiques!!

To be fair that was the first I landed on. It's probably a rogue one when Gary McPeter was having a bad day.

7:49pm. Jack messages Chloe

Crikey. Yeah, let's hope so. I really wish you hadn't sought that out. I didn't need to see that.

9:15pm. Chloe messages Jack

Ooh here's another!

Attic Priory Gazette 8th September 2014

Gary McPeter writes:

'... In the opening sequences of The Attic Priory Players' production of 'West Side Story', Tony played by Christian Schmidt promises the audience that:

'Something's coming, something good, if I can wait.

Something's coming, I don't know what it is, but it is gonna be great'

The audience waited. Not much came and when it did it was far from great. By the end of the evening, those audience members who were still awake had witnessed the wanton demolition of one of the greatest musicals ever composed.

The curtain lifted to reveal a beautifully lit scaffold set. We would later realise that this was the moment the show peaked, and it would be too kind to describe what followed as a spiralling kamikaze nose-dive into oblivion.

The orchestra threatened to rescue this production but even they, under the skilful baton-ship of James Starling could not stem the tide of relentless mediocrity.

When one thinks of Bernstein's West Side Story, one thinks of its racing, breathless, dynamic score. Close your eyes and you will almost certainly be able to visualise two street-hardened gangs slugging it out on the baked sidewalks of New York. Unfortunately, theatre etiquette dictates that eyes should remain open. What the audience were treated to was a performance from a gurning Christian Schmidt who managed to turn in a performance so devoid of gravitas you could have been forgiven for thinking he wasn't present on stage at all. The only clue he was still there was the sound of him honking his way through 'One Hand, One Heart'.

Anita played by Jo-Ann Pinchley-Cooke drifted aimlessly about the stage, missed a crucial entrance, and didn't look the slightest bit interested in her lover Bernardo, an orange-faced shambles played by Tim Waddle.

The two gangs tried their best but ultimately it was just twelve out-of-condition men mincing about some scaffolding. At one-point mid-rumble, they were collectively scared by a rogue note from the horn player.

Amongst the carnage, credit should go to Molly Grant as Maria. She gave an assured performance and coped admirably with the demanding vocal score.

West Side Story runs nightly until Saturday 13th September.'

9:28pm. Jack messages Chloe

Gee Officer Chloe. Thanks for that. Not feeling any better about this whole am-dram thing. This is terrifying. Please stop.

9:32pm. Chloe messages Jack

You're welcome. By the way I wouldn't bandy the term 'am-dram' or 'amateur' about if I were you. The Attic Priory Players seem to hate that. They refer to themselves as 'non-professional'.

10:05pm. Jack messages Chloe

Isn't that the same thing?

10:07pm. Chloe messages Jack

Well yes.

I can only think the psychology behind it is that the reader will only focus on the word 'professional'.

It'd be interesting to get Jung's take on it.

C

10:12pm. Jack messages Chloe

Well I'm not getting paid so as far as I'm concerned, it's amateur. In fact, I've had to stump up £50 just to be in the bloody thing. Brains spouted some nonsense about how the actors wouldn't be insured if they hadn't paid their 'subs' as he called it.

We might be putting that to the test: I caught a glimpse of a couple of men with beards helping Trevor Thwacker make a start building our set. It's all looking a bit Heath Robinson. There's a man in the cast called Brian Barrowman who by his own admission is carrying a bit of timber (meaning he's chunky not that he's helping build the set). I hope he's paid his subs cos there's no chance the upper level of scaffolding is going to support him.

10:17pm. Jack messages Chloe

Brian is friends with Bill Freynolds (think Statler & Waldorf). Unlike Brian, Bill is quite small, that is except for his Adam's apple, which would give Cristiano Ronaldo's a run for its money.

Then there's Val; I don't think I've told you about Val. Val is a transgender person. She has the worst language of anyone I know (including Mike). Val has a fantastic speaking voice which cuts through the room. It's also a good two tones lower than mine; a fact she was quick to point out to me. Val is someone my Mum would call a snazzy dresser. She has a no-expense-spared, stylish approach. She's going to be an ally I can tell, and when I've got to know her better I'm going to quiz her on her make-up technique since currently she tends to paint her bright blue eyeshadow well beyond what would normally be considered the acceptable extremities of an eyelid.

At the start of yesterday's rehearsal, Donald and Christian Schmidt were demonstrating a 'trust exercise' - y'know, those things you're made to do on work away days by a facilitator who sells it to you as an 'ice breaker'. Anyway, Schmidt and MacMary were balancing a scaffolding plank between them (which I think was supposed to prove they could trust each other while working as a team), when this big voice boomed out from the back 'Fuck me! We've got two weeks until opening night. Can we just get on with the shitting thing!?' It was Val.

She incurred the wrath of Mary MacMary but Val just shrugged and frowned her big clown face back at her. It was water off a duck's back. I think we're going to get on well. Jack

10:25pm. Chloe messages Jack

'Noises Off'

10:26pm. Jack messages Chloe

Sorry?

10:27pm. Chloe messages Jack

'Noises Off'

10:29pm. Jack messages Chloe

Right. You've just repeated the same thing. If the addition of speech marks was intended to make it clearer to me what you're on about, it hasn't.

Forget the speech marks; if anything, it looks like there should be an apostrophe somewhere but not sure where. What are you banging on about?

PS There's a green stain on the ceiling right above my pillow. Green! What sort of liquid/creature/food could possibly leave a green stain?

7.

10 days 'til curtain up

7:14am. Jack messages Chloe

How could you leave me hanging after last night's exchange? I didn't sleep a wink. I was still staring at my phone at 2am waiting for the word 'typing..' to appear at the top of the screen. When I did drop off, I woke with a start from the noise of my phone clattering to the floor. It was 4am.

Jack

8:14am. Chloe messages Jack

Oh dear. Sorry. I fell asleep.

PS It could be ectoplasm (on the ceiling). That's the logical explanation. Failing that it'll be avocado.

C

8:17am. Jack messages Chloe

Er... 'Noises Off'?

Jack

8:20am. Chloe messages Jack

It's a play; well a farce really. You know... one bedroom door opens at the precise moment another slams shut. The sort of play that has a synopsis that ends '... hilarity ensues'.

There's a Frederick in it which I'm guessing is you. He kisses a woman called Brooke which has got to be Jo-Ann Pinchley-Cooke. Right?

C

8:21am. Jack messages Chloe

Wrong. Very wrong.

J

PS I kept awake for that?! You used to be fascinating. Have you fallen in with the wrong crowd?

PPS Stop messaging me cos I need to learn my lines. Donald wants 'books down' next week.

8:24am. Chloe messages Jack

Got many lines?

8:26am. Jack messages Chloe

134

55

8:27am. Chloe messages Jack

Crikey. That's a lot. Are you worried? I mean, you have the worst memory of anyone I know.

8:28am. Jack messages Chloe

I'm not listening.

I'm learning my lines.

Or had you forgotten?

J

8:33am. Jo-Ann Pinchley-Cooke messages Jack

Hey babes. I'm down at the theatre. My mobile massage business is really taking off, so I thought I'd put some leaflets in the foyer.

Anyway, I overheard Trevor Thwacker swearing cos Dick Rump hadn't ordered more nails. I told him I'd check with you cos you'd be likely to have loads. 50mm galvanised mean anything to you?

Jo-Ann xxxxxx

Btw, it's singing tonight. A bit nervous about it. Apparently, you did a cracking singing audition so I might lean on you for moral support.

8:36am. Jack messages Jo-Ann Pinchley-Cooke

Hey back.

Yeah, I probably didn't make it clear the other night, I'm not a carpenter so I don't have a stock of nails.

I'm having a bit of quiet time today – trying to learn my lines.

Jack

PS Don't worry about the singing. You'll be fine. Pretend you're drunk and doing karaoke. That's what I do. Seems to work.

8:39am. Jo-Ann Pinchley-Cooke messages Jack

Bloody hell Jack. That's a brilliant idea. I'll come to The Hunter's and get spice racked before rehearsal. You're staying there, right? You can join me. Lol. Gotta fly!

J-A xxxxxxx

8:45am. Chloe messages Jack

Jen's just messaged and accused me of giving her the wrong number for you. She said you haven't been replying. Just saying...

C

8:49am. Jack messages Chloe

:

Jx

8:50am. Jack messages Chloe

I didn't mean to put that kiss!!! I never put a kiss. That was a mistake. Please disregard it.

Jack

8:53am. Chloe messages Jack

Oh my, I'm all a flutter.

What can I look forward to next?

Can I expect roses?

Will you climb my balcony?

Make me a compilation CD?

Tell me I'm your soul mate through the medium of 'Steve Wright's Sunday Shite Songs'?

Put the bins out for me?

Or... were you thinking of Jen when you typed your kiss? I think you were.

Or... Miss Pinchley-Cooke with her many kisses?

A packet of pickled onion flavoured Monster Munch says she uses LOL and LMAO a lot too. Katie's the same. She messages like a teenage girl in 2005.

Vigorous snogs

Chloe

8:59am. Trevor messages Jack

Hi mate. Trevor Thwacker here. You sat next to me at The Hunter's the other night.

Word has it you're a carpenter. Nice one. You kept that quiet. You don't happen to have any galvanised round head nails in your bag do you? 50mm or 75mm or anything in-between? It'll save me the hour round trip into Great Huckingford. That blonde bird said she was going to ask you, but then cleared off.

If you want to lend a hand anytime, I could do with someone with your skills. The rest of them are next to useless. Arty types. Don't like getting their hands dirty. The only one who's any good is that Val bird. She turns up proper dolled up too. Classy bird that one. Anyway if you could let us know about the nails.

Cheers mate

Trevor

Where did you get your work gilet from? Could do with one of them meself.

9:05am. Tiny messages Jack

Howdy partner. Tiny here.

Would have knocked on your door but didn't like to in case you had a lady friend with you?

Which is fine obviously... if you had a lady friend with you?

Tiny x

9:07am. Jack messages Tiny

Hi Tiny. I think you forgot to put in your message what you were going to knock on my door to ask me.

Jack

9:09am. Tiny messages Jack

Hahahahahaha. Yeah. I'm such a scatter cushion. Jo-Ann messaged me to see what time I was opening. Said she wanted to come for drinks here at 6. She said you'd be joining her and asked for that table for two in the window. I'll get Mel in early to work the bar.

Thing is, will you be eating? If so, I'll get the chef to start a bit earlier. Won't do the lazy git any harm.

Tiny xx

9:15am. Jack messages Tiny

Hi Tiny. No, it's fine thanks. I won't need to eat. Your excellent breakfast has kept both my stomach and arteries nicely full.

Cheers

Jack

9:25am Jen messages Jack

Hi Jack. Jen here. Not sure you got my last message. Still laughing about ten-pin bowling. A bit disappointed you didn't get in touch to reminisce. I guess you've been busy settling in. You were so funny that night. And very naughty!

Jen xxx

9:27am. Jack messages Trevor

Hi Trevor. I think there's been a misunderstanding. I'm not a carpenter so don't have any nails. Sorry.

Jack

PS I got my jumper from 'PerfectHomeStore' in Upper Lungton. £19.99.

9:29am. Jack messages Chloe

Chloe. What the hell happened when we went ten-pin bowling? I remember being drunk. That's it.

Jack

PS This is urgent!

PPS You were right. Female bar person.

9:30am. Jack messages Chloe

Have you turned your phone off?!?

1:33pm Kitty Cooper messages Jack

Ciao Jackie boy! It's Kitty from The Attic Priory. I'm head of costumes and trust me my little chickpea it's not as glamorous as it sounds. It's mostly hanging things up and altering costumes. Lol

Actors are so picky you wouldn't believe. The boys are the worst. You'd think it'd be the girls but no. That Christian Schmidt is a right Prima Donna. Everything has to cling to that boy, or he gets his Calvin Klein's in a right twist. I've seen his body. It's not toned; he just doesn't eat much. If you waved a sausage in front of his face he'd go into anaphylactic shock. Ooh hark at me using big words!

The boy's obsessed about his appearance. I wouldn't mind but I thought I'd left egotistical actors behind when I retired from head of costumes at Bristol Old Vic. Oh and don't believe a word Graham Knott tells you about HIS professional career. He'll tell anyone who'll listen that he was a Director at the RSC. Director my arse! It's a load of old tosh. He was Director of FINANCE, but he leaves the 'finance' bit out!! Hark at me bitching!

Anyway, gotta run, got to make a veil out of gauze. You could cut your hand on the material, it's a right load of old tat. Still, it'll be good enough for that stuck up bison MacMary.

Talking of costumes love, will you be at rehearsal tonight? If so. I need to measure you up (so to speak!!).

I'll warm the tape up darling.

Au Revoir my lovely,

Kitty x

1:35pm Jack messages Jo-Ann Pinchley-Cooke

Quick question... Is Kitty the costume person male or female?

Jack

PS How come absolutely everyone has my mobile number?

1:56pm Jo-Ann Pinchley-Cooke messages Jack

Lmao! Hahahaha

You might want to get someone other than Kitty to hold the end of the tape when you get your inside leg measured!! I'll come with you and do it if you like? Lol.

Looking forward to later. I might be 10 minutes late. Oh and we need a strategy for skittles night.

Jo-Ann xxxx

2:00pm Jack messages Jo-Ann Pinchley-Cooke

So, Kitty is a man?... or a woman?

Strategy? Isn't the strategy to drink your own bodyweight in lager and knock down as many skittles as possible?

Jack

2:08pm Jo-Ann Pinchley-Cooke messages Jack

It's hard to describe Kitty. I think you should wait and see.

Not bowling strategy! Coupling up strategy! You have to play in couples. You don't want to get stuck with Mary MacMary or Trevor or Howard Cobham as your bowling partner.

Jo-Ann xxxx

Oh. and Tiny has every cast member's phone number. Part of her job as prompt is to ring everyone on show nights to make sure everyone is fit and well, not asleep and not forgotten it's a performance night. Trouble is, by the time she's got her words out, she's made everyone 20 minutes late. Lol.

3:22pm. Trevor messages Jack

Hi mate.

Could you do me a favour and message Mel the barmaid and ask her if her phone's off?

Trevor

3:46pm. Jack messages Trevor

Hi Trevor. Um... if her phone's off she won't get my message until she switches her phone back on. I take it *you've* tried messaging her?

Jack

3:48pm. Trevor messages Jack

Yes mate. No response. That's why I reckon her phone is switched off.

3:51pm. Jack messages Trevor

Right... maybe best to wait until she switches it on? She'll get your message then? Assuming it's not urgent. Is it something urgent?

Jack

3:53pm. Trevor messages Jack

Nah nothing urgent. I was just going to ask her if she wanted a lift into town before her shift like.

Cheers mate.

Oh best say Trevor wants to know. She might think it's odd if you ask her.

3:57pm. Jack messages Trevor

I'm a bit confused Trevor.

Do you want me to message Mel to ask her if her phone is off (even though it seems likely her phone is turned off)?

... Or... did you still want me to ask her that question about going into town (even though it's likely her phone is turned off)?

Jack

4:05pm. Trevor messages Jack

Yeah. Thanks mate.

4:07pm. Jack messages Trevor

Right. Okaaay... If I could just run by you exactly what you want me to say so I'm clear... How's this... 'Hi Mel, I'm Jack and I reside in one of the rooms upstairs at the pub. Trevor thinks your phone is off so has asked me to message you – it would appear that phones are sometimes reachable by selected mobiles even though they appear switched off to others. I must admit this is news to me. Anyway, would you like Trevor to give you a lift into town before your shift starts?'

4:08pm. Trevor messages Jack

Christ it's a bit long-winded but yeah that'll do.

Personally, I wouldn't start it with 'I'm Jack'. You sound like that fella who sent that tape pretending to be The Yorkshire Ripper.

Cheers

Trevor

4:10pm. Jack messages Trevor

I haven't got her number.

4:12pm. Trevor messages Jack

Bloody hell. Really? 07865 546329

4:14pm. Jack messages Mel

Hi Mel. Jack here (I'm in the next play at the theatre and currently staying in one of the rooms at The Hunter's).

For reasons I've stopped trying to apply logic to, Trevor has asked me to message you to see if you want a lift into town (with him – I'm to make it clear it's with him and not me). Anyway, I'll probably catch you in the bar later.

Thanks

Jack

4:22pm. Trevor messages Jack

Hi mate. You hear anything back from Mel yet?

Trevor

4:23pm. Jack messages Trevor

No. Nothing.

4:24pm. Trevor messages Jack

I reckon her phone must be off.

4:25pm. Jack messages Jo-Ann Pinchley-Cooke

Hi Jo-Ann. You know you mentioned a strategy for coupling up at tomorrow's Skittles? I feel a pressing need to be prepared. Tell me more...

Thanks

Jack

4:35pm Jack messages Chloe

Chloe! Soooooo... 10 pin bowling! What occurred?

J

4:48pm Jack messages Chloe

FFS. WHERE ARE YOU?

IS YOUR PHONE OFF?

WHY ARE EVERYONE'S PHONES OFF?

OH GOD I'VE TURNED INTO TREVOR.

4:48pm Chloe messages Jack

There's no need to shout.

My phone's been on all day.

4:50pm Jack messages Chloe

What?!! Why in God's name didn't you reply to all my messages?!!

4:55pm Chloe messages Jack

I refer The Right Honourable Gentleman to his earlier comment made at 8:21am in which he said:

'Stop messaging me cos I need to learn my lines.'

Chloe

PS Also there's this thing called work that sometimes requires me to do things other than message you.

PPS How did the line learning go? Get much done?

5:05pm Jack messages Chloe

I had a few interruptions. I managed to get two lines cemented in.

The first was 'Hi. I'm Frederick'

The second was 'no'.

J

5:10pm Chloe messages Jack

Awwww. I'm so proud!

What's your cue line for when you say 'no'?

C

5:13pm Jack messages Chloe

?

5:15pm Chloe messages Jack

What's the line that precedes yours?

If you don't know what it is and who says it, how will you know when to launch in with your 'no'?

I was in a musical once where this guy in our cast shouted 'hello' five times. He was too early on four of them, missed the place where he should have said it, realised he should have said it and yelled it out while another character was mid-way through singing his ballad.

C

5:18pm Jack messages Chloe

I wish I'd met you earlier. That would have been a great night out.

Jack

5:20pm Chloe messages Jack

I'm sorry you didn't get to mock me earlier in my life.

What happens in situations when someone badly cocks up on stage, is the whole cast rallies around the poor actor to reassure them that the audience will never have noticed.

Fact is EVERYONE will have noticed (except for the Director - they don't usually have a clue what's going on).

Chloe

5:25pm Jo-Ann Pinchley-Cooke messages Jack

Hey lover (I can call you that cos you're my lover in the play. Well, one of them lol).

So…skittles…what happens is everyone stands up and tosses a coin. If you toss a tail, you sit down. If you toss a head, you stay standing. It keeps going until two people are left with heads. They are then partnered-up. Then we repeat the process until everyone has a partner.

Jo-Ann xxxxx

5:27pm Jack messages Jo-Ann Pinchley-Cooke

Right. OK.

Sounds like a lot of tossing.

Hang on. What if you have 5 people left standing and 4 of them toss a tail? You'd have one person left on their own. Do you start the whole thing again?

What time does the evening start? It could be hours before a ball is bowled. Maybe we should ask Tiny to open early.

Jack

5:29pm Jo-Ann Pinchley-Cooke messages Jack

Lol xxxx

5:32pm Jack messages Jo-Ann Pinchley-Cooke

What if there's an odd number of people to begin with? Is there a contingency for that?

5:35pm Jo-Ann Pinchley-Cooke messages Jack

Lol. It happened last year. Christian Schmidt offered to make up a threesome with Donald and Mary MacMary. Christian can be such an arse licker at times. I have no idea what the other girls see in him.

5:37pm Jack messages Jo-Ann Pinchley-Cooke

Sorry… so what are the tactics to get in the right couple and more importantly to avoid getting in the wrong couple?

Surely, it's down to chance?!

5:39pm Jo-Ann Pinchley-Cooke messages Jack

Oh you just cheat.

Make sure no-one can see your coin. If Trevor or Mary or Donald or Christian are sitting on a head (so to speak lol), then just say you have a tail and sit down. And vice versa.

5:41pm Jack messages Jo-Ann Pinchley-Cooke

I think I may find this difficult. I'm a man who struggled to learn two lines today.

Do you go to the lengths of identifying someone you want to be with, or do you just make sure you avoid the annoying ones?

5:43pm Jo-Ann Pinchley-Cooke messages Jack

A bit of both

Xxx

5:44pm Jack messages Jo-Ann Pinchley-Cooke

Right. I think I get it.

Thanks

Jack

PS Do you have a thigh gap?

5:46pm Jo-Ann Pinchley-Cooke messages Jack

Hmmmmm... I'm pretty sure no one has ever asked me that before!

I'll be over for our drink in a bit so you can judge for yourself! lol

Jo-Ann xxxxxx

6:05pm Jack messages Jen

Hi Jen! Nice to hear from you. Sorry I haven't been in touch, but it's been kind of manic here since I arrived. I'll be in touch properly soon. Hope you're OK.

Jack

11:15pm Jack messages Chloe

Back from rehearsal. Knackered. I've come straight to bed.

Could be difficult sleeping though, Tiny and Mel have turned the karaoke machine on. It's just the two of them. Mel's pretty good, she should be in the show. Tiny's not great (unless she's singing 19 by Paul Hardcastle).

8.

Saturday 19th January

9 days 'til curtain up

5:46am Chloe messages Jack

Hey Daniel Day Lewis, how was rehearsal last night? Sorry I wasn't awake.

8:06am Jack messages Chloe

Woah! You were up early! You never get up that early (unless you're going on holiday). Are you ill? Oh wait, are you still up from the night before? That'll be it. Nice going. Good night?!

8:08am Chloe messages Jack

Had drinks with Katie and passed out on the sofa. I think I was drinking Bailey's. I have no idea why. I HATE Bailey's and now I'll be tasting it for days. Why have a drink that tastes like a pudding? I woke up early, feeling queasy.

8:12am Jack messages Chloe

Get yourself down to Pimpernel's for a fry up. We always used to do that, remember? Cured most of our hangovers, that place did.

Rehearsal was mixed. James Starling did some singing with us. Some people really can't sing at all - the blokes mainly. James asked me what my vocal range was. I told him I didn't know which was a mistake. He made me sing Happy Birthday (again), over and over, but higher each time. You look a right idiot when it gets to the bit where you're supposed to insert the person's name whose birthday it is. What are you supposed to do, make a name up? Pick someone who's in the room and hope it's their birthday? All this was running through my head on the first go through and in the end, I decided to plump for what I thought was the lesser of three evils: 'Happy Birthday dear Aurghh Aurghh…' Bloody humiliating. Christian Schmidt was sniggering. Dunno why; that reviewer was right about the gurning. When Schmidt sang later in the evening, he looked like a giraffe trying to snag an apple off a branch that was just out of reach. He was sticking his chin that far in the air I thought Bruce Forsyth had joined us. I reckon you could pull a bloke in off the street, and he'd make a better sound.

8:15am Jack messages Chloe

Anyway, Happy Birthday was getting higher and higher until James abandoned that and just asked me to sing a scale. I wanted to point out that we could have saved a lot of time and personal anguish if this approach had been taken from the start.

Turns out I'm a tenor. James was pleased with this because he said the group didn't have one. Christian Schmidt flew into a rage at this and protested that he too was a tenor and is categorised as such by all the other theatre groups he performs with. James hit back by telling him he was barely a baritone. Tim Waddle made some comment about balls dropping which didn't really make any sense but drew a few nervous laughs anyway.

8:17am Jack messages Chloe

I've learned that the vocal ranges for men are bass, baritone and tenor. For the women it's alto and soprano. Only two choices for women which seems a bit unfair. Which one are you? Let me guess…Alto?

8:19am Jack messages Chloe

The surprise of the night was Val. Val sings soprano, and she has the most beautiful voice. After a couple of pints in the pub afterwards, I plucked up courage, leaned into Val and quietly suggested that she could lose her slightly deep speaking voice by just singing her everyday conversations. She roared a huge belly laugh, told me I was a genius and then punched me on the arm so hard I thought I was going to hit the canvas. You know me, I bruise like a peach. That arm's going to be tender for weeks.

J

PS Are we all going away again this year? Spring? If you like, I'll get some brochures and come up with some possibles.

PPS There's an old couple staying here. She's nice but he's odd. He does this small cough before talking. Every time! I don't know how it doesn't drive his wife batty. Everything he does is attention-seeking, whether it be an exaggerated sneeze or reading aloud from his newspaper. I'm at breakfast now and he's buttering his toast so loudly, I had to check it wasn't a cat flaying a scratching post. It's kind of amusing watching them try to understand what Tiny's saying though.

8:22am Chloe messages Jack

Wow. Someone's grumpy this morning! I take it the kissing didn't go well last night. What happened? Did you accidentally dribble? Or nibble? Or did you both lean heads to the same side and knock the girl's teeth out? If Jen comes up to visit, you should practise some more on her.

Chloe

PS Brochures?! Jack, you're 32 not 300! I know you're old fashioned and it's lovely (sometimes) but you must be the only person walking this planet under the age of sixty, who still visits a travel agent to get armfuls of brochures. Just look online like everyone else.

PPS Funny you should mention a holiday though, Mike and Katie mentioned it last week at the quiz. They're up for it. Connor said he needed to check. Check what, I'm not sure. The man lives alone and as far as any of us can tell, we're his only social group (apart from Ravi – let's not forget Ravi).

PPPS I could be way off the mark here, but I don't think giraffes eat apples from trees Jack.

8:25am Jack messages Chloe

I've just read your message three times and I'm as sure as I can be that, within the context of kissing, you just typed the sentence 'If Jen comes up to visit, you should practise some more on her'.

I'll be frank, it's the *'practise some more'* part of the sentence which is troubling me.

I'm telling myself that when you typed 'practise *some more'* you meant that *as well* as kissing Jo-Ann, I could get *more* practise by kissing someone *new* – the example you've given being Jen?

I'm also telling myself that your choice of Jen was a person randomly plucked out of the air by you, simply in your haste to finish your message?

In addition, I'm choosing to assume that by using Jen as an example, you were merely being practical since I have no relationship with Jen?

Accordingly, I'm deducing that if such a *'practise'* were to take place at an unspecified point in the future, it would be my *first** kiss with Jen?

Furthermore, a reasonable interpretation on my part is that you only selected Jen as a possible candidate for kissing practise because, being two unattached adults, we could both approach said kissing practise without any historic emotional attachment of any sort?

To summarise, any kissing entered into would NOT be '*more*' practise with *Jen*, rather '*more*' practise overall Yes?

J

*pay particular attention to the word '*first*'. If you scanned my message quickly, please take time to digest it and make sure you understand the context. There's no sub-text to worry about.

PS I'm fully aware that in my message, I've inserted several question marks where normally I wouldn't. I wanted to make sure that my sentences were written as questions because QUESTIONS REQUIRE ANSWERS!

8:27am Chloe messages Jack

Is that all you did last night? Sing Happy Birthday? Isn't the show on in a couple of weeks. You're being very calm about it. I'd be canning myself.

8:32am Jack messages Chloe

It'll be OK, I think. I'm not due in the office until after the show week, so I'll have my days to try and get to grips with it. We've 'blocked' some of it (I think that's the right word?). Y'know... enter there, sit down there, stand up, say your lines, exit there. I got a bollocking for writing notes in my script in pen. You're supposed to write in pencil because the scripts go back to the rights holder after the show. No one tells you these things. They expect you to know! Upstage, downstage,

stage left, stage right. I blame you; at no point did you tell me I'd be learning a new language.

Oh, and Christian Schmidt accused me of 'upstaging him'. I only stepped forward to retrieve my pen off Donald's desk.

8:35am Jack messages Chloe

James taught us 4-part harmony. No one was getting it, so he quickly shaved that to 2 parts and when that still sounded naff, we switched to singing in unison which was only marginally better.

By the time we'd done all that and some blocking there was no time for kissing practise or much else for that matter. I glanced around and everyone was looking nervous (apart from Val). One girl who looks constantly haunted by the whole thing was staring into space while making confetti from her script. I don't think they'll be getting the deposit back on that one.

8:37am Jack messages Chloe

A slightly tiddly Jo-Ann slurred her way through one of her songs and seemed pleased with it. James didn't look convinced.

Oh, and Trevor's wife pitched up midway through rehearsal. She was fuming. Not sure why; no one was. Trevor ducked out of rehearsal and came back in ten minutes later, all flustered and red-faced.

8:38am Jack messages Chloe

But... there's some light relief later, it's skittles night at The Hunter's. The skittles bit sounds easy. It's the selection process to determine bowling partners that's daunting. Think Champions' League draw: names spread between 4 bowls, a seeding system no one can understand and endless permutations of competitors who can't be drawn together for various reasons. And…much like the Champions' League draw, I fear the process of picking partners tonight will take about three hours, after which I'll find myself in the 'group of death'. There's always a group of death: the group that the washed-up footballer who's making the draw, raises his eyebrow at, chuckles, and shoots a knowing look direct to camera.

Jack

8:50am Chloe messages Jack

Are you playing football or skittles later?

C

8:51am Jack messages Chloe

Oh, I forgot. I got measured up for my costumes last night by the most flamboyant man in the world. He's also the roundest person I've ever met. Round as a beach ball.

It was an education. When he talked about other men, he generally referred to them as 'she' or 'her'. E.g. 'hark at *her*', 'get *her*', 'if *she* thinks I'm making *her* a suit from scratch *she* can think again'.

Have you ever heard anyone refer to another man as she or her? It's baffling.

8:54am Chloe messages Jack

Connor often calls you a twat. Does that count?

9:08am Jack messages Chloe

I now know what a thigh gap is. Jo-Ann showed me hers in the bar last night. I had to ask her to point to where I should be looking. She was wearing gym legging things so it was easy to spot. I reckon it's about 2cm at its widest. She told me it's the Holy Grail for women and asked me what I thought of it. I didn't know what to say, panicked and blurted out something inappropriate about drinking from it and finding everlasting life. We talked about the show and tactics for tonight's skittles evening.

Mel shouted over that she'd got my message (that's a long story involving Trevor). Jo-Ann wanted to know what I was messaging Mel for. Halfway through explaining, Tiny shouted over 'I didn't mean to pry about female companions being in your room'. Jo-Ann now thinks I'm running a harem upstairs. I assured her that I hadn't been sneaking women upstairs and don't have any plans (or more importantly, offers) to.

9:11am Jack messages Chloe

I admit to being slightly awkward around someone as attractive as Jo-Ann. I find I get a bit unnecessary and struggle to concentrate. It's unlike me to feel awkward (not Robot Wars-contestants-awkward); felt the need to add perspective there; those poor bastards can't look Philippa Forester in the eye without clamming-up.

Luckily, my coping mechanism kicked in last night with Jo-Ann and I focused on two things:

a. The table. It was unbelievably sticky. I couldn't lean on it, put my hands on it or rest my beer on it without coming away with a thick, snail mucus-like substance all over me. If you could somehow harness or bottle it, you could rock up on Dragons' Den with a product capable of mending space stations. Duncan Bannatyne would still say he was out though. Is it me or did he never invest?

b. I've forgotten what (b) was.

9:15am Chloe messages Jack

Duncan Bannatyne hasn't been a dragon for about ten years. My God Jack, sometimes I think you should have been born in a different era. Victorian. You're like something out of a Dickens novel. You and Jen should get it on. Marriage for the two of you would be turns around the grounds, recitals on the pianoforte, a collection of exotic plants in the glasshouse and sex with your clothes on.

9:17am Chloe messages Jack

You know that guy who Jen lived with for a couple of years? We're going back a bit here, but you must remember? The one who worked at The Skipton Building Society? Well Connor claims that Jen wouldn't pee in front of him. I mean that's properly Dickensian right? Apart from anything else, who has time to wait patiently outside until tinkle-time is over (I don't call it that, I'm just projecting what Jen might call it). What was that bloke's name? The peeing thing could have been why they split up. Oh wait, no. It's because she's mental.

9:20am Jack messages Chloe

How did Connor find that out? Was he employed as their bathroom attendant? Always on standby with a hand towel and some aftershave?

Jen's OK really. She's just a bit insecure and needy. Actually no, you're right, she's mental. Do I need to remind you that I'm still waiting for your account of our ten-pin bowling night? I've had to fob Jen off with a 'holding message', promising I'll message properly soon. So hurry up. What happened? I fear it's something bad. It is, isn't it? I need to know by the end of the day.

She said I was 'naughty'.

Jack

PS Katie told me once, that while she was in the bath, Mike came into the bathroom, sat on the toilet, and took a dump. He didn't even say anything. Just sat there and got on with it. He was there for the long haul too – took his mountain bike magazine in with him. Katie said she just lay there in the candlelight, glass of wine in hand, utterly incapable of speech.

PPS (b) thigh gap; that was the other reason I couldn't concentrate. It just came back to me.

9:28am Chloe messages Jack

Tell me if I've got this right... you saw a thigh gap for the first time and things got sticky?

C

PS Katie's never mentioned that to me before. I'd kick him out - on the street. That's rank.

9:35am Jack messages Chloe

Two years of dancing around each other in the bathroom? I can't get my head around it. Are you positive you've got that right? I wonder if Jen allowed her fella to be in the bathroom if she was taking a shower? (normal, not golden).

J

PS When I first brought Elvis home all those years ago, I didn't get naked in front of him for a couple of days. I can't explain why. I got past it though.

9:38am Chloe messages Jack

I think you're in danger of over-analysing Jen's bathroom regime.

C

PS Awww I miss Elvis. He was fab. You were all shook up when he died though. Will you get another cat do you think? If you do, I'd be more inclined to come and visit.

PPS Do you think skittles is a good idea? I'd have thought you'd be steering clear of any sort of bowling for a while...

10:17am Tiny messages Jack

Hi Jack. Tiny here. I'm finalising numbers for tonight's skittles. You're coming, aren't you? Is it just you or shall I put you down for a plus one? Can't wait. I'm going to do a bit of food. I'll be keeping it simple; burgers and chips.

Tiny xx

10:19am Jack messages Tiny

H1 Tiny. Yes, I'll be along later. I don't have a girlfriend though, so it'll just be me. Can't beat a burger. Excellent work!

10:20am Tiny messages Jack

Oh that's a shame. Is it a case of just not meeting the right girl?

Cate Wilson is single if you can put up with the skin complaint. Herr eczema is frightful.

10:21am Jack messages Tiny

Is Herr Eczema an ex-husband?

10:28am Tiny messages Jack

No, it's a skin complaint. You can get cream for it, I think.

Tiny

10:32am Jack messages Tiny

Right. Thanks.

Jack

PS It's not so much a case of struggling to find the right girl, as only having been here one week! Crikey Tiny, I'd have to be a fast mover to have snagged myself a girlfriend this quickly!

10:36am Tiny messages Jack

I'll keep my ear to the ground for a girlfriend for you. I'll get Mel on the case too. I'm pretty sure Mel's seeing a fella but she's dead cagey about it; doesn't tell me anything. Still, she's good at matching people up. She uses crystals and astronomy.

10:40am Jack messages Tiny

Don't fret about the girlfriend thing Tiny. I haven't got time for one anyway what with this show! See you later.

Jack

PS I think it's astrology. Astronomy is Brian Cox. Astrology is Russell Grant.

PPS Come to think of it Russell Grant looks a bit like Kitty. I knew Kitty reminded me of someone.

11:57am Christian Schmidt messages Jack

Hello Jack. Donald gave me your number. If you're at the skittles later, could we have a chat? Nothing heavy.

Christian

12:45pm Dick Rump messages Jack

Hi Jack. Dick Rump here. I mainly look after the lighting and sound at the theatre but I'm helping put the programme content together on this one. Howard Cobham usually does it but he's got all sorts of other stuff going on. Going to go for a three colour A5 format. A4 just gets a bit pricey y'know. Sykes's in Bamburgh do a great job with the printing. The chap that owns it used to do a bit of choreography for us until we ended up with that clog-wearing hippie Robin Olsen.

Any time before 21st Jan will be sound.

Cheers

Dick

12:48pm Jack messages Chloe

Chloe.

A quick survey for you.

In your opinion, in the amateur theatre society you perform in, which of the following would you say are consistently displayed amongst its members?*:

    a. Insecurity

    b. Forgetfulness

    c. Disorganised thinking

    d. Delusional Schizophrenia

    e. Poor grooming and hygiene

    f. Stupidity

*(feel free to apply a ranking from 1-10 with 10 placing the cast on a spectrum and potentially a danger to others):

12:58pm Chloe messages Jack

    a. 10

    b. 8

c. 8

d. 9x2

e. 9

f. 8.5

1:05pm Jack messages Dick Rump

Hi Dick.

Thanks for getting in touch.

In your message, I think you may have omitted to say what it is you want from me by the 21st .

Cheers

Jack

1:20pm Dick Rump messages Jack

Hahahaha. Sorry.

Your Biog.

Cheers

1:22pm Jack messages Chloe

The word 'Biog' mean anything to you? Someone called Dick just messaged me, asking for mine. Is it a typo? Does he want my toilet? That's kinda niche.

Jack

1:28pm Chloe messages Jack

A better definition of niche is what you and Jen did with the shot glasses at ten-pin bowling.

Chloe

PS I think Dick wants you to write your biography for the programme; a piece about how thrilled you are to be appearing in the show etc. Sometimes people mention their jobs, that sort of thing. They're always dull. I doubt the audience ever read them. Oh and they'll want you to write it in the third person. Y'know 'Jack is pleased to be kissing Jo-Ann Pinchley-Cooke…'

1:35pm Jack messages Chloe

Jack's familiar with third person writing. Jack often writes in the third person when referring to his acquaintance Chloe. e.g. 'Jack used to like his friend Chloe'.

Jack

PS Jack has a rehearsal at 4pm, so Jack is going to have a quick nap now.

PPS Jack senses that his friend Chloe has issues with Jo-Ann Pinchley-Cooke, especially when it comes to her kissing Jack (which she hasn't done yet).

1:41pm Chloe messages Jack

Chloe knows where Jack is staying. Chloe plans to sneak into Jack's room while he's snoozing and tattoo 'I love Jen' on his butt.

1:44pm Jack messages Dick

Hi Dick

The 21st is the day after tomorrow for the biog. OK, well I'll get something to you. I might have to keep it short.

Cheers

Jack

2:41pm Jo-Ann Pinchley-Cooke messages Jack

Donald has told me I've got to rehearse in my costume from now on. I spend the whole show in a bloody basque! He reckons I need to be comfortable with it and that it's best for everyone. Best for him more like! He's such a perv. Anyway, can you keep him away from me? He's way too touchy-feely. And that Tim Waddle. And Trevor.

Don't forget our strategy later at skittles! We'll make a fab pair!

Jo-Ann xxxxxxxxxx

3:45pm Jack messages Jo-Ann Pinchley-Cooke

I can't promise I'll be able to protect you but at least you don't have to worry about me: I only have eyes for Val.

Christ, I'd better get a move on.

Jack

3:46pm Jo-Ann Pinchley-Cooke messages Jack

LMAO xxx

6:34pm Jack messages Chloe

Well, that was an interesting rehearsal. Donald insisted that Jo-Ann wear her costume throughout this afternoon's rehearsal so she'd 'feel comfortable in it'. She wears a basque for pretty much the whole show. She'd have been more comfortable being lowered into the lion enclosure at Whipsnade. As it happened, the whole thing backfired. A sweating Donald clearly couldn't concentrate and earned a rebuke from Mary. Trevor came up to the rehearsal room and explained he needed to sit in to make sure his set 'reflected the briefs' (yup, he used the plural). At one point in the show, Jo-Ann has to get herself into the pose of Rodin's 'Thinker'. Tim Waddle took it upon himself to slide in behind her and, after placing her hand on her chin, bent her over slightly at the waist. It was all a bit unseemly. The end result was that the rehearsal was largely a write off. Skittles in a minute. Need to get ready.

6:45pm Chloe messages Jack

Good luck!

PS Sliding in behind someone to help them get into position… hmmm… sounds an awful lot like you teaching Jen how to bowl the other week. If I'd been in Jen's position, I think I'd have felt compelled to get a pregnancy test afterwards.

PPS Unlike Miss J-A P-C, I don't think Jen was uncomfortable with it. She was a very willing pupil.

PPPS I'm pretty sure you even winked when you told her which fingers went in which holes.

6:49pm Jack messages Chloe

What?!!! I wouldn't do anything that cringeworthy.

This is a wind-up. I don't remember any of this.

6:51pm Chloe messages Jack

It's probably best that way. Hopefully Jen will be hazy about it too. Although at some point, she'll get a reminder from the dry cleaners to pick her top up. At this juncture, some of the night's shenanigans might come rushing back to her.

Do the words SHOT GLASSES, BRA, BOXERS... mean anything to you?

6:54pm Jack messages Chloe

What?!!!

NO THEY DON'T!

6:56pm Jack messages Chloe

Oh wait…

6:57pm Jack messages Chloe

I've gotta get downstairs.

WE NEED TO TALK ABOUT THIS LATER!

Don't get tired. Drink plenty of coffee. Keep lights bright. Play upbeat music. You need to help me put a message together for Jen. In fact you can draft it while I'm skittling. Aim for a grovelling apology but ensure it's clear that it was just a high-jinx night and that there shouldn't be any obligation on either party to develop what was a bit of drunken flirting into anything more permanent i.e. make it clear and say sorry but keep it light.

Thanks.

J

7:02pm Chloe messages Jack

I think I've grasped the briefs.

C

PS … oh wait… no, that was you.

7:05pm Chloe messages Jack

How about…

Hi Jen. I think I may have been overly 'playful' the other week at ten-pin bowling. When I asked you to see if you could remove a shot glass from my boxers and ONLY touch glass and no skin, you failed. As such, I now demand that we be made husband and wife, purchase a dog, and buy a small holding in the countryside.

Xxxxxxx

7:14pm Chloe messages Jack

Or…

Hey my little cupcake. After you retrieved the shot glass from my boxers and invited me to do the same trick but with the glass inside your bra, I can't look at a bottle of Jägermeister or a coat hook, without thinking of you. It's driving me crazy. Say you'll be mine?

Xxxxxxx

7:28pm Chloe messages Jack

Or…

You've *bowled* me over.

Grab yourself a *turkey*.

Xxxxxxx

(not sure about the italics – it reinforces the points nicely but could be seen as patronising)

7:35pm Jack messages Chloe

No, no and no (and yes, no, I dunno).

7:38pm Chloe messages Jack

If I'm to drink endless cups of coffee to stay awake for midnight chats, I hope your repertoire gets better.

No wonder you don't have a girlfriend.

Chloe

7:42pm Jack messages Chloe

Skittle selection underway. It turns out I'm no good at cheating.

7:43pm Chloe messages Jack

You're being too hard on yourself - you cheated on Deborah Long without her finding out… oh wait, or was that Mike?

C

7:44pm Jack messages Chloe

My first coin toss got away from me and landed at Kitty Cooper's feet. While I stooped to retrieve it, he made a noise like only Kenneth Williams in his pomp, could. By which time everyone could see that my coin was a head.

Jack

PS I never cheated on Mike.

7:46pm Chloe messages Jack

So, who's your bowling partner? J-A P-C?

C

7:47pm Jack messages Chloe

No. Trevor. At which point, I should have bailed from the evening (and my life).

Jack

7:49pm Chloe messages Jack

Good retort. Much better. A return to form. I'll have another coffee so I'm ready for you later.

(winks/snogs/bra fumbles)

C

7:52pm Chloe messages Jack

Oh, talking of bra fumbles, do you remember showing off to Jen that you could undo her bra with one hand through her top? It took you fifteen attempts but you eventually managed it.

I mean, to be fair, you've done the bra thing to me too (just before my speech at MY WORK AWARDS CEREMONY!).

C

PS I now wear ones with three hooks – take that as a deterrent.

7:54pm Jack messages Chloe

I don't remember doing that on bowling night.

I do remember doing it to you on your awards night and you not having chance to do it back up.

You adopted the weirdest pose when you were speaking to the room; slightly hunched over, shoulders forward, arms bent, with your elbows tucked in at your sides. It was the best impression of someone water divining I've ever seen. That, or a hunchback playing the castanets.

Jack

PS When's this year's awards? I'll put it in my diary.

7:56pm Chloe messages Jack

Any more of that and I'll be clamping my diary shut on *your* castanets!

(scratch that – that sounded a bit weird).

Ewww

C

8:04pm Jack messages Chloe

Breaking News! J-A P-C is crap at cheating too! She's ended up with Tim Waddle. He's stood next to her explaining what constitutes a good bowling action. There's a lot of knee bending going on. Jo-Ann is hopeless at telling her face NOT to do what her brain is thinking. She's looking at him like she's been handed an ice cream with a turd poking out, instead of a flake.

Jack

8:10pm Chloe messages Jack

Personally I've always preferred Mister Shitty to Mister Whippy.

Chloe

8:22pm Jack messages Chloe

Tim Waddle (the creepy Rodin guy) has the most ridiculous flourish to his bowling action. Upon releasing the ball, he contorts himself so one of his ears is about 3cm off the surface of the lane, while performing a full body twist, culminating with one leg pointing vertically toward the ceiling (complete with pointed toe).

On the last round, I wasn't the only one who suspected he may have followed through. Glances were exchanged. The room fell completely silent on Waddle's next turn. People held their breath. Literally held their breath.

Jack

8:25pm Jo-Ann Pinchley-Cooke messages Jack

Hey Jack. Look across the room. I'm doing my best impression of Tim Waddle bowling. Hahahahaha. Seriously, how bloody embarrassing getting paired with that!

What went wrong? We completely screwed up the coin toss! You got Trevor and I got Waddle.

I'm going to have to get very, very drunk.

You up for after-hours drinks? If so, I'll have a quiet word in Tiny's ear.

Talking of Tiny, have you noticed a slight stutter in her bowling action?

Jo-Ann Xxxxxxxx

Btw, in the last round, Christian knocked all the skittles down and Donald rushed over to congratulate him. He did that thing that old people do to the top of children's heads. You know, the awkward ruffle of hair. Anyway, Christian's 'hair' slipped. Did you catch it?

8:30pm Jack messages Jo-Ann Pinchley-Cooke

Hi.

I didn't catch it (or see it). How did I miss that? Must have been monumental; much like the butterfly that flaps its wings in Kansas causing an earthquake in China, Christian's hair shifts, and it triggers a plague of deadly frogs somewhere in Borneo.

Your Waddle impression is uncanny! Don't let him catch you copying him! On second thoughts, let him catch you, it might spice the evening up a bit.

PS Has Howard Cobham had a stroke? He just stands there and drops the ball from waist height. On his last go, it took a full 10 seconds for the ball to make its way to the skittles. I timed it. When it reached, it sort of kissed the far-left skittle, making it rock gently before it settled back in its upright position. What an anti-climax. I reckon on his next go I could make it to the toilet and back before the ball reaches the other end!

8:32pm Jo-Ann Pinchley-Cooke messages Jack

For a number 1 or 2?

8:35pm Jack messages Jo-Ann Pinchley-Cooke

2 (and a shower).

9:15pm Jack messages Chloe

Shit! There's been a bit of drama here. I'm on my way to hospital with Val. She's had some sort of an episode. She was fine one minute, then as she was bowling, there was a 'fuck!' as she dived forwards, ball still in hand and slid down the alley, dress up round her armpits, billowing like a parachute. Unlike a parachute, it didn't slow her down though, mainly because Tiny had oiled the lane that afternoon. No one's quite sure if she's hurt from her tumble or whether she had some sort of seizure pre-tumble.

I wouldn't mind but Trevor and me were joint first after an hour's bowling.

9:18pm Jack messages Chloe

I volunteered to go in the ambulance with Val to the hospital. She thought it was lovely of me but I'm fairly sure everyone else was suspicious that I'd taken advantage of the situation to escape from Trevor.

9:20pm Jack messages Chloe

Oh, and Christian Schmidt who'd earlier teamed up in a three with The MacMarys (again) was subsequently yanked from his cosy group and paired up with Trevor. He looked none too pleased about it. Got to go, Val's started hallucinating and the ambulance crew are looking (mildly) concerned.

Jack

9:22pm Chloe messages Jack

Bloody hell. That sounds awful. Keep in touch. Hope everything works out.

Chloe

10:09pm Jen messages Jack

Hey Jack. Surprise!! Where are you? I'm stood outside your place, but I don't think you're home and I'm bloody freezing my shot glasses off here! Hahaha

Jen xx

10:09pm Jack messages Jen

Hi Jen

Er…my house in Hammersmith?

10:11pm Jen messages Jack

Hahaha. You're so funny. No! Priory Lofty or whatever it's called. Left work early. Took me bloody ages to get here. Why is it so cold here?! Where are you? Come get me. I'm gasping for a drink and a radiator!

xxx

10:13pm Jack messages Chloe

To say I have somewhat of a situation here would be an understatement. Henry Kissinger would feel out of his depth with this one.

J

10:16pm Chloe messages Jack

Are you at the hospital yet?

Hope everything's OK?

What situation?

Chloe

10:18pm Jack messages Chloe

Hard to believe my night could get any worse right?

WRONG!

'How wrong', I hear you ask?

Try this on for size…

JEN HAS TURNED UP

TO NORTHUMBERLAND

TO MY HOUSE

Jack

PS Keep drinking coffee. Add vodka. You ain't going to bed yet lady.

PPS Pray for me.

10:19pm Chloe messages Jack

Oh, this is priceless! It's like a fairy-tale! Hahahahaha

PS I'll open a sauvignon to celebrate!

10:21pm Jo-Ann Pinchley-Cooke messages Jack

Hey. Hope Val's OK?

Hugs

Jo-Ann xxxxxx

10:23pm Jo-Ann Pinchley-Cooke messages Jack

OMG. Tim has just SOILED HIMSELF!!!!!

Before his ball had reached the skittles he scurried off like one of those ridiculous long-distance walkers: taking fairy steps at a hundred miles an hour while clenching his butt cheeks together.

WTF?!!

Hugs

Jo-Ann xxxxxx

10:23pm Jack messages Jen

Hi Jen. Er... cool.

Thing is, my house wasn't ready to move into so I've taken a room at the local pub – which is great by the way.

Problem though – I'm on my way to hospital (long story) and not sure when I'll make it back to the pub. The cast of the show I'm rehearsing for, are having a skittles night in the bar. You'll have passed the pub; right by the village green – The Hunter's Arms. Head there, thcy have a real fire, you'll soon warm up. It's quite late, I take it you were going to stay the night? If so, do you want me to book you a room at the pub? I'll ring the landlady if you like? I'm afraid there's nothing else for miles. Let me know.

Jack

10:25pm Jen messages Jack

Hospital? God are you OK?!

Yes I'll need to stay at least one night. Thanks.

Or should I come to the hospital?

Jen xx

10:27pm Jack messages Jen

Yeah I'm fine, it's my friend who we called the ambulance for.

No, don't come to the hospital, it's miles away!

I'll get you booked in at The Hunter's. When you get there ask for a woman called Tiny. Tell her you're my friend.

It'll probably be a really late one at the hospital, so I'll see you at breakfast? 9am?

Jack

10:28pm Jen messages Jack

That's amazing. Thanks Jack. I owe you.

See you tomorrow

Jen xxx

10:30pm Jack messages Jo-Ann Pinchley-Cooke

Hey Jo-Ann

Tim Waddle! Hilarious!!!

I want to hear the full story tomorrow (plus any other gossip).

We're at the hospital. Val seems a bit better. They're just taking her to find a bed now.

I'll keep in touch.

Jack

(Tim Waddle - hahahahaha)

10:32pm Jack messages Tiny

Hi Tiny

I tried ringing but I'm guessing you were skittling! A friend of mine from London has turned up out of the blue. I've sent her to the pub. Could you sort a room out for her?

Cheers

Jack

10:42pm Tiny messages Jack

Hi Jack

No rooms left I'm afraid. Trevor took the last one. The old couple are in Petunia, I've put Trevor in Palm and you're already in Pansy.

Tiny

10:44pm Jack messages Tiny

Trevor? What?! Can't he just get a taxi home? Otherwise my friend has no chance of finding a room tonight.

10:47pm Tiny messages Jack

Not that simple. Trevor's wife's kicked him out. I think he was caught showing Mel his wood store (if you catch my drift).

Anyway, don't worry, I've told your 'friend' she can bunk in with you. I've given her the spare key. She's up there now. Gotta go, it's my turn to bowl!

Tiny x

10:53pm Chloe messages Jack

What's happening? Everything OK? I'm getting a bit squiffy here.

10:58pm Jen messages Jack

Turns out we'll see each other before breakfast!!!!

Wow! I don't think I've ever seen so much chintz! Springy mattress though. Thanks for telling Tiny I could stay in your room. You're my hero! I think I'll head down to the bar, sit in front of the fire, and get a few drinks down me – it's been a long day!

Hope your friend is OK.

See you later

Jen xxx

(No snoring! Or being naughty!)

11:05pm Jack messages Tiny

Hi Tiny

I feel the need to point out she's a friend and not a 'friend'.

Also, it didn't seem relevant before but is my bed king, double or queen-sized?

11:08pm Tiny messages Jack

All I know is that it was ex-show home. All the bedroom furniture is. It's made slightly smaller so as to make the rooms look bigger apparently.

Got to run, some idiot's made a right mess of the Gents'

Tiny x

Someone just likened Kitty Cooper to a bowling ball and he flounced off in a huff.

11:12pm Jack messages Jo-Ann Pinchley-Cooke

Hey Jo-Ann

Thought you'd like to know, Val is settled in a nice ward. The only bed available was on a men's ward but the nurse has assured me if Val has to stay beyond a couple of days they'll find her a different bed. There are just three others (two are asleep and the third seems to think he's a visitor, despite his nurses insisting he gets back into bed). Val must be feeling better cos I just told her that Tim Waddle shat his pants and she laughed so hard it woke the sleeping patients up. She got a ticking off from the nurse. She's currently trying to add a harmony line to the beeping machine she's hooked up to. I think James Starling would be proud.

To say Val's nurse is the no-nonsense sort would be doing her an injustice. She's terrifying. The sort that, despite being obese, lectures you about the need to lose weight.

It's a bit worrying though that Val lost consciousness for that short while. They're going to run some tests tomorrow. Apart from that she seems fine.

Could you let the others know?

Thanks

Jack

PS I'm sorry we screwed up the partnering. You got a crap deal Hahahahahaha

11:17pm Jo-Ann Pinchley-Cooke messages Jack

Thanks hun. Why don't we team up at next Saturday's treasure hunt?

Jo-Ann xxx

11:19pm Jack messages Jo-Ann Pinchley-Cooke

Treasure Hunt? As in *car* treasure hunt? First I've heard of it. Will there be a coin toss? If so, I'll practise. I'm not getting into a confined space with Trevor. And I'm definitely not sharing a car with Waddle Fart-Pants.

No sir-ee.

Jack

11:31pm Jack messages Chloe

I just used 'No sir-ee' in a message. Is there something wrong with me?

Jack

11:33pm Chloe messages Jack

Darn tootin'.

C

11:36pm Jack messages Chloe

Val's asleep so I'm heading back. Back to a bed which has Jen in it.

Wish me luck.

Jack

11:42pm Chloe messages Jack

Er... run that by me again. For a moment there I was convinced you mentioned (all casual-like) that Jen is in your bed.

Yup I've looked back and re-read. Jen, it would appear, is waiting in your bed. I hate to ask the obvious but...

HOW?

WHEN?

WHY?

WHY?

WHY?

Chloe

PS WHY?

11:44pm Jack messages Chloe

Forget that. What does one do in this situation? Top and tail? Or back-to-back?

Jack

11:48pm Chloe messages Jack

You're asking me as if this is something I do regularly. Frankly, I resent the insinuation.

Chloe

11:52pm Jack messages Chloe

It'll be OK. She messaged me and told me not to be naughty.

11:55pm Chloe messages Jack

When someone says, 'don't be naughty', what they're really saying is 'it's OK to be naughty', 'I want you to be naughty', 'please be naughty', 'I'll be naughty back', 'I'll be your naughty nurse' etc.

Chloe

11:58pm Jack messages Chloe

What if she's naked?

12:01am Chloe messages Jack

For Christ's sake Jack, she's not going to be naked. We're talking about the woman who wouldn't pee in front of her live-in boyfriend. Just get back to the pub and get on with it.

12:03am Jack messages Chloe

I'm not mad about the phrase 'get on with it'.

Jack

12:05am Chloe messages Jack

How about 'Get on it'?

hahahahaha

Chloe

PS If Jen's lying facing into the middle of the bed, it rules out the back-to-back option. I know I'm stating the obvious but forewarned is forearmed as they say.

PPS I bet Jen has a nice ass. Let me know.

12:07am Jack messages Chloe

I'm not listening. STOP MESSAGING!

Jack

1:04am Jack messages Chloe

Right… I'm back… and I'm in bed…

1:05am Jack messages Chloe

… so far, so good.

1:06am Jack messages Chloe

CHLOE! Why aren't you responding?

J

1:08am Chloe messages Jack

At 12:07am you messaged me saying 'STOP MESSAGING'.

I'm getting mixed signals here.

Chloe

PS Which way is she facing? Into you or away from you?

1:10am Jack messages Chloe

Away. It's all fine.

J

1:11am Chloe messages Jack

Is she naked?

1:11am Jack messages Chloe

What? No! I dunno! I didn't look. I just slid under the sheet, with stealth. Commando-style.

1:12am Chloe messages Jack

What? So *you're* naked?!

1:14am Jack messages Chloe

What? No!

Oh bollocks, I've left the light on in the bathroom!

Hang on…

1:15am Chloe messages Jack

FFS. Shambles. I'm dealing with an amateur here.

Chloe

1:16am Jack messages Chloe

SHE'S NAKED!

1:17am Chloe messages Jack

WHAT?! NO WAY!

1:19am Jack messages Chloe

YES WAY!

NAKED!

1:21am Chloe messages Jack

Alright! No need to panic. You've seen naked women before. I mean you've seen ME naked for Christ's sake!

1:24am Jack messages Chloe

What?! No I haven't! When?

1:25am Chloe messages Jack

In the sauna in Austria when we went skiing. My towel dropped.

C

1:27am Jack messages Chloe

I didn't know your towel had dropped. I didn't see anything.

J

1:29am Chloe messages Jack

Really? Thank God for that. It was January and I was carrying a few winter pounds.

C

PS To be honest, now I come to think of it, I'm a bit offended you didn't notice.

1:31am Jack messages Chloe

We're getting SIDE-TRACKED here.

I don't know if you've forgotten, but there's a naked Jen in my bed!

1:33am Chloe messages Jack

Are you absolutely sure she's naked?

1:34am Jack messages Chloe

Course I'm bloody sure! I know what a naked woman looks like!!

J

1:35am Chloe messages Jack

What happened to stealth?!

1:36am Jack messages Chloe

I didn't think I needed to be so careful. She was asleep. I couldn't help noticing – first her neck, then her bare shoulders, then her bare back and then her bare butt.

1:37am Chloe messages Jack

What's her butt like?

C

1:38am Jack messages Chloe

I dunno! I didn't shine a torch on it!

J

1:39am Chloe messages Jack

I mean, is it flat, or bubble shaped? Is she tanned?

C

1:40am Jack messages Chloe

What?! I'm not sure. Flat maybe. Yes flat (I think). Looked reasonably tanned. Hard to say.

1:41am Chloe messages Jack

It's probably a flattering light. Get a picture.

1:42am Jack messages Chloe

I'M NOT GETTING A PICTURE!

1:43am Jack messages Chloe

SHIT! She's stirring.

1:44am Chloe messages Jack

Are you sure that's the only thing stirring right now?

C

1:45am Jack messages Chloe

If she wakes up, I'll just tell her I'm messaging the cast to update them on Val's condition.

Jack

1:46am Chloe messages Jack

You could do. Or you could just tell her you're messaging me.

Are you ashamed of me now?

Yesterday you were sending kisses and putting my bins out (that sounded wrong).

What's changed? Has this fair maiden stolen you from me? I'm sure my heart will break!

1:48am Jack messages Chloe

Yeah, yeah, yeah.

I'm being careful. Jen's the jealous type! You said so yourself!

J

1:51am Chloe messages Jack

I did? Oh, yeah, I did.

1:52am Jack messages Chloe

Have you never seen 'Dangerous Women Who Kill'?

J

1:53am Chloe messages Jack

Is that the one where you've got a clear 20 minutes when the adverts come on? (5 minutes of adverts followed by 15 minutes where they recap the 15 minutes you watched before the adverts started?).

C

1:54am Jack messages Chloe

Yes.

1:55am Chloe messages Jack

Yes. Once.

C

1:57am Jack messages Chloe

Oh God, she's moving again!

J

1:58am Chloe messages Jack

Bloody hell Jack, she's not Aileen Wuornos!

2:01am Jack messages Chloe

New approach – I'm going to turn my phone off and pretend to be asleep. I'll be pretending cos there's no chance I'm going to get any actual sleep.

2:03am Chloe messages Jack

Well no. Not if the praying mantis you've jumped into bed with has anything to do with it.

2:04am Jack messages Chloe

Funny.

Night Chloe.

J

2:05am Chloe messages Jack

Night Jack.

C

PS Get a picture before you turn your phone off.

2:06am Jack messages Chloe

No.

J

PS I did see you naked.

PPS I was too gentlemanly to comment at the time.

2:07am Chloe messages Jack

Really?

C

2:08am Jack messages Chloe

Yes.

Why the italics?

J

2:08am Chloe messages Jack

I'm whispering.

C

2:08am Jack messages Chloe

Right. Good idea… Thanks.

I'm going now.

Definitely.

Night.

2:09am Chloe messages Jack

Night.

C

2:10am Jack messages Chloe

PS - you have a decent enough butt.

J

2:10am Chloe messages Jack

Awww thanks.

PS – I know.

Chloe x

9.

8 days 'til curtain up

9:03am Chloe messages Jack

Hey. Any funny business happen last night? I'm picturing you both lying there looking content while smoking cigarettes and telling each other how wonderful it was.

9:08am Jack messages Chloe

I got virtually no sleep!

9:12am Chloe messages Jack

Awww, sorry.

C

9:14am Jack messages Chloe

No need. You misunderstand. The woman was insatiable!

Forget prudish. Nothing prudish about her whatsoever!

I'd get out of bed, but I fear my legs would be too wobbly to support me.

9:15am Chloe messages Jack

Nice try but it ain't April 1st

9:17am Jack messages Chloe

Put it this way, if anything happened, it was without my knowledge.

9:19am Chloe messages Jack

Pretty sure that's a criminal offence. But then, failing to stay awake during a woman's advances should also be a criminal offence.

So, what's happening right now? Is she facing you? Is she looking at you all starry-eyed? Has she let the covers deliberately slip, so her forbidden fruit is only just concealed?

Right now, I bet you're telling her that you're messaging the group (again).

C

9:22am Jack messages Chloe

None of the above. She's not here.

We'd originally agreed to meet for breakfast at 9am before bed-sharing was imposed on us. I'd best haul my ass out of bed and go and catch up with her. I'll message you later.

Jack

PS And don't think I don't know how much you're enjoying all this.

9:25am Chloe messages Jack

'All work and no play make Jack a dull boy.'

9:28am Jack messages Chloe

Shit! Shit! Shit!

9:28am Chloe messages Jack

Is that an instruction? A bit weird. Besides, I'm usually a once-a-day girl. Don't think I've ever managed three.

9:29am Jack messages Chloe

I just burst in on Jen peeing!

I shouted 'SHIT! SORRY!' and bolted.

9:29am Chloe messages Jack

What did Jen say?

9:29am Jack messages Chloe

She didn't *say* anything.

She *screamed* 'SOMEONE PEEING HERE!'.

Oh, and she was still NAKED!!

9:30am Chloe messages Jack

Don't suppose you got a decent view of her butt? She'd be sitting down I suppose. Unless she was doing the crouch hovering thing? No, she wouldn't be doing that, it's not a public toilet.

9:31am Jack messages Chloe

Can't help but think you're failing to grasp the gravity of this situation.

Jack

PS She's mortified I've seen her weeing, but it appears she's not bothered about me seeing her naked!

WTF?

9:32am Chloe messages Jack

There was something I meant to say just now but I've forgotten what it was. I think it was important. And helpful.

No, it's gone. Sorry.

9:32am Chloe messages Jack

Hahahahahahahahahahahahahahahahahahahahahaha

(It just came back to me)

PS hahahaha

9:33am Jack messages Chloe

I've shouted through the door to her that I'm heading down for breakfast. How many times do you think I need to say sorry? I'm up to seven already but it doesn't feel enough.

9:34am Chloe messages Jack

It's your room and your toilet. I'd have turned it around and blamed it on her. Tell her you're shy, tell her you've never seen a naked woman before and now you're traumatised.

9:35am Jack messages Chloe

I can't.

J

9:36am Chloe messages Jack

Why not?

C

9:38am Jack messages Chloe

Well…a few months ago, I may have blurted out that I'd seen you naked in a sauna.

J

9:41am Chloe messages Jack

Right.

OK…I'm struggling to imagine how any conversation would suddenly reach a relevant point where you'd dive in with your naked-Chloe-in-the-sauna-story. What on earth was the trigger that made you think of me?!!!

C

9:44am Jack messages Chloe

A plate of biscuits was handed round, and the only ones left were two marshmallow teacakes and a chocolate ring.

Jack

9:47am Chloe messages Jack

As ice goes, the slither you're skating on right now is very, very thin.

Chloe

PS I'm curious. When you told your Chloe-naked-in-the-sauna story, how did you describe me?

9:51am Jack messages Chloe

I remember exactly what I said:

'Seeing Chloe that day, in all her radiant beauty reminded me of Proverbs 3:15 *She is more precious than rubies; nothing you desire can compare with her.*'

The room, paused for reflection and I added: 'and contrary to popular belief, the tattoo of an exclamation mark on her left butt cheek, is not there to serve as a warning, but to cleverly disguise the presence of a small mole (and to distract from the lack of a thigh gap).'

Jack

PS I think it was rubies. It might have been rabies.

9:52am Chloe messages Jack

Funny.

I don't have any tattoos.

9:53am Jack messages Chloe

I know. What can I say? I felt the story could do with some embellishment.

J

9:54am Chloe messages Jack

I'm not happy that you thought my body needed to be 'embellished'.

C

9:55am Jack messages Chloe

Alright Aphrodite, no need to get jealous.

PS I'm at breakfast now. The old couple aren't around. I'm hoping they've gone home, so it frees up a room.

9:56am Chloe messages Jack

Who's jealous!!?

And of who?!?

Jen??! With her tanned, lean, neat ass?

Christ, you're right. I am jealous.

C

10:04am Jack messages Chloe

Damn! Tiny just said the old couple merely had an early breakfast. They're here for at least one more night.

10:06am Chloe messages Jack

Which one did you take?

10:07am Jack messages Chloe

?

10:09am Chloe messages Jack

Which biscuit did you go for?

10:11am Jack messages Chloe

None. Didn't fancy any of them.

J

PS I hovered momentarily over the chocolate ring, but it looked as if someone had already had a go at it, so I passed.

10:13am Jack messages Chloe

Jen's just appeared in the breakfast room. Clothed. I'll message later.

J

10:17am Chloe messages Jack

Meh. I may be free later, I may not.

C

10:27am Christian Schmidt messages Jack

We didn't get to talk last night. Could you come to the theatre fifteen minutes early tonight?

11:14am Jack messages Christian Schmidt

Hi mate.

Yeah I'm not sure. I'm taking afternoon tea with The Queen and afterwards I'm meeting Sandra Bullock for a couple of pints in The Hunter's. I'm also scheduled to present a lifetime achievement award to Noel Edmonds so it's kind of a busy day.

I'll do my best.

Cheers

Jack

11:16am Christian Schmidt messages the cast & crew

Cast and crew,

I'm sure I don't need to remind you that in less than two weeks' time, we will be performing the show in front of a paying audience. Therefore, I request that everyone make an effort to get to rehearsals on time. Also, if at any point during a rehearsal you are not required to be acting, singing or dancing, you should remain quiet and afford your fellow actors the respect they deserve.

Christian

11:16am Jack messages Christian Schmidt

The audience has to pay?

Jack

11:17am Jo-Ann Pinchley-Cooke messages Jack

Hey dude. Did you just get a message from Christian?

Jo-Ann xxxxxxx

PS Sorry you didn't make it back in time for drinks last night. We missed you.

PPS Who was that girl in the bar with the cute ass? She seemed to know you.

11:18am Jack messages Jo-Ann Pinchley-Cooke

I got two messages!

In the first, he said he wanted to meet with me to discuss something.

In the second, which I suspect is the one you've also received, he told me to be quiet and punctual.

J

11:20am Jo-Ann Pinchley-Cooke messages Jack

Who does he think he is?! He's not part of the production team. What an arse.

I think we're doing the kissing tonight. I'm not wearing that bloody basque again though. It was proper pinching me in places a girl doesn't want to be pinched.

Oh I might be a bit late; my hair stylist has shifted my appointment back half an hour.

J-A xxxxxxx

11:22am Jack messages Jo-Ann Pinchley-Cooke

I hope you've cleared your hair appointment with our new attendance monitor! Otherwise you risk being picked off by Sniper Schmidt.

11:23am Tiny messages Jack

Hey lover boy. Have you had the message from Christian?

Just when I thought he couldn't get any more of an dickhead…

11:24am Jack messages Tiny

Yes I did.

Shall we all turn up about 6 minutes late?

Jack

11:24am Tiny messages Jack

YES! Where have you been all my life?!

11:25am Jack messages Tiny

I was supposed to meet you twenty years ago but my poor timekeeping, as highlighted in the group message, means I'm running a bit late.

11:27am Jack messages Val

Hey, Val. How're you feeling today?

Any idea what time visiting hours are?

Jack

11:28am Jack messages Val

Now I think of it, that was a stupid message from me. You're probably not allowed your phone. I'll pluck up some courage and ring your nurse.

Jack

PS I'll ring anonymously and use a burner phone so she can't trace the call.

11:30am Val messages Jack

HAHA. I have my phone. It's the only thing keeping me sane. I've been doing some on-line clothes shopping this morning. I've bought a new frock. You know that one Liz Hurley wore that time with the safety pins? It's like that, but orange. I've put your name and the pub down as the delivery address. Hope that's OK.

Visiting is 2:30pm but don't worry about coming all the way over here darl. They're definitely keeping me in tonight but there have been mutterings from the doctor about going home tomorrow if my bastard bloods come back OK.

Val

Oh, who won the skittles?

11:32am Jack messages Val

I don't know, I'll find out.

I'll see you later, probably around 3pm.

Do you want anything?

Jack

11:33am Val messages Jack

Heat magazine and some sanitary towels (but only if you have time).

Val x

11:34am Jack messages Val

Er… Okaaay.

Right you are.

Jack

11:35am Jack messages Chloe

Val wants me to bring her some sanitary towels. Discuss.

Jack

11:37am Chloe messages Jack

Bloody hell. Could it be she's had a gender-change operation sometime in the past? Would that mean periods? Sounds unlikely. I dunno.

Chloe

11:39am Jack messages Chloe

Nope. Tiny told me she hasn't, and Tiny wouldn't get something like that wrong. She knows everyone's business.

J

11:41am Chloe messages Jack

Did you ask Val why she wanted them?

C

11:43am Jack messages Chloe

No, of course not!

141

11:44am Chloe messages Jack

Why not?

11:46am Jack messages Chloe

I don't know. She's in hospital isn't she. And I don't want to look stupid.

Jack

11:48am Chloe messages Jack

You don't think turning up to an all-male ward in a hospital while waving a packet of sanitary towels above your head will make you look a tad stupid?

11:51am Jack messages Chloe

Fair point. I'll ask her.

12:13pm Chloe messages Jack

This seems to be taking a while. What did she say?

C

12:16am Jack messages Chloe

I'm still composing the message. It's not easy.

12:21pm Chloe messages Jack

What are you struggling with? – do you need help with your name?

For crying out loud! Just ask her what she needs them for. It's not difficult.

C

12:25pm Jack messages Val

Hi, Val. Me again. Look, this is probably a really stupid question… I know that you're a woman… and women from time to time need things that women need… it's just that some women need things more than other women need them… I'm not saying that those women who need them less, are any less womanly because of it… no… not at all… the rate of consumption of things that women need should not be an indicator of femininity… in fact, I've heard it said that women who need fewer of these things are generally happier for it…

Jack

PS Why do you need the sanitary towels?

12:27pm Val messages Jack

They're on my list of props for the show I'm to appear in after this one.

Val

12:28pm Jack messages Val

I'll see you at 3pm.

Jack

12:30pm Jack messages Jo-Ann Pinchley-Cooke

Hey Jo-Ann

Who won the skittles last night?

Jack

12:32pm Jo-Ann Pinchley-Cooke messages Jack

Hi babes.

Trevor and Christian.

Technically I reckon half the trophy is yours. Lol.

It looked like the trophy might have been heading my way until skid-marks Waddle let it all go.

Jo-Ann

(So…who's the girl? You didn't say you had a girlfriend).

12:36pm Jack messages Jo-Ann Pinchley-Cooke

She's not my girlfriend, just a friend from London. She just turned up out of the blue yesterday! There weren't any rooms free because Trevor's staying at the Hunter's now (via his wife's boot). Jen's had to bunk in with me and it's all a bit awkward to be honest.

Jack

PS Would you sleep naked next to a bloke who is just a friend?

12:38pm Jo-Ann Pinchley-Cooke messages Jack

Yeah, OK. When? Today? It'll need to be before five. My place or yours? Lol

Seriously you can stay in my spare room if you'd rather not share with your friend.

Jo-Ann

12:41pm Jack messages Jo-Ann Pinchley-Cooke

Thanks, but I'm not sure your boyfriend would approve!

Jack

12:43pm Jo-Ann Pinchley-Cooke messages Jack

Who says I have a boyfriend? Have you been Facebook-stalking me Jack? Naughty! LMAO

Jo-Ann xxxxxxx

12:45pm Jack messages Jo-Ann Pinchley-Cooke

No! Erm, I think someone mentioned you were in a relationship. I'm not on Facebook.

J

12:47pm Jo-Ann Pinchley-Cooke messages Jack

My boyfriend had to go. Too boring. Always talked about traffic lights. Lol

Jo-Ann

(So there's no boyfriend to beat you up if you still want the spare room for a couple of nights).

12:49pm Jack messages Jo-Ann Pinchley-Cooke

Traffic lights? That's an odd thing to be obsessed with.

I think my friend Jen is only here for one more night, so I think I'll stick it out at The Hunter's. Thanks for the offer though. You're a pal.

J

12:51pm Jo-Ann Pinchley-Cooke messages Jack

No worries.

My ex worked for the council as a traffic-light sequencer. He thought it was fascinating. Trouble is, no one else did.

Jo-Ann

3:08pm Jack messages Chloe

Hi my little teacake.

At the hospital. Val's asleep. I've found out from her scary nurse that she's being allowed home tomorrow. They couldn't really find anything wrong. Her iron levels were down a bit but that's pretty much it.

Anyway, I've been meaning to ask you; is it considered good acting to stamp your foot just as you're delivering a line? Maybe it's something they teach at the RSC or something?

Jack

3:10pm Chloe messages Jack

Hi Tampon-boy.

I've not heard of this. Why?

Chloe

PS You never told me why Val needed sanitary towels.

3:11pm Jack messages Chloe

They're a prop for her next show. Makes sense. We've been asked to source some of the smaller personal props ourselves for this show.

Jack

PS You haven't got a tobacco pipe by any chance?

3:14pm Chloe messages Jack

Bent billiard, Lumberman, Horn, Diplomat, Oom Paul or Gourd Calabash?

3:16pm Jack messages Chloe

Just a normal chimney type.

3:17pm Chloe messages Jack

No, sorry.

C

3:20pm Chloe messages Jack

I'm drumming my fingers on the coffee table while waiting for you to explain the foot-stamping.

'Impatient' from London.

3:23pm Jack messages Chloe

I think I've mentioned the guy in the cast called Brian Barrowman. He's about seventy years old (give or take). He has this thing where he stamps his foot just prior to delivering a line. In fact two of the cast do it. Bill Freynolds is constantly at it too. I assumed it was what professionals do; like a way of alerting the audience that they're about to speak.

No one else seems to have noticed. The two of them have a scene together with a rapid-fire exchange of dialogue. By the time they've got through it you feel like you've sat through a performance of 'Stomp'.

I say rapid-fire; it's not really, on account that neither of them can remember their lines. There's a lot of staring at each other and willing the other on to grasp a line and run with it.

When Bill Freynolds *does* remember a line, he adds an 'h' or more accurately an 'hur' to the front of most of his words, mainly to ones that begin with a consonant e.g. h'Now then my h'child, go get me my h'trumpet.

3:28pm Chloe messages Jack

If that's a line in your show, I'm not coming to see it.

Chloe

PS The foot stamping is weird. I've not come across that before. Ask Donald 'Where's Yer Troosers' what he thinks of it.

3:33pm Chloe messages Jack

What I *have* come across is actors (again, usually older actors) who sort of 'sing' their lines. They add a serious dose of vibrato with a nasal quality and extend all vowels. Hard to type an example but think of a sheep with a cold saying the word 'yes' but holding on to the word for two full seconds and in a pitch two tones up from normal speaking voice.

It sounds like something an old Shakespearean actor might do. Y'know, like Simon Cowell.

C

3:36pm Jack messages Chloe

Simon Callow.

I don't think Simon Cowell has done Shakespeare any more than Simon Callow has done X-Factor.

Jack

3:49pm Chloe messages Jack

Tomato / Tomato.

(that doesn't really work in a message)

Tomaydo / Tomardo.

(better)

3:51pm Jack messages Chloe

Let's call the whole thing off.

PS Yes Bill Freynolds AND Brian Barrowman both sing their lines!

3:52pm Chloe messages Jack

I was bored earlier. Had two no-shows for a house viewing in Tooting.

I used my time wisely though. I found a much kinder review on the Attic Priory Players' website.

Gary McPeter reviews The Attic Priory Players' production of Miss Saigon. 13th April 2009.

'Why does Saigon never sleep at night?' asks US Marine, Chris, played by The Attic Priory Players' very own Christian Schmidt.

Three reasons for Saigon's insomnia immediately spring to mind:

Firstly, as impressive as the helicopter sound effect was, the deafening roar of rotor blades was unleashed on an unsuspecting audience at least five scenes too early, rendering Schmidt's musings about a solo saxophone (which was curiously accompanied by a flute) completely inaudible.

Secondly, further sleep-deprivation was to come for Saigon, when, during Kim's beautiful heart-wrenching 'The Movie in my Mind', something worked loose on Trevor Thwacker's multi-level set causing the complete collapse of Kim's bedroom. Even the band's percussionist couldn't compete with the cacophony of noise, as a dozen or more scaffold poles rained down around a somewhat startled Kim, played by Jo-Ann Pinchley-Cooke. Not to be outdone, the bed's metal headboard waited a full two minutes before deciding it too wished to be at ground floor level.

Thirdly, an exhausted Saigon lost its battle for sleep owing to what must be the poorest attempt at 'The Morning of the Dragon', the world of theatre has ever seen. Admittedly, the song has a fiendish time signature, but this can be no excuse for the seemingly random assault of a cymbal by the deranged drummer. While three bare-chested, overweight men in pantaloons attempted acrobatics (with the inevitable tearing of at least one hamstring), the band made such a poor fist of the score, that the audience could have been forgiven for thinking they'd paid to listen to a five-year-old with a hammer, erect a flat-packed shed.

Staging a musical of the magnitude of Miss Saigon was never going to be straightforward and The Attic Priory Players deserve a measure of credit for tackling it head-on.

Ultimately though, more was bitten off than could ever be chewed.

If a helicopter had landed in the car park during the interval, the theatre exit doors would surely have succumbed to the stampede of those seeking to escape their misery in search of something better elsewhere.

I can't have been alone in thinking 'Why God, Why?'

Miss Saigon runs nightly until 18th April.

3:55pm Jack messages Chloe

What will it take to get you to stop? I'll do anything.

3:57pm Chloe messages Jack

Are you quoting Jen from last night?

3:58pm Jack messages Chloe

Hilarious.

Right, I think I'll come away from the hospital now. Val's snoring is getting embarrassing. There's a family gathered around a patient's bed opposite and they're virtually shouting to make themselves heard.

I've left Val's props in her bedside cabinet.

Jack

3:59pm Jen messages Jack

Hi Jack. Wondered if you wanted to grab a Sunday roast with me in the pub before your rehearsal?

Jen x

4:02pm Jack messages Jen

That's a great idea. Sorry I haven't spent much time with you. I'm just leaving the hospital now, so I'll see you in the bar at about 5:15pm?

I'll probably have a quick wash and brush-up in the room first if you want to make use of the bathroom 'uninterrupted'. Again, sorry about that!

Jack

4:05pm Jen messages Jack

Hey silly. No harm done. I hope you're OK with me sleeping au naturel. I can't bear to be clothed in bed.

I was a bit chilly in bed last night though... any suggestions…?

Jen xx

PS Shall I ask Tiny to keep a couple of roasts back for us? What's your meat preference?

4:09pm Jack messages Jen

Not pork.

4:12pm Jack messages Chloe

My relationship with Jen is moving on apace. We're having a roast dinner together before my rehearsal.

4:13pm Chloe messages Jack

Will there be stuffing?

C

4:14pm Jack messages Chloe

Remind me again why I'm friends with you?

4:16pm Tiny messages Jack

Hey Valentino. Your girlfriend has been telling us how good you are at undoing bras. Mel wants you to have a go at undoing hers cos she reckons you'll have no chance.

Tiny

(Might be best to do it when Trevor's not around though. He's like a lovesick puppy with her at the moment).

4:18pm Jack messages Tiny

By all accounts I'm actually pretty rubbish at undoing bras but please thank Mel for her interest.

Jack

PS Jen isn't my girlfriend.

PPS Stop serving her alcohol – I'm worried about what else she might say.

PPPS I don't mean to be horrible but what the hell does Mel see in Trevor? Mel's a really pretty girl. Bright too. I can't work it out.

4:21pm Tiny messages Jack

No one can understand it. I'll tell you something for nothing though, Mel's well chuffed that you think she's pretty! I've also told her that Jen isn't your girlfriend.

You're full of surprises!

Tiny

Oh, it's a dancing rehearsal tonight! Can't wait!

4:24pm Jack messages Tiny

It's OK for you Tiny, you're our prompt, you don't have to dance! Try not to watch me, I'm a terrible dancer! I don't mind jigging about now and then but not in front of other people. I'm more of a 'private dancer' - y'know like Tina Turner.

4:27pm Tiny messages Jack

Really? From memory, Tina Turner's private dancer wore very little and danced for money with the aid of a pole.

Like I said, you're full of surprises.

Tiny

4:29pm Jack messages Tiny

Oh yeah. I've never really thought about the lyrics before now. I'm not that type of dancer.

Jack

4:31pm Tiny messages Jack

Pity.

6:34pm Jack messages Val

Hey Val. Didn't want to wake you earlier. Hope you're still feeling lots better.

To answer your question, Christian and Trevor won the skittles. It's probably best that way. They can both feel important for five minutes.

Jack

PS Oh, assuming the doctors are still happy for you to come home tomorrow, I'll come and get you. I'll ring the hospital first thing to get an idea of a time.

6:36pm Jack messages Chloe

Dinner was OK. Everything's been smoothed over from this morning. Will be heading over to the theatre in a bit. Christian Schmidt has requested a meeting with me. No idea what it's all about.

I've told Jen she may as well come and watch the rehearsal, otherwise she'll be stuck in the pub on her own, and frankly, the less she talks to Mel the barmaid right now, the better.

We're to learn a dance at tonight's rehearsal; can't say I'm looking forward to that. Reading aloud is one thing but dancing is quite another. What are you up to later?

Jack

6:39pm Chloe messages Jack

Please say you'll video yourself dancing?! Get Jen to record it on her phone.

What type of dancing?

Contemporary? Tap? Ballet? Ballroom? Square? Barn? Morris? Ice?

6:42pm Jack messages Chloe

Dunno. Probably not ice, although I'm getting quite adept at skating whenever I go to the cast toilet. Did I tell you our toilet is outside? The path to it is a death trap whenever the outside temperature gets anywhere close to zero. Yesterday, the toilet itself froze up. It wouldn't flush. It wasn't too much of a surprise since there was ice on the inside of the walls. The toilet building must be breaching at least twenty health and safety regulations. To reach it, you have to go through the wood store (pause to pray there isn't a fire), then strap your skates on to negotiate the path, before heading inside and holding your breath. Makes Indiana Jones' crusades look like a walk in the park.

Jack

PS There will be no video footage of dancing.

6:50pm Chloe messages Jack

I don't remember Harrison Ford whining about having to walk to a toilet.

Keep in touch; there's a lot that could go wrong tonight both at the theatre and in your bedroom. Hahahaha

Chloe

PS Have you snogged Jo-Ann Pinchley-Cooke yet?

6:52pm Jack messages Chloe

In rehearsal or on my own time?

6:53pm Chloe messages Jack

Either!

6:55pm Jack messages Chloe

No.

6:57pm Chloe messages Jack

Well get on with it.

PS to answer your earlier question, I've decided to learn a language so I'm heading to the college in a bit.

6:59pm Jack messages Chloe

Good idea, though we both know you won't stick at it.

What's the language? Spanish? I bet it's Spanish!

7:02pm Chloe messages Jack

German.

7:04pm Jack messages Chloe

Ahhh, the language of love.

7:05pm Chloe messages Jen

Hi Jen. Hope you're having a great time Oup t'North. Jack says it's been lovely to have a familiar face there with him. Between me and you he was a bit peed off with the estate agent and the mix up over his new house not being ready. Honestly, I think he's very touched you made the effort to travel all that way to see him. It's such a pisser you can't stay longer. Tonight's your last night, isn't it? What a pity.

Butt anyway, Jack says that you're heading to rehearsal with him later. They're learning a wee dance. Do me a favour and video Jack dancing on your phone.

Thanks

Chloe

PS What's the show? Jack's been coy about it and given me a right load of ball cock.

7:12pm Jen messages Chloe

Hi Chloe. Lovely to hear from you. Jack was certainly surprised when I turned up yesterday! You should have seen the look on his little face!

To be honest I wasn't sure if I was treading on your toes? You two have always been close and I was never sure if you'd been an item in the past. Or if you wanted to be an item at some point in the future?

Anyway, I'm rambling now. I've got to get going if I'm to make this rehearsal. We have to get there early for some reason. No idea what the show is, Jack hasn't told me anything about it. Will let you know later.

Jen

(Not sure about videoing Jack though. It feels a bit mean).

7:18pm Chloe messages Jen

Jack and me? Hahahaha hahahaha

Not happening - Jack still thinks it's acceptable to wear a fleece. Also, a couple of years ago, he flirted with the idea of joining CAMRA; you know, that club for bearded, social misfits who sit about talking about warm beer.

I told him in no uncertain terms that our friendship would be over if he went down that route. He doesn't even drink ale. In his quest to find a new hobby, he eventually landed on competitive duck herding.

Have fun later.

Chloe

PS Jack and me hahahahaha

7:46pm Jack messages Chloe

There's a nun sat watching our rehearsal.

There's been no explanation as to who she's with, or why she's here.

J

7:47pm Chloe messages Jack

Right. That IS odd.

C

PS Ask her if she's actually climbed *every* mountain, or if she's been fibbing.

7:48pm Jack messages Chloe

The Choreographer is here. Robin Olsen. Bit of a hippie. Long greasy hair in a ponytail. He's wearing those shoes that have a compartment for each toe; the ones that are more like a sock. I'd heard of them but never seen anyone actually wearing them. He's also wearing a lightweight scarf with tassel things on it. You know me, I have a mistrust of indoor scarf-wearers. Seems like a nice fella though.

Jack

PS He seems to be in no rush whatsoever which is making Donald and Schmidt extremely twitchy.

8:34pm Chloe messages Jack

Guten Abend!

Mein Name ist Chloe.

Ich bin sehr attraktiv und Ich habe fantastische Titten.

C

8:40pm Jack messages Chloe

I'm nervous for lesson two.

8:42pm Chloe messages Jack

What's the dancing like? Is it difficult?

C

8:44pm Jack messages Chloe

We've paused to 'catch our breath' as Robin put it. I'd argue it wasn't really necessary since the dancing comprised of going around in pairs in a circle with a bit of weaving in and out.

If you pushed me to pin a style of dance on it, I'd go for 'walking'.

Jack

PS A couple of the others do a bit of a tap routine. The rehearsal room is carpeted.

PPS Robin has worse personal hygiene that Trevor.

PPPS Progress! Robin has a key to the bar and he's more than willing to use it.

8:49pm Chloe messages Jack

Is the nun still there?

C

8:52pm Jack messages Chloe

Yes. Still no idea why she's here or who asked her along.

8:54pm Chloe messages Jack

Are any members of the cast outwardly Catholic?

C

8:56pm Jack messages Chloe

Yes. Bill Freynolds is clutching his rosary beads and is about to perform an exorcism on Christian Schmidt.

What do you mean *'outwardly Catholic?'* WHAT ARE YOU TALKING ABOUT?!

8:58pm Chloe messages Jack

ALRIGHT! Holen Sie sich Ihre Knickers nicht in einer Wendung!

Chloe

9:00pm Jack messages Chloe

Chloe. Here's the thing… using translation software on your phone probably isn't the best way to learn a new language.

Jack

9:02pm Chloe messages Jack

Arschloch.

C

9:03pm Jack messages Chloe

Gotta go back in. Remind me to tell you about my meeting with Christian Schmidt!

Jack

9:15pm Jen messages Jack

Who does the nun belong to?

Jen

PS You're rocking the dance moves.

PPS That looked to be quite a lengthy kiss with your leading lady. Is it supposed to last that long?

10:15pm Jack messages Chloe

We're all back at the pub. Christian is in a mood. He volunteered to be the show's 'Dance Captain'. Robin told him it wasn't necessary but then asked Bill Freynolds to write all of our moves down in case anyone forgets them.

I saw Bill's written record of our moves. It consisted of hundreds of circles, squiggly lines and arrows. It looked like a hybrid of the ancient male and female gender symbols. I'm going to recommend Val adopt it as her own.

Jack

10:17pm Jack messages Chloe

Tim Waddle has started to wear a black polo necked jumper and a trilby. It's very Steven Berkoff. I've found out that Tim is a director as well as an actor and apparently he's unimpressed that Donald gets all the directing gigs. It all stems from when Tim cast Cate Wilson instead of Mary MacMary in a production of Shirley Valentine. Since then, Tim hasn't been allowed to direct anything. It's proper playground stuff this! It's brilliant!

J

PS Gotta go. Trevor is doing a pretty good Willie Nelson on the karaoke machine.

PPS Tiny had an aborted attempt at 'Titanium'. It was more Norman Collier to be fair (you'll need to google him).

10:18pm Jack messages Chloe

When you google him, be sure to focus on the faulty microphone part of his act. His other joke was to impersonate a chicken.

Jack

10:20pm Chloe messages Jack

Seriously, how do you know this stuff? We're virtually the same age and I've never heard of most of your 'cultural' references.

10:24pm Val messages Jack

You're an angel Jack. Thanks for coming by today. Sorry I was asleep. I was completely bolloxed. I won't get any shuteye tonight now; I'm not kidding, the bloke in the bed opposite is snoring like a twattin' walrus!

Val

10:28pm Jack messages Val

How awful.

Val, you've done lots of shows with this group, right? Have you ever seen a nun hanging around the theatre?

10:30pm Val messages Jack

That'll be Pete.

10:32pm Jack messages Val

You're going to have to give me more to go on…

10:34pm Val messages Jack

It's just the theatre ghost. It's a bit misleading because people used to say it was a monk, hence they called him 'Attic Priory Pete'. But then it was agreed that it was actually a woman they'd seen floating about the place. For some reason no one thought to change her name from Pete. I'd have thought

Raphaella or Pam would have been better…you know, something biblical.

Val

10:37pm Jack messages Val

Right… thing is, this was a real person. Sat down, not floating.

A real nun.

J

PS Are you still on those sedatives they gave you yesterday?

10:39pm Val messages Jack

Right. No, I've never seen a nun. I've never seen the bastard ghost either come to think of it.

10:41pm Jack messages Val

OK. Thanks for your help.

10:43pm Val messages Jack

We have lots to catch up on tomorrow. Tiny messaged me to say that:

1. Trevor is playing happy families with Mel.

2. Christian Schmidt is angry about lateness.

3. Your girlfriend has turned up!

I've only been in hospital one day!

Val

10:47pm Jack messages Val

1. Yes (which I find weird).

2. Yes. Very angry.

3. A woman *has* turned up who *isn't* my girlfriend*.

Jack

*I don't have a girlfriend in the same way that I'm not a carpenter.

10:51pm Val messages Jack

Carpenter? What are you on about? You're a strange one. Hahaha

Val x

11:41pm Jack messages Chloe

In bed. All is well.

I developed a system: Jen goes to the bathroom, clothed. Then, she comes back into the bedroom but, before she gets undressed for bed, I go into the bathroom. I spend long enough in there to allow Jen to get herself into bed. I then ask if it's OK to come out. When it's safe, I return to the bedroom, strip down to my boxers and get into bed too.

Jack

11:45pm Chloe messages Jack

Stand aside Alan Turing, there's a new problem-solver on the block.

Chloe

PS What will you give the World tomorrow? A step-by-step guide to climbing stairs?

PPS 'step-by-step' hahahahaha

11:47pm Jack messages Chloe

I just felt skin on skin.

11:48pm Chloe messages Jack

Which part of *Jen's* skin on which part of *your* skin? (This is crucial).

11:49pm Jack messages Chloe

I don't know.

11:50pm Chloe messages Jack

You must know what part of YOUR skin you idiot.

11:51pm Jack messages Chloe

Oh yeah. Course. My back.

11:52pm Chloe messages Jack

So…. You're facing away from Jen?

11:53pm Jack messages Chloe

No I'm facing *towards* Jen. A third person in the room must have touched my back. OF COURSE I'M FACING AWAY!

11:55pm Chloe messages Jack

You'd make a terrible hostage negotiator. No patience.

11:57pm Jack messages Chloe

So…?

11:58pm Chloe messages Jack

So, what? What body part? If you can't work that out Jack there's no hope for you.

I'll simplify it for you.

If her head isn't further down the bed than yours then we can rule out her head and shoulders. It won't be a hip, knee, or foot unless she's an ex-performer with Cirque du Soleil. It won't be a hand because you'd know if it was a hand and there would probably be stroking.

That leaves two options. One of which is an elbow.

Chloe

PS Being pedantic, it's technically three options (and only one of those is an elbow).

PPS Did you ever watch Twin Peaks?

12:00am Jack messages Chloe

Again, why did we become acquainted?

J

12:02am Chloe messages Jack

Because, when you marry Jen, I will give the finest best man's speech out of everyone you know. Mike would think he was hilarious but would in fact be tedious, Katie would be too soppy, and Connor would spend the entire wedding breakfast testing his pulse only to arrive at the conclusion he couldn't go through with it.

C

12:04am Jack messages Chloe

I'll ask the nun to marry Jen and me.

Jack

12:05am Chloe messages Jack

Good idea.

Turn over.

You may now kiss the bride.

Night.

C

12:06am Jack messages Chloe

Night.

J

10.

7 days 'til curtain up

7:44am Chloe messages Jack

It troubles me that you wear boxer shorts.

C

7:47am Jack messages Chloe

I always like to wear something in bed, in case an intruder breaks in, or I'm taken ill.

J

7:49am Chloe messages Jack

No! I mean no one wears boxer shorts these days, whether they're in bed or not. It's jockey shorts now. Tighter fitting so you're not flopping about all over the place. I'm amazed you can still buy boxers.

C

7:53am Jack messages Chloe

I haven't needed to buy any for years. I've owned the pair I'm wearing now from just before I graduated 10 years ago. They're still in great nick.

7:55am Chloe messages Jack

Don't you have the same wallet from when you were like twelve or something too? Why the fascination with keeping stuff until it's obsolete?

C

PS Getting back to boxer shorts in bed, are you worried an intruder might judge you if you're naked? I can reassure you; I don't think they'll pause to mark you out of ten before they cosh you over the head and pinch your wallet.

7:57am Jack messages Chloe

Don't distract me; in my head I'm trying to reverse the bathroom process from last night. I think I'm the one who needs to go to the bathroom first, but I need to wait until Jen's awake. Does that sound about right?

J

7:59am Chloe messages Jack

What difference does it make? You've got your sixty-year-old boxer shorts on, so you're nicely covered up. Just get up and go about your day.

C

8:03am Jack messages Chloe

Are you OK? You seem a bit spikey. If you're missing your best friend don't worry, I'm sure he'll be back for weddings, funerals and birthdays that end in a zero.

Talking of spikey, Christian Schmidt asked me for that chat yesterday. He wanted me to adjust how I was performing a few pages of script. He was adamant it would improve the production.

8:05am Chloe messages Jack

Did he suggest you didn't come on stage?

8:08am Jack messages Chloe

YES! How the bloody hell did you know that? Has Tiny got your number? She has everyone's number. Christ is nothing sacred?!

8:12am Chloe messages Jack

Er... I didn't know. I was joking.

C

8:15am Jack messages Chloe

Right. Well, your comedy routine needs work. I don't think it's ready for an audience.

So, Schmidt said to me that he thought two of our scenes would be 'harder hitting' if he were alone on the stage. He said it would create a connection between him and the audience and explained that it was important for the audience to feel empathy with his character. He mentioned some words like 'gravitas', 'centre stage', 'owning the space', 'dry ice' and 'palm of his hand'.

I told him the last of his phrases was too much information but if he thought it was in the best interests of the show, then I'd give it a whirl.

It's a win-win. He gets to be important, and I don't have to learn the lines for those scenes. I'll just pin them up and shout them from off stage. Twelve lines chalked off! Well eleven really, one of them is 'Ah'.

8:22am Chloe messages Jack

The more I hear about that man, the more I dislike him. He sounds like a complete narcissist. We need a plan to keep his ego in check.

8:26am Jack messages Chloe

I'm all for that. I had the idea of a mock kidnapping.

Us: ski masked-up.

Him: blindfolded, bundled into the back of an unmarked rental van and left in the middle of a field of cows; ones who've just had calves - the protective type. At the very least there'll be screaming and cow shit.

8:29am Chloe messages Jack

It's a bit 'A-team'. Also, I'm struggling to work out which part of the kidnapping is 'mock'.

My main worry with your plan is that I think it has the potential to backfire by appealing to his sense of the dramatic. I can see him twisting the story and dining out on it for years. *'... I was held captive for a whole month longer than Terry Waite and in a fouler smelling environment... the thought of my adoring public holding candle-lit vigils was the only thing keeping me going on those cold, lonely nights while surrounded by vicious beasts... everything seemed hopeless… on the brink of giving up… tried singing just to keep my spirits up... when suddenly, BAM! unexpected release'* etc. etc.

8:31am Jack messages Chloe

I hear you. How about:

Old folks' home. A lunchtime. 'Christian Schmidt sings The Musicals'. That's one audience right there that won't hold back. No reason to be polite when you're eighty-five and way down the pecking order for the communal TV remote. *Bargain Hunt? Piss Off!* Random shouting-out or staring into space is commonplace in those places. That'd break him. You don't recover from that.

8:33am Chloe messages Jack

Children In Need Fund Raiser. One night only in the main house. Christian Schmidt and his jazz band take requests for charity. Songs are auctioned. The audience picks songs from a list that Schmidt doesn't know about. For the list, I'm thinking:

Anything from the musical Hair

'Hair Down' by SiR ft. Kendrick Lamar

'Hairdresser Blues' by Hunx

8:34am Jack messages Chloe

'Whip My Hair' by Willow Smith

8:35am Chloe messages Jack

'Let My Hair Down' by Nelly Furtado

(not to be confused with 'Let Your Hair Down' by MAGIC!)

8:36am Jack messages Chloe

'Cut My Hair' by The Who

8:37am Chloe messages Jack

'Bangs (I Got Bangs)' by Hovey Benjamin

8:38am Jack messages Chloe

'Hairspray Queen' by Nirvana

(this should carry a reserve price of £25)

8:39am Chloe messages Jack

'The Haircut Song' by Ray Stevens

(£30)

8:40am Jack messages Chloe

'Bad Hair Day' by Bizaardvark

(also £30)

8:42am Chloe messages Jack

'I Am Not My Hair' by India.Arie ft. Akon

(£35 upping the ante)

8:43am Jack messages Chloe

'Bobby Got a Shadfly Caught in His Hair' by Sufjan Stevens

(£40)

8:44am Chloe messages Jack

'I Think I'm Going Bald' by Rush

(£75) and Christian takes some disadvantaged kids to see a donkey in a field.

8:45am Jack messages Chloe

Please tell me you flirted with including 'Hair I Go Again' by Aerosmith?

8:46am Chloe messages Jack

I did. It didn't make the cut.

8:47am Jack messages Chloe

Very droll.

There's Whigfield. But that only works if it's a Saturday.

Jen's woken up. I need to concentrate on how I extricate myself from the bed to the bathroom to the breakfast room. It's the 3 B's.

8:48am Chloe messages Jack

4 B's

Boxers (falling out of).

PS I'm buying you pants for your birthday.

8:49am Jack messages Chloe

Wow, new pants. I can't help but feel the spark's gone from our relationship.

PS Did I tell you, Christian put a notice up in the theatre?

8:51am Chloe messages Jack

Nein.

8:52am Jack messages Chloe

Yup. It was headed up 'HOUSE RULES!'.

8:54am Chloe messages Jack

By pinning that up, presumably he was championing the genre of electronic dance music characterized by a repetitive four-on-the-floor beat and a typical tempo of 120 to 130 beats per minute?

8:55am Jack messages Chloe

That's what I thought.

But no, the poster went on to list things we must all strive for, for the show to be a success. We've been left in no doubt that failure to adhere to the list will result in a ticking off (best scenario) or death.

8:56am Chloe messages Jack

What's on the list?

8:57am Jack messages Chloe

There were lots of ultimatums on there; too many to remember, but in the main it was demanding punctuality and requesting that lines be learned.

He attempted to soften it by adding (in a 6-point font) 'and then we can all achieve something wonderful together, something that we can be proud of'.

8:58am Chloe messages Jack

The man has time issues. Steal his watch.

8:58am Jack messages Chloe

I daren't, It might be Nazi gold.

9:02am Chloe messages Jack

I did a viewing yesterday where the couple I was showing the house to reeled off things they didn't like about it. They were ALL fittings and the like that the present owner will be taking with her. I pointed this out but still they came back at me with 'I'm not sure about the curtains', 'oh dear, those cushions don't work with that sofa', 'we'd have to change the table and chairs' etc. etc.

YES, YOU WOULD BECAUSE THEY WON'T BE THERE WHEN YOU MOVE IN *(WHICH YOU WON'T BE DOING, BECAUSE YOU'RE TIME WASTERS!)*.

9:04am Jack messages Chloe

I'm going to put you in touch with Herr Schmidt so you two can work on your anger issues together.

J

PS I don't think Christian is German actually. I mean, there'll be an ancestral link obviously.

9:10am Jack messages Jen

Hey lazy bones! I'm down having breakfast if you're up and about yet? No worries if not, it must have been exhausting watching all that frenetic, athletic dancing at rehearsal last night hahaha

Jack

9:15am Jen messages Jack

Hi! I'm having a cheeky lie-in. What have you got planned for today? Wondered if you wanted to head to the beach? It's freezing I know but bracing is good sometimes!

Jen xx

9:18am Jack messages Jen

That sounds like a good idea. It'll be a nice thing to do on your last day. What time? 10:00am? I've got my walking gear in the car, so I don't need to come back up to the bedroom!

Jack

9:20am Jen messages Jack

Ooh spoil sport!

Jen xx

Btw you owe me. Chloe asked me to video you dancing last night. I said no. x

9:22am Jack messages Jen

Chloe's crafty. She asked *me* to ask *you* to video it and I said no too.

She'll be massively disappointed. An embarrassing video is just the sort of thing she loves to trot out at my birthdays in front of guests. Hahahaha

Oh, I need to pick Val up from the hospital at some point today, but I'll call the ward from the beach to find out a time.

See you downstairs at 10:00am.

Jack

9:30am Jack messages Chloe

Hey Martin Scorsese. Your current film project didn't get off the ground!

Jack

9:32am Chloe messages Jack

Alright Gene Kelly, keep your ballet tights on.

9:35am Tiny messages the cast

Good morning my children. Below is a link to a video of last night's dancing. Robin asked me to film and circulate it as an aide memoire.

(It was the best night I've had in ages! Haha)

Tiny xx

PS Tim, those trousers have come up nicely.

PPS Jack, I've sent the link to your sister.

9:38am Jack messages Tiny

Sister?

Jack

9:42am Tiny messages Jack

Oh Jack, you're priceless. I wish I had a sister like yours, she really looks out for you. I told her she should come up here as soon as she's able.

Tiny x

9:45am Jack messages Tiny

How do you have my *sister's* number?

9:48am Tiny messages Jack

I run the mailing list. She joined it a few days ago. We had a lovely exchange. She said you'd said nice things about me, and I told her you're really sweet to everyone here. She was so worried about you moving here on your own you know. I think she was relieved when you decided to join our group. I reassured her that I'll look after you when your girlfriend goes back home.

See you later at rehearsal.

How's Val doing by the way?

9:52am Jack messages Tiny

Val's doing much better thanks. I'm hopefully picking her up later to take her home.

Jack

9:54am Jack messages Chloe

Do the words SISTER, MAILING & LIST mean anything to you?

Jack

9:55am Chloe messages Jack

Mebbe.

9:55am Jack messages Chloe

I have image rights. If that video ever makes it into the public domain, you'll be hearing from my lawyer.

9:57am Chloe messages Jack

What's your lawyer's name? You don't have one, do you? No one has, yet in any given TV crime series, suspects always say 'if you have any further questions, I want my lawyer present'.

I've only ever used a solicitor for moving house, and I'll use one when I get divorced from my husband. What I don't have is a criminal lawyer on speed dial who I'm on first name terms with.

(and neither do you).

Kisses

10:03am Jack messages Chloe

You've never owned your own house and to my knowledge you don't have a husband to divorce. Having said that, you're a danger to society and it's only a matter of time before my Private Dick gets some dirt on you, so I'd think about 'lawyering up'.

10:05am Chloe messages Jack

So many gags...

10:07am Jack messages Chloe

I should point out that the only reason I'm still messaging right now is because Jen is late. She was supposed to meet me at 10am. We're going for a walk on a beach.

10:09am Chloe messages Jack

Ooh how romantic. Will you hold hands? Both dressed entirely in white? Glen Medeiros following behind, strumming his guitar while singing 'Nothing's Gonna Change My Love For You'? Maybe a horse without a rider will gallop past while you're skimming stones. Then, without warning, a rogue breaker chases you both back up the sand a few metres and you cling onto each other while laughing. Your salty, bronzed bodies and tousled hair, backlit by a golden, setting sun.

Chloe

PS Shortly after, Jen gets stung by a jellyfish, and you have to pee on her foot. She can't watch. Glen stops singing, the sun goes behind a black cloud and the horse pulls up to take a dump.

10:12am Jack messages Chloe

I've just had a gander at the rehearsal video. I reckon I look pretty loose. Nonchalant, almost. Tim Waddle on the other hand looks a bit rigid, and frankly out of his depth.

10:15am Chloe messages Jack

Christian seems to have different moves to everyone else. Is this deliberate?

10:18am Jack messages Chloe

Yes. He convinced Robin that his character is too much of a free spirit to conform to group choreography.

J

PS Where the hell is Jen? She's late!

10:20am Chloe messages Jack

I'm sensing the first cracks in this relationship. It always starts this way; barely perceptible annoyances that, before long become intolerable. A blunt instrument to the back of the head swiftly followed by a call to your lawyer.

10:23am Jack messages Chloe

She's here. A bit dressed up for the beach!

11:52am Trevor messages Jack

Catherine Zeta Jones (in Zorro).

12:16pm Jack messages Trevor

Hi Trevor. I think you just messaged me by mistake (I hope).

Jack

12:19pm Trevor messages Jack

Yeah. Sorry mate.

12:22pm Jack messages Val

Hi Val! I've just spoken to the ward sister and she says you're good to go! There'll be a load of form-filling and the hospital pharmacy need to make you up some drugs first, so she reckons if I swing round about 3pm that won't be far off. See you later.

Jack

12:25pm Val messages Jack

You're my hero! Can't wait to get out of this devil's arse hole of a place. There are some right oddballs here. We've a new fella on the ward who right now is playing an imaginary piano.

Val xxx

Oh, I'll ask Mel to look out something fresh for me to wear. She has a key to my place. I'll ask her to pass the outfit to you if that's OK.

12:28pm Jack messages Val

Yeah course. No worries

12:32pm Jack messages Chloe

I picked up some holiday brochures yesterday.

Wasn't sure what you guys had in mind, so I got a good range:

1. Wales – 'Cottages for Connoisseurs'

2. Switzerland - 'Swiss Wheels' (Cycling Holiday)

3. Greece - 'Sea and Sail' which also carries the strap line 'All Aboard for your very own Aegean adventure'

4. Germany - 'Rhine River Cruises' (River Boat)

5. Australia - 'Aussie Rules' (Motor Home Rental in Australia)

6. Italy - 'Pasta Salt' (a collection of cuisine-based specialist holidays in Italy)

7. Africa

12:59pm Chloe messages Jack

1. It'll rain

2. Not with Mike's piles

3. Connor gets sea-sick (remember Mallorca?)

4. See above (also I felt the brochure title was self-explanatory)

5. Too far, too hot & too full of Australians

6. Katie's diet consists entirely of fish fingers, nachos and Maltesers

7. Africa? This is very broad. Please expand. What is it mainly? Safaris? Blood diamonds?

1:05pm Chloe messages Jack

Also, did you not think to get something more mainstream I dunno… like Spanish Hotels?!!!

1:08pm Jack messages Chloe

The African one is helping to put water supplies into villages and things like that.

1:12pm Chloe messages Jack

So, no then.

1:15pm Jack messages Chloe

They had one called 'Magic Mallorca'. That was hotels and villas.

1:18pm Chloe messages Jack

Why didn't you take that one!!??

1:20pm Jack messages Chloe

I couldn't carry any more. I'd already had to put 'Very Vietnam' back.

1:23pm Chloe messages Jack

'Very Vietnam'?

Why would you call a brochure that? I'm assuming it's a brochure for holidays solely in Vietnam, therefore it makes no sense to add the word 'very'. It's either Vietnam or it isn't. It'd be like saying 'I've just bought a car and it's very Porsche'.

1:25pm Jack messages Chloe

Are you sure you didn't mishear Porsche? Said quickly or mumbled, 'Porsche' sounds a lot like 'posh'.

What you heard makes no sense.

1:28pm Chloe messages Jack

You're 'very beachy' right now.

1:31pm Jack messages Chloe

That's quite good.

J

PS What did you message me for again?

1:32pm Chloe messages Jack

I didn't.

1:33pm Jack messages Chloe

Well, when you remember what it was you wanted to ask, just message me. Gotta dash. I'll need to go and drop Jen off before heading to the hospital. The rest of the cast have been summoned to the theatre to help paint Trevor's set.

Hmmm… Val… or set painting? Talk about Hobson's Choice (that's not our play by the way).

1:35pm Chloe messages Jack

Cobblers!

2:07pm Jack messages Chloe

I'm getting quite the reputation. Mel just handed me some clothes for Val and then asked me to try to undo her bra (while clothed obviously). I tried pointing out that I'm not in the habit of undoing women's bras and that I didn't consider it a party trick (which is what Tiny has labelled it as).

She insisted. And said it had to be one-handed.

I spent two minutes fumbling about like an idiot. Finally, she turned around, smirked, winked at me and whispered, 'it's a front-loader'. What is it with women and their bras? I suppose they know men are scared of them. Have power. Will wield.

Anyway, I steeled myself and snapped the bugger open on the first attempt. Three fingers (well, two fingers and a thumb).

I accompanied the moment of success with a high pitched 'ta-da' which in hindsight was a bit lame.

Jack

2:11pm Chloe messages Jack

Y'know highly skilled musicians or sportspeople or adventurers who achieve success despite having to perform under great pressure and weight of expectation? Well, ordinary folk tend to be attracted to such people. I know I am. Maybe it's because they seem out of reach to us mere mortals. Perhaps it's because we are painfully aware of our own inadequacies and choose to compensate by imagining ourselves with trailblazers who inspire and entertain in a way we can't. It can be a physical attraction, intellectual attraction, or a combination of both. Age tends not to be a barrier. Generally speaking, talented people are irresistible.

Personally, I go weak at the knees when I think of greats at the top of their game, like Andrea Bocelli, Rafael Nadal, Jeff Buckley, Steve McQueen, Barrack Obama, Sir Edmund Hilary, Matisse, Neil Armstrong, Ben Fogle…

What I don't have in my portfolio of attractive high achievers, is a pioneer of underwear tricks; one who will stop at nothing to conquer a bra clasp.

2:15pm Jack messages Chloe

Ben Fogle?

He'd be shite at undoing a bra.

3:11pm Jack messages Chloe

At the hospital. There's a search on for Val's suspender belt. Three more nurses have joined the hunt which can't be an efficient use of NHS resources. One of the search party asked Val where she'd last seen it and must have regretted asking when Val barked back 'around my waist!'.

3:14pm Chloe messages Jack

Has she still got her stockings?

3:15pm Jack messages Chloe

Dunno. They've just whipped off her *surgical* ones. I'm not getting involved. She's calmed down a bit now. She's trying to flog tickets for our show. Credit to the nurses who, despite clearly having no intention of coming along, are making all the right noises.

3:28pm Mary MacMary messages Jack

Hi Jack.

Mary here. Has Christian been telling you to do scenes differently than we agreed? If so, I'll have his guts for garters. I only found out because Tiny has scratched some lines from her script because she says she won't have to prompt on those anymore.

I'M the director of this production, not Christian bloody Schmidt-Face! (Well, Donald is technically but he runs everything by me, and I advise him on all artistic matters).

Can I ask, what are the changes he's asked you to make?

Mary

Oh, and how are you finding the process darling? Everything OK?

3:32pm Jack messages Mary MacMary

Hi Mary.

I don't want to cause any bother. I'm an inexperienced first timer, so am more than happy for others to point me in the right direction, which is why I took on board what Christian suggested.

He just suggested I should shout my lines from the wings for a couple of scenes. No drama.

I'm enjoying being in the show. There's a lot to take in in such a short time but hopefully that won't give me time to worry about it!

It's all great. Everyone's been really welcoming.

I'll see you later at rehearsal.

Jack

3:34pm Mary MacMary messages Jack

No drama?! No drama?!! Too bloody right there'll be no drama, because that brown-nosing prick will have shoved his skinny arm halfway down the show's throat and ripped the heart out of the bastard thing. He only got the part because he's male, under forty and in possession of his own teeth.

I'll give him drama! For a start off he can stop camping about the place. He's playing a coal miner, not bloody Liberace.

Don't you worry Jack, you're doing great. If he tries to give you any further 'tips' on how to perform your role, I want you to come to me.

Or Donald.

But preferably me.

3:38pm Jack messages Mary MacMary

Right. OK. Thanks.

I'm not sure if this is relevant to your inquiry, but Christian mentioned that he intended singing an extra song at the end of the show. It's not scripted but he thought it would be a fitting finale. Is that the sort of thing I'm to tell you?

Jack

PS Is there a witness protection scheme available?

3:42pm Mary MacMary messages Jack

EXTRA SONG?!

He'll be lucky if I don't strip him of the ones he's got! James Starling's always telling him to keep on the note. Same note?! Same bloody octave would be a start!

Mary

5:07pm Jack messages Chloe

Back at The Hunter's. Jen's stuff's still here. She's probably building herself up for a teary goodbye.

I took Val home. Her front garden is a bit like her face; it looks like an office paintballing away-day has happened in it. I've never seen so many pots in such a small space. There must be seventy or so, all different (bright) colours. Come the summer, when they contain plants, it must be quite the psychedelic trip. She also has sparkly comedy and tragedy theatre masks nailed to her front door.

Talking of colours, when we got into the car, Val asked me what I thought of her make up. I asked her if I could be honest with her and suggested that she could try more subtle tones. I told her that I'd heard women talk of a smoky eye shadow for example. She seemed excited to try it.

Jack

5:12pm Chloe messages Jack

In my experience, international fashion consultants don't wear gilets, tend to have more than one client, and don't usually specialise in circus clowns.

The day I come to you for fashion advice is the day I kill myself.

Chloe

PS I shall say this only once… It's nice you're looking out for Val. I'm guessing it's not easy for a trans person to be accepted in a rural northern village (that's Val, not you).

PPS That said, you're still second on my list entitled 'friends to potentially cull'.

5:14pm Jack messages Chloe

Who's top?

5:15pm Chloe messages Jack

My parents.

5:17pm Jack messages Chloe

I thought you disowned them years ago.

5:19pm Chloe messages Jack

I did. I decided to re-own them on account there could be an inheritance. No point cutting my nose off etc. etc.

Come to think of it, they should probably be promoted to second on my list. You're now demoted to top – unless you can think of something you can offer me in return for being my friend? (except the thing that's just popped into your head – no one wants that).*

Chloe

*(except Jen) (and Mel) (and probably Tiny)

Gosh, you're quite the gigolo these days.

5:23pm Jack messages Chloe

… and Mary MacMary. I have a feeling she wants to take me under her wing (or into her bosom) and teach me new things. I sincerely hope she means things like stagecraft.

I must ask her if she regrets having taken her husband's surname and if she resents Donald for having that surname in the first place. It might explain her stroppy disposition.

It's like the father of those Neville brothers who played football. Neville Neville. I'm going out on a limb here but if a sweepstake was held to guess the baby's name, I wouldn't be picking Neville. Neville would be below Hannibal and Adolf.

Maybe if you inherited a great surname like 'Spangle' it'd be different – 'Spangle Spangle', or 'Skedaddle Skedaddle'. But 'Mary MacMary' and 'Neville Neville'? No, no, no. A thousand times no.

Jack

5:35pm Chloe messages Jack

Have you ever considered changing your surname to 'Shit'?

Chloe

5:37pm Jack messages Jen

Jen's gone home. You know what, I'm going to miss having a naked woman next to me. She does have a great butt. And she laughs at my jokes. The peeing thing is unfortunate though.

Jack

5:45pm Jack messages Chloe

What? No witty retort?

Jack

5:47pm Chloe messages Jack

I thought my retort was very witty. I can't help it if my brand of humour is too sophisticated for you.

5:49pm Jack messages Chloe

Oh shit!

5:50pm Chloe messages Jack

Finally! Christ, it wasn't that hard a gag to grasp.

5:52pm Jack messages Chloe

No! No! No!

Shit!

My

Message

Went

To

Jen

5:55pm Chloe messages Jack

What message?!

5:58pm Jack messages Chloe

The one that was meant for you, but I sent it to Jen by mistake.

Oh bollocks.

This isn't good.

6:00pm Chloe messages Jack

I haven't seen it.

6:02pm Jack messages Chloe

I KNOW! Because I sent it to JEN!

6:03pm Chloe messages Jack

Alright, calm down. It's probably not as bad as you think. What did you say?

6:05pm Jack messages Chloe

I said she had a nice butt and that I was going to miss having a naked woman in my bed. Then there was a bit about peeing.

6:07pm Chloe messages Jack

Oh, that is bad. Did you recall it?

6:08pm Jack messages Chloe

What?! You can do that?! HOW?

6:09pm Chloe messages Jack

Wait, maybe that's email. I forget.

6:10pm Jack messages Chloe

CAN I RECALL IT?

PS This is not a time for casual suggestions. I need facts, not hunches!

6:14pm Chloe messages Jack

Yeah, thought so. Just googled it. You can't recall a message. If you'd have emailed her you could have done. There's a lesson there I suppose.

6:16pm Jack messages Chloe

Great. Thanks Aesop.

6:45pm Jo-Ann Pinchley-Cooke messages Jack

Hahahahaha Excellent! Bloody EXCELLENT!!!

Jo-Ann xxx

6:47pm Jack messages Jo-Ann Pinchley-Cooke

Er thanks.

What is? (excellent).

Jack

6:49pm Jo-Ann Pinchley-Cooke messages Jack

Christian's poster. Don't be coy. Hahahaha

Brilliant.

J-A xxxx

6:51pm Jack messages Jo-Ann Pinchley-Cooke

Right. I have a feeling I'm about to let you down, which is something that doesn't appear on my 'to do' list today.

Much as I'd like to take credit for whatever fate has befallen Christian's poster, I can't.

What's happened to it?

Will he be cross?

6:53pm Jo-Ann Pinchley-Cooke messages Jack

He's here! Cross?! He's bloody raging. He ripped it down, but I got a photo.

J-A

6:55pm Tiny messages Jack

10/10 Jack. As a piece of art, Christian's poster will now forever hold a special place in my heart.

Tiny

6:57pm Mel messages Jack

Hi Jack. Was that your idea to staple-gun the wig to that poster? Bloody genius. The way you've styled it so that the words 'HOUSE' & 'RULES' now look like a pair of eyes is Damion Hirst-esque. Knocks Hirst's shark tank shite into a tin hat.

Mel

6:59pm Jack messages Jo-Ann Pinchley-Cooke

I've just received the photo, thanks.

While the wig is impressive, what really caught my eye was the addition of inspirational quotations at the foot of Christian's list of dos and don'ts.

For instance, whoever scribbled 'There's nothing like new hair to make you feel confident and beautiful':

   a) Has been reading too many self-help books.

   b) Is Val.

7:03pm Jack messages Tiny

Hi Tiny. The poster enhancements are nothing to do with me I'm afraid. Very funny though.

Jack

7:05pm Tiny messages Jack

You weren't responsible for:

'Having long hair makes me feel like a princess'?

7:07pm Jack messages Tiny

Nope.

Although I'd have been proud to have been the one who added 'What's that you say? Be punctual? Sorry, I can't hear you over the volume of my hair'.

Jack

7:09pm Trevor messages Jack

Having a bet with Mel here about this poster.

I've bet her a... (well I can't say what I've bet her) that you're the brains behind:

'Invest in your hair. It's the crown you never take off (well except to wash it)'.

Let me know mate.

Trevor

7:11pm Jack messages Trevor

The wanton vandalism of Christian's poster is not my doing I'm afraid.

Jack

PS I'm guessing you won't be getting Catherine Zeta-Jones later now.

7:13pm Trevor messages Jack

No. More's the pity.

Trevor

Oh, I'll need the staple-gun back mate. Got some canvasses to fix to some scenery flats. Cheers.

Trevor

7:14pm Jack messages Tiny

By the way you'd have known if I'd contributed to the gratuitous sabotage of Christian's poster because you'd be reading:

'I used to be thinner than my hair'.

7:22pm Jack messages Chloe

Christian's poster has been subjected to various graffiti attacks. I've been sent a photo.

7:26pm Chloe messages Jack

Haven't you got a rehearsal tonight? Have you seen the time?

7:27pm Jack messages Chloe

Oh shit! Speak later!

J

8:12pm Jen messages Jack

Awww. That's lovely. I just stopped to get some petrol and saw your message. I was a bit blue about leaving but that's given me a real pick-me-up.

I'll come back up again soon; maybe for the show if I can get away.

Next time I'll come for longer so we can see a lot more of each other!

You're so lovely.

Jen xxxxxx

PS I've always liked my bum.

PPS I told you not to worry about the bathroom incident, silly.

8:30pm Jack messages Chloe

Break time. Jen saw my message. She saw it when she stopped for petrol; petrol and a wedding magazine judging by how thrilled she is that I complimented her.

Jack

PS I was only four minutes late to rehearsal and no one important noticed because Mary MacMary was in the auditorium yelling at Christian.

8:35pm Jack messages Chloe

Dick Rump just swanned over to remind me I was supposed to give him my biog today. I apologised and assured him I'd write it tonight and send it to him first thing tomorrow.

If you're not too busy learning how to ask where the library in Stuttgart is, could you send me an example of the sort of thing Dick will be expecting from me? Thanks.

Jack

PS Tim Waddle's rubber soled shoes tonight were making a sound not unlike his bottom on skittles night. Lots of sniggering. It's childish, everyone knows it's childish, but somehow it's still funny.

8:39pm Chloe messages Jack

Is Tim 'Hosenscheisser' Waddle aware of his comedy shoes?

8:41pm Jack messages Chloe

No I don't think so. He's been too busy practising moving a chair from one side of the stage to the other. He told me that in the hands of a skilful actor, a chair can represent a weapon, or a lover; it can be a dance partner or a window; a tree or a washing machine. I asked him if it could be a toilet. He said that I was making the classic mistake of thinking of a chair as something you sit on.

8:43pm Chloe messages Jack

Does he sit on it?

8:44pm Jack messages Chloe

Yes.

8:46pm Chloe messages Jack

Right. Why does he move it? Does it become a tree or a washing machine?

8:48pm Jack messages Chloe

No. When Tim sits on it, it's a chair at a desk. He then moves it so it's in place for the next scene where it transforms itself into a chair at a dining table, at which point Mary sits on it.

Jack

8:49pm Chloe messages Jack

When's this show on?

8:49pm Jack messages Chloe

Gotta dash.

J

10:14pm Dick Rump messages Jack

Hi Jack

Do you have access to email? If so, can you send your programme biog direct to the printers' tomorrow? I've got to meet someone to pick up some new lighting gels so I'm not going to be around.

Just a few pointers:

Try and keep it short – not like that berk Schmidt who feels he needs to list every role he's ever done complete with venue and running dates.

Try and avoid bigging yourself up too much. Tim always refers to his 'critically acclaimed performance in…'

Write it in the third person. Don't ask me why; it must be bleeding obvious to anyone reading it that the cast member has written it themselves.

Don't try to make it funny. The average age of our audience is about seventy-eight. No one will get it.

Finally, I know you'll make sure everything is spelled correctly because you're clearly a bright lad, but can you pay particular attention to punctuation. Howard Cobham normally proof-reads everyone's biog and he's an absolute stickler for grammatical correctness. He'll come down on me like a tonne of bricks if one slips through the net.

The man is even obsessed with poorly constructed graffiti. Only yesterday he revealed that the public toilets in Lower Grapple had the words 'GAY'S OUT' scrawled on the wall. He wrote to the council to report it. While he acknowledged that in all probability the graffiti was an attempt at an offensive homophobic slur, Howard protested that taken at face value, the graffiti must be referencing a woman called Gay, who had either gone out or come out.

Howard suggested to The Council that the same author may be responsible for messages written at Brackley Tunstead's public toilets ('Ive seen Sharons' Tit's') and at Hurlingham railway station toilets ('Jame's cocks's tiny').

Cheers

Dick

PS the email address is graham@sykesbamburgh.co.uk

10:27pm Jack messages Dick Rump

Hi Dick.

Thanks for that info. I'll be sure to email my biog first thing in the morning.

Jack

PS Where *is* Howard these days? I haven't seen him for ages.

10:29pm Dick Rump messages Jack

He's doing some work for the community.

10:54pm Chloe messages Jack

I thought writing your programme biog would prove tricky since I don't have context of what your show is about, but actually, it's been remarkably easy. You've no need to make any changes, just submit it as it is below:

Jack is a southern person who has learned to read aloud. He also knows how to sing and dance. When Jack isn't doing these things, he likes to spend time with his colouring books and crayons. Jack is good at colouring-in, and he usually keeps within the lines. Jack has a girlfriend called Jen. Jack and Jen like to go to the beach together to look for shells.

Jack has seen Jen's bumpa, her wabbers and her cooter.

Jack is very much looking forward to playing Frederick.

10:58pm Jack messages Chloe

I think your attempt suffers from being too intellectual. This reads better:

This is Jack's first foray into non-professional theatre, a venture that has proved challenging and somewhat nerve-wracking!

Accordingly, Jack would like to take this opportunity to thank his acquaintances Katie Shaw, Mike Jordan, Connor Reid and especially Chloe Walker, for their support. Not a day has gone by without a helpful comment or constructive criticism, all done with an unswerving patience and sensitivity. Jack assures them that he will not forget their contributions in a hurry.

By day, Jack is a human cannonball so is well used to meeting obstacles head-on.

11:03pm Chloe messages Jack

Hmmm. I don't think it says enough about you. It's lovely that you've seen fit to mention your friends, but this is YOUR special moment. How about:

Jack is honoured to have been chosen to play the role of Frederick in this ground-breaking production.

Jack has had to overcome a great deal of adversity in his relatively young life. For Jack, getting up on stage is all part of the healing process and he'd like the audience to know:

'He decided long ago

Never to walk in anyone's shadow

If he fails, if he succeeds

At least he'll live as he believes

No matter what they take from him

He hasn't shat his pants like that bloke called Tim'

11:15pm Jack messages Chloe

Houston, we have a problem because while you made a valiant attempt, I fear it comes across a bit sentimental. I think today's audiences are more theatre-savvy, so I feel it needs to be more relevant:

Jack is no stranger to the theatre. He's been three times. Once to see Shakespeare's 'Henry IV Part II', once to see 'The Seagull' by Chekhov and once to see 'Ashes to Ashes' by Harold Pinter.

Jack hopes tonight's audience will have also seen those three plays because, by comparison, tonight's production will seem gripping and hilarious.

Jack can next be seen in London's West End in a revival of the taut political thriller 'That'll sponge out – Bill Clinton, The Musical'.

11:25pm Chloe messages Jack

I take your point, but I feel it's important to give your audience a glimpse into the real Jack, his hopes, fears, insecurities etc.:

I think it was the famous philosopher Ludwig Wittgenstein who wrote 'I don't know why we are here, but I'm pretty sure it is not to enjoy ourselves'.

Jack can't speak for the audience, but he would like it pointed out to Mr Wittgenstein that he has enjoyed himself immensely.

By day, Jack works as a bomb disposal expert, and he brings those skills to this production where he diffuses a bomb in the shape of a chair.

11:29pm Jack messages Chloe

At the risk of prolonging this exchange to a point well past my bedtime, I'd like to offer an alternative; one which casts an image of me as an ambitious individual, who will use The Attic Priory Players as a stepping-stone to greater things:

At thirty-two years young, Jack is a late comer to the world of theatre. Despite this, Jack is looking forward to developing his skills and hopes for a rapid rise through the ranks of non-professional theatre.

Jack reminds any sceptics, that stage and screen legends such as Robbie Coltrane, Luciano Pavarotti, John Candy, William Shatner and Freddie Starr all started out small before going on to be very, very big.

Jack returns to the stage later this year in the tap-dancing extravaganza 'Best Foot Forward! – Douglas Bader The Musical'.

11:32pm Chloe messages Jack

You haven't mentioned Jen in any of those attempts. In my experience, people usually thank their partners.

11:35pm Jack messages Chloe

I think you're confusing this with The Academy Awards.

11:38pm Chloe messages Jack

Jen would win 'best supporting butt'.

Gute Nacht kleiner Insektenpenis.

Chloe x

11:40pm Jack messages Chloe

Gute Nacht an Sie und Ihren großen Damengarten.

Jack

11.

Tuesday 22nd January

6 days 'til curtain up

8:23am Jack messages Chloe

I meant to say, last night, Mrs Brains brought pork pie along to our rehearsal. Just pork pie, nothing else. It looked suspiciously like the platter that the treasurer sneezed on at the Brains' house and I wasn't the only one to think that. Tim Waddle, Donald MacMary and me all shot conspiratorial glances at each other. For that brief moment, we were allies.

While we hesitated, Christian Schmidt and Trevor dived in and helped themselves.

J

8:35am Chloe messages Jack

Ewww. What with The Hunter's lax cleaning regime and snuff-boy not being able to keep the snot in his nose, it's a wonder you're still alive.

Chloe

PS If you do die from a horrible bacterial infection, could I have your T'Pau album?

8:37am Jack messages Chloe

Sure, if Mike hasn't ransacked my storage unit and sold everything on eBay.

8:42am Chloe messages Jack

I've already removed anything of value.

8:47am Jack messages Chloe

I spotted a curious thing in the theatre foyer last night. In a far corner there's a small statue of the theatre's patron. It's none other than TV wildlife legend Terry Nutkins. You've heard of him, right?

8:49am Chloe messages Jack

The fella with the zany hair? Yeah, I've seen re-runs of The Really Wild Show. Why's he their patron?

8:51am Jack messages Chloe

I don't know. I'm not sure where he hailed from, but this might have been a favourite spot; there's loads of wildlife up here and he was big on sea lions. It's a fairly rubbish statue because the sculptor has given his hands all ten digits.

Everyone knows Nutkins lost part of two fingers after he was attacked by an otter. Thing is, Terry Nutkins died a few years back, I remember watching it on the news and feeling sad about it. BUT above his statue is a piece written by the theatre in a tense that suggests they still think he's alive.

8:53am Chloe messages Jack

Right. Maybe no-one's told them.

8:55am Jack messages Chloe

Possible. But wouldn't they put two and two together having not seen him for all those years, or received any communication from him, or cheques?

8:57am Chloe messages Jack

Maybe, but the theatre treasurer's off his tits on snuff so it's not massively surprising he hasn't noticed.

9:01am Jack messages Chloe

Yeah, I guess. Why would he have been patron of a theatre in the first place? He was an animal lover. Surely, he'd have put his name to an otter sanctuary or something.

9:03am Chloe messages Jack

I don't know Miss Marple. Why is it important?

9:05am Jack messages Chloe

Well, it's Nutkins isn't it! He was brilliant. He even pitched up on Countryfile a few years ago. Craven looked positively out of his depth.

Jack

PS It's a crap statue too. I mean, you can tell it's him, mainly because of the hair (and the brass plaque with his name on it). It's not a great likeness though (not as bad as that Cristiano Ronaldo one they unveiled at Madeira airport, obviously).

9:08am Chloe messages Jack

I take it you've learned your 134 lines then.

9:09am Jack messages Chloe

Hmmm, Donald had a word last night and suggested I was a little bit behind with my lines. I'd better look at them today.

J

PS Tim Waddle does this slightly strange thing of looking at my forehead while delivering his lines. What's that all about?

9:11am Chloe messages Jack

Does he do that right after you've delivered a funny line of your own?

9:13am Jack messages Chloe

I decided to make all my lines funny. My line in Act 1 scene 3, ('Nurse! We're losing him!') will bring the house down.

(Yes, he does).

9:15am Chloe messages Jack

I believe that the looking-at-the-forehead thing was originally taught as a technique to prevent an actor from corpsing. There are various reasons why an actor might get a fit of the giggles:

1. The other actor has just delivered a funny line (very unlikely) because even if the script is funny, amateur actors will somehow contrive to rip all the humour out of it, usually because of the wrong intonation or painfully slow speed of delivery.

2. The other actor has tripped over while making their entrance (relatively common).When this happens, the actor who hasn't tripped, ALWAYS rallies round the stricken actor, and starts to brush-down their clothing (because that's what they believe would happen in a real-life situation). The tiniest giggle

from the audience at this juncture can trigger uncontrollable laughter from one or both actors, who henceforth should deliver their lines to the forehead opposite. By minimising eye contact, it's sometimes possible to stop the laughter between actors from escalating.

3. An actor on stage has fluffed a line badly - fluffed it in such a way that the line takes on an entirely different meaning (extremely likely).

I saw a local group present The Full Monty. One of the characters had the line 'I'll be the laughing-stock of Buffalo if I chicken out now!'

The line that the actor actually delivered during the performance was 'I'll be the chicken stock of Buffalo...'. Hard for anyone to keep a straight face after that. The forehead technique won't help you there. To be fair it was the highlight of an otherwise laborious production.

Chloe

PS I was in a production once where an actor forgot his own character name. It was South Pacific. The actor in question began his line 'If my name's not Commander…' but couldn't finish it because, beyond his rank, he'd forgotten who he was supposed to be. What followed took an eternity, as the man doggedly repeated the line while banging his fist on the table in front of him, presumably in the vain hope his name would come back to him. It didn't. One by one, the other actors, (while stifling laughter) gradually drifted off stage.

9:17am Jack messages Chloe

So… what you're saying is, if I want people to stop looking at my forehead, I should stop being so funny.

9:18am Chloe messages Jack

On reflection, I think it's more likely that your big forehead is fascinating.

9:22am Jack messages Val

Hi Val! Still feeling well, I hope.

Know anything about the statue in the theatre foyer?

Jack

9:24am Val messages Jack

Hi Jack

I feel bloody great thanks. I'm still laughing about that shite wig stuck to Christian's poster! What a tonic that was last night! It's a good job he didn't catch you defacing it!

The Terry Nutkins statue? What about it?

Val

9:26am Jack messages Val

Nutkins just seems like a bit of a strange patron for an arts establishment to have, that's all.

Jack

PS I'm glad you're still feeling fine and dandy.

PPS I didn't contribute to the enrichment of Christian's poster. I know this because I wasn't there.

9:28am Val messages Jack

Oh, he's a great patron. He always finds time to chat to you.

Val

(has anyone told you about the guy in the audience, who always falls asleep? To make matters worse he always sits on the front row. He comes to see every show. Mel usually runs a book on whose lines he'll fall asleep during first).

9:30am Jack messages Val

Christ! That's a bit soul-destroying having someone nod-off mid-dialogue! How long into the production is it before he tends to take his nap? I only ask because I'm on stage in the first scene so I'm worried the betting on me might be heavy.

Jack

PS My money's on Tim Waddle. His monologue in scene two (the one about the camel in the desert) is probably the most depressing piece of theatre I've ever witnessed.

9:33am Val messages Jack

He was asleep before the end of the overture in the last show.

Val

9:35am Jack messages Tiny

Hi Tiny,

Have you ever met the theatre's patron?

Jack

9:38am Tiny messages Jack

Hi. Yes, three or four times. Lovely man.

Tiny

9:40am Jack messages Tiny

Terry Nutkins, right?

9:41am Tiny messages Jack

Yes, well I'm not sure of his surname. I just know him as Terry. There's a statue of him near the bar.

9:43am Jack messages Tiny

When you met him, did you notice how many fingers he had?

9:44am Tiny messages Jack

What? Oh Jack! Hahahahahahaha.

Tiny

Btw, has Mel messaged you about helping her pick out a dress for the after-show party? Val told her you do a bit of fashion consultancy and have a great eye.

9:49am Jack messages Chloe

I think I'm about to increase my client-base to two for my fashion consultancy business.

J

9:51am Chloe messages Jack

I hate to point out the obvious, but businesses usually get paid for their work.

Chloe

PS Who's the blind person you'll be helping?

9:53am Jack messages Chloe

It's not definite yet, but the rumour is that Mel is looking for some fashion advice.

J

9:54am Chloe messages Jack

I took you shopping once when I was buying a dress for my works do, remember? You were rubbish. You just sat there and stared at your phone looking disinterested. In your defence, you did grunt occasionally when I appeared from the changing rooms and sashayed around a bit.

This will be the end of your friendship with Mel.

C

PS John Prescott has more fashion sense than you.

PPS What does Mel look like? She doesn't act, so isn't on the Attic Priory Players web page.

PPPS Give me her surname. I'll look her up on Facebook.

9:55am Mel messages Jack

Hey Jack! How goes it?

Look, I need to buy a new dress for the after-show party, but I could do with someone coming with me to tell me if I look fat or frumpy – that sort of thing. You seem like a man with his finger on the fashion pulse. Say you'll come with me?! Pleeeease?! I'll buy you lunch.

Mel xxx

9:57am Jack messages Chloe

And there it is! The official request has come through for my services.

Jack

PS I don't know Mel's surname (and even if I did, if I told you, I'd have to kill you).

PPS Mel is very attractive. There are a few tattoos and piercings going on. I'm not usually mad about those as you know, but Rooney Mara had some in that dragon film thing, and I've always fancied her.

Jack

9:59am Jack messages Mel

Hi Mel.

Yeah, sure. Sounds like fun.

When did you have in mind? If it's tomorrow I'll have to be back for my 3 o'clock with Vivienne Westwood (she has a new line she wants to run by me and frankly, going by the initial sketches, I'm not at all convinced).

Jack

10:02am Mel messages Jack

Hahahaha

You free today? 12pm? I was thinking Alnwick. They have some good shops, and it isn't too far away.

Mel xxx

10:04am Jack messages Mel

Yep. 12pm is good for me. You can test me on my lines while I'm driving.

Jack

10:05am Mel messages Jack

Yaaay!

I'll see you outside the pub at 12pm.

This is gonna be a blast.

Mel xxx

10:08am Chloe messages Jack

What will you wear?

Whatever it is you'll need to explain that it's retro chic.

10:12am Jack messages Chloe

Head to toe in camouflage. I'll pair it with my distressed boots and the fedora I 'lifted' from Kitty's hat box. I shall use the words 'daaahling' and 'ciao' a great deal.

10:13am Chloe messages Jack

Oh lord. That poor girl.

Chloe

PS Just how attractive? Prettier than Jen?

10:15am Jack messages Chloe

Yes. And I doubt there are any inhibitions with bodily functions.

Jack

10:16am Chloe messages Jack

Is Mel prettier than *me*?

Oh God is *Jen* prettier than me?

C

10:18am Jack messages Chloe

You've used up all your questions.

Wow you're insecure today. Are you having an ugly day? Are your elbows looking fat?

10:20am Chloe messages Jack

You've used up all your questions.

10:52am Tiny messages Jack

Hi Jack

I'm trying to firm up numbers for our group theatre visit tomorrow. Did you want to come?

Tiny x

10:55am Jack messages Tiny

Hi Tiny

I haven't heard anything about this. What's the itinerary?

Jack

10:57am Tiny messages Jack

Honestly Jack, it's been on the group's Facebook page for days! I noticed you hadn't responded to say whether you wanted to come so I thought I'd message you to make sure.

It's an amateur production of 'Beauty and the Beast' by The Criterion Choral Society. Nice small theatre, if a bit grubby. There's still space on the minibus. You should come, it'll be a giggle. The minibus leaves the pub car park at 12:00pm tomorrow. £14.50 which includes your ticket and minibus. We're booked in for a pre-show lunch at Giuseppe's.

Tiny x

10:59am Jack messages Tiny

Hi Tiny

Yeah, that sounds great. Count me in. I'll give you the cash later.

Jack

PS I'm not on social media. My 'sister' tends to give me edited highlights.

11:03am Jack messages Chloe

Tiny has just accused an establishment of being 'grubby'. It's a bit rich. Yesterday, I found a rogue sock and while I was looking for its partner, I came across what can only be described as a mound of fuzzy, toxic looking organisms. I didn't dare disturb it for fear it was playing a vital role in the earth's ecosystem.

Also, there hasn't been any soap in the Gents' toilets for days now, which is alarming given the tsunami that materialised from Tim Waddle's bottom last Saturday.

I'm not convinced the wearing of a Hazmat suit here would be adequate protection.

Jack

11:05am Chloe messages Jack

Is it more or less rank than Mike's old flat?

When considering your answer, keep in mind that his flat was visited by an environmental health officer following complaints from tenants in the adjacent flats. He didn't seem the slightest bit embarrassed that his sink's U-bend was supporting more than three hundred species of aquatic life.

Chloe

11:08am Jack messages Chloe

It was only one neighbour who complained, and I think it was around the time Mike was going through his 'Ian Dury and The Blockheads' phase. 'Hit me with your Rhythm Stick' played on a loop for three weeks finally caused his neighbour to snap.

Jack

1:03pm Jack messages Chloe

The hunt for a frock is going well.

Jack

1:04pm Chloe messages Jack

Please tell me you haven't called it that.

Chloe

PS I hope you're offering more than an occasional grunt to that poor deluded soul.

1:18pm Jack messages Chloe

You underestimate me. I learned a lot from my shopping expedition with you.

For instance, I know now that when offering your opinion on an outfit, you need to do it promptly and decisively. The worst thing you can do is pause after you've been asked, 'what do you think?' If you pause, you may as well say 'it looks shite'.

1:20pm Jack messages Chloe

I've decided to be up-front. But I've also got some lines prepared that make me look both intelligent and sensitive.

After Mel emerged in the first outfit, I immediately said 'If I'm honest Mel, you can do better; it flattered to deceive on the hanger.'

She replied 'I'm glad you said that cos it doesn't feel right'.

'It's just not you', I said. 'You need something that shows everyone who the real Mel is.'

After giving me the thumbs up, she disappeared behind the curtain and reappeared in a dress that had a two-inch-wide gap down its front, all the way from her neck to her waist. She made a joke about me not being able to undo her bra because she wasn't wearing one. I made her twirl around in it eight times before reluctantly declaring it unfit for purpose.

1:22pm Jack messages Chloe

I told her that while I was too gentlemanly to stare at her cleavage, she couldn't expect the same courtesy from Tim Waddle and Trevor. I had to correct myself because I'd forgotten Mel and Trevor were an item (Mel then corrected *me* because they aren't anymore – there was too much scaffold prattle in the pillow talk).

Gotta go. Mel's asking for help in the changing room.

1:23pm Chloe messages Jack

'Help in the changing room'… that old chestnut!?! Purlease!

C

1:27pm Jack messages Chloe

She needed help getting out of her dress.

1:28pm Chloe messages Jack

Help getting out of a dress she was barely wearing in the first place?

I can't believe she's played the *'ooh I need help getting out of my dress'* card. We've all tried that one!

Chloe

1:30pm Jack messages Chloe

You didn't try it when I was giving you fashion advice in Primark.

J

1:30pm Chloe messages Jack

I was going to, but you'd wandered off to the lingerie section.

1:32pm Jack messages Chloe

Anyway, you'd have been proud of me in the changing cubicle. Not only was I chivalrous and averted my gaze, but I spotted the next outfit she'd cued-up to try on. I saved her the bother. It was a very nice turquoise jump-suit, but I explained that while she'd undoubtedly look a million dollars in it, it was an impractical proposition given the number of toilet trips needed at a party. There'd be too much faffing about. She told me I was amazing and could be so much more than a carpenter.

1:34pm Chloe messages Jack

At this rate, she'll be going home with nothing.

1:46pm Jack messages Chloe

Nah. I've told her that while she's trying on her final outfit, I'll have a scout round and pick out a couple of things for her to try.

1:48pm Chloe messages Jack

This'll be interesting. Do you even know what size she is?

1:49pm Jack messages Chloe

In a dress or underwear?

1:49pm Chloe messages Jack

[Chloe raises an eyebrow and does her best disdainful look]

1:50pm Jack messages Chloe

Dress: 8

1:51pm Chloe messages Jack

Bitch. I hate her. She's not your type. Get out now. Run.

1:57pm Jack messages Chloe

There's a bloke 'helping' his girlfriend. He's such an amateur. She just paraded in front of him, clearly pleased with what she'd just seen in the changing room mirror. It should have a been a slam dunk – an immediate 'Wow. Yes. Buy it!' But no. He paused then offered the wettest 'er… yes… nice' but said it with an upward inflection that screamed uncertainty. She told him he didn't sound sure, whereupon he overcompensated by sounding too enthusiastic. She wasn't buying it (his pretence or the dress). I forecast a journey home conducted in complete silence.

1:59pm Chloe messages Jack

How's the line learning going?

2:13pm Jack messages Chloe

Heading for a drink in a minute. I've brought my script, so I'll ask Mel to test me.

2:14pm Chloe messages Jack

The ultimate dream date.

Chloe

PS Did the dress-buying end in failure?

2:17pm Jack messages Chloe

No, quite the opposite. Mel's at the till now. I found her a lovely peacock-blue floaty number (the assistant told me it was called a maxi dress). It fit her a treat. I told her she looked graceful yet sexy, and when paired with her Dr Martins the overall look was one that oozed elegance but with a smattering of authority. She said it was perfect, felt fabulous in it, and couldn't wait to wear it to the party.

2:19pm Chloe messages Jack

Don't tell me, she said she couldn't thank you enough…

2:21pm Jack messages Chloe

She's buying me lunch. I told her that was thanks enough.

Jack

PS I think your attitude must have been wrong when I went shopping with you. This was a breeze.

Jack

2:25pm Chloe messages Jack

Within twenty minutes you'll have told her that:

1. Your ears are only nice and flat to your head because your Mother took the time to make sure they were folded back against your head when you slept as a toddler.

2. Tennis shouldn't be an Olympic sport.

3. Wearing sunglasses impairs a person's hearing.

4. Fish don't have an ageing gene.

2:28pm Jack messages Chloe

Who leaked these revelations to you?

2:28pm Chloe messages Jack

You did. Within twenty minutes of meeting me.

2:29pm Jack messages Chloe

Right. It's nice that you remembered them.

Jack

PS While I'm line-learning, eating and generally having a good time, get your thinking cap on… in the shows you've appeared in, have you ever had a narcoleptic amongst the audience?

2:40pm Jack messages Val

Hi Val

Out of interest, when was the last time you *saw* Terry Nutkins?

Jack

2:45pm Chloe messages Jack

In the shows I performed in, no member of the audience *entered* suffering from narcolepsy.

Chloe

2:50pm Jack messages Chloe

Thank God for that.

J

2:55pm Chloe messages Jack

A few have died mid-show over the years though. Two in one production – A Tom Stoppard from memory.

When the ambulance service receives a call from our theatre, they just head round the back to where the scenery doors are. It's easier to get a body out.

We lost one audience member during the song 'Some Things are Meant to be' from Little Women. It added a poignancy to a show that up to that point had been severely lacking in it.

3:00pm Jack messages Chloe

I'm starting to think I should be receiving danger-money. Talking of mild peril, we've been asked to arrive early to the theatre tonight to 'walk the set'. Trevor has announced that, bar a bit of painting, it's finished. I caught him boring the nervous girl; he was assuring her it ranked in his top five finest set creations.

All I know is it'll be a brave person to be the first to step onto it. I'm going to advocate someone who hasn't got many lines, just in case. I plan to arrive late.

Jack

3:12pm Chloe messages Jack

Good plan. How was lunch?

How long did you go before telling Mel that the Trans Volcanic Bunchgrass Lizard only lives long enough to mate once?

C

3:17pm Jack messages Chloe

38 minutes. Lunch was good thanks. Still drinking. Mel's been gone a while; I hope she's not ill. That woman can certainly drink. It's going to have to be a taxi home. One of the upsides of having a company car is you don't care where you leave it. That said, I'd hazard a guess that Alnwick isn't a hot bed of crime and I'm not sure how attractive a Vauxhall Astra would be to the criminal underworld, but as far as I'm concerned, they can do their worst.

3:19pm Chloe messages Jack

Have you got around to telling her about your hideous skin disease?

C

3:19pm Jack messages Chloe

No. Because I don't have a hideous skin disease.

3:20pm Chloe messages Jack

Oh, hang on, is that not you? I was just chatting with Tiny and somehow it came up.

3:22pm Jack messages Chloe

Did it. Really.

Jack

PS Mel started to show me her tattoos. She said there were more 'miscellaneous ones' but they weren't for showing in the pub. One tattoo on the underside of her wrist comprises a serpent and a lotus flower. Any idea what that means?

3:23pm Chloe messages Jack

It means you're going to be late to rehearsal.

4:39pm Val messages Jack

Last year, I think.

Val xx

5:17pm Jack messages Val

?

5:18pm Val messages Jack

That Terry fella. Last year. Lady Windermere's fan. What a pile of old shite that was.

5:19pm Jack messages Val

Was he alive? Did he have 10 (complete) fingers?

5:22pm Val messages Jack

Have you been drinking?

5:24pm Jack messages Val

I cannot lie. I have. With Mel. If I'm late, (when I'm late) will you cover for me? You'll come up with something plausible.

Cheers Val. I owe you.

Jack

7:18pm Jack messages Chloe

It's tense here.

7:19pm Chloe messages Jack

Why? What's wrong. Is your serpent not playing ball? Try and relax, it happens to a lot of men. I'm sure she'll be patient. Don't take too long though, doesn't her shift start in 10 minutes' time? Think of Jen, think of England, think of the girl you left behind (Blackadder II episode 3 – 'Potato').

7:21pm Jack messages Chloe

It's tense at the *theatre*!

7:22pm Chloe messages Jack

You're not doing it in the wood store? Crikey, you've gone up in my estimation (sorry for using the word 'up' there. It was insensitive of me and purely unintentional).

7:23pm Jack messages Chloe

Funny. Hilarious. It must be *laughter* that your audiences are dying of.

7:24pm Chloe messages Jack

Thanks. I'm thinking of trialling my act at Edinburgh this year. You can come if you like. I'll need flyers handing out.

7:28pm Jack messages Chloe

It's tense because there's a bloke from the Health & Safety Executive here and judging from the noises he's making and the fact Trevor's head looks like it might explode at any minute, I'm concluding things aren't going well.

Things got off to a bad start when Phil (the Health & Safety guy) stepped off the ladder onto the first level of scaffolding, at which point the other end of the plank sprung up and clattered back down again. The only thing that prevented it from being a reconstruction of a Laurel and Hardy sketch was the plank didn't rear all the way up and hit Phil in the face. Phil found two ladders that weren't tied on, half a dozen scaffold clamps that weren't even tightened up and a hammer hooked carelessly over a handrail. I fear he's going to insist the cast wear hard hats which given there's a coal mining angle to the show, wouldn't be a complete disaster.

Jack

PS It might stretch credibility if Mrs Harper wears a hard hat in her kitchen while looking into the open casket that contains the body of her dead husband.

7:33pm Chloe messages Jack

Bloody hell Jack. Be careful up there!

Chloe

PS How late were you?

7:35pm Jack messages Chloe

A fashionable thirty-five minutes late.

It was OK though because Val covered for me with:

'Jack's going to be late. He's biffing Mel'

Jack

PS I wasn't 'biffing Mel'. I did put her to bed though, she was hammered. I had to carry her, so I was pleased she's an 8.

7:37pm Chloe messages Jack

Alright, no need to go on about it!

7:38pm Jack messages Chloe

What are you? 10? 12? I'm trying to think back to me giving you that piggyback. I'll give you the benefit of the doubt and say you're a 10.

7:40pm Chloe messages Jack

I'll give you the benefit of my fist in a minute.

I'm a 10. In everything. Always.

(unless there are concurrent store promotions on merlot and pot noodle).

C

7:42pm Jack messages Katie, Mike & Connor

Right guys. Chloe's 30th. Present idea.

A case of wine, six pot noodles and a blouse (size 12).

Jack

7:52pm Jack messages Chloe

This rehearsal's fast becoming a non-event. Safety guy has only just left. Donald sent the nervous girl up to walk about on both upper tiers. The poor girl was on her hands and knees. Entrances and exits are going to take about ten minutes. I've no idea how they plan to get the coffin up there; there's clearly no room. The cast are going to take it in turns to stand still in various places while Dick Rump focuses the stage lights. So far, there seems to be a lot of red lights which would be fine if the show was set in Amsterdam or Hades.

7:57pm Chloe messages Jack

Is your show 'The Hired Man' by Howard Goodall?

It's set in Victorian England. The sort of show that's described as 'gritty'. It has miners in it. I saw an amateur production where the lead character (hard as nails farm labourer and coal miner) was flouncing about with a brand new stainless-steel Spear and Jackson spade in his hands.

Classic fayre.

8:02pm Jack messages Chloe

Nope. Our show has been written by a local historian with music by our rehearsal pianist; a quiet man who looks as if he's straight from 'One Flew Over The Cuckoo's Nest'. Wears a grey cotton tracksuit top and bottoms. No stripes or logos. Oh, and he never speaks.

8:05pm Chloe messages Jack

Oh Lord. Does your show have a name?

C

8:07pm Jack messages Chloe

'One night in Barcombe.'

It's a hard-hitting show set in the 1920s about the men and women who lived in the region of Bardon Mill. It focuses on the lives and loves of two families, both touched by tragedy.

8:09pm Chloe messages Jack

It sounds like a show that would be described as 'character driven' (i.e. nothing happens).

8:11pm Jack messages Chloe

Oh no, there's lots to keep the audience entertained; the Northumberland accents for one. Professor Higgins would be struggling to pinpoint some of the dialects, and I'm convinced Tim Waddle thinks the show is set in Cornwall.

If the show's music were a game of scrabble, two hours' worth of notes have been shoved in a green bag and emptied onto the floor. To say the tunes sound random would be an insult to 'chaos theory'.

Our most convincing coal miner is Val.

Christian Schmidt has picked out a waistcoat for himself that should be accompanied by a snooker cue, not a shovel.

Tim Waddle has made his own miner's helmet from a colander and an elasticated head torch.

The nervous girl enters on a bicycle that's gold coloured and labelled '*RAPTOR*'.

The chair that isn't a chair is made of faux wicker and borrowed from The Brains' conservatory.

Jack

PS Book early to guarantee disappointment.

8:13pm Chloe messages Jack

Does the nervous girl have a name?

8:13pm Jack messages Chloe

I don't think so, no. I'll ask.

8:15pm Jack messages Chloe

It's Charlotte. I've told her she should come down the pub with us after rehearsals. Outside of rehearsals we never see her.

8:16pm Chloe messages Jack

Smart girl.

8:18pm Jack messages Chloe

Christian just clapped his hands to get everyone's attention and ordered us to spend our time learning our lines rather than standing about chatting. Val's retort was immediate: 'What are you going to be doing Dennis Taylor, practising your shitting break-off?'

8:19pm Chloe messages Jack

He'll be incurring the wrath of Mary if he isn't careful.

8:20pm Jack messages Chloe

She gave him daggers and is now berating Trevor for losing us rehearsal time through his incompetence.

J

PS Tiny shouted something to the room. Everyone looked to Tim Waddle for a translation; even he was flummoxed but suggested it was something to do with helping people with their lines. Everyone scattered leaving me with Tiny. I said thanks and she's just run off to get her script (at least I think that's what she's done). Yesterday morning I ended up with a pineapple as part of my cooked breakfast. I didn't challenge it.

8:23pm Chloe messages Jack

Talking of Tiny, I took your advice and googled Norman 'two-jokes' Collier. I couldn't decide which part of his act I preferred. I'm erring towards the chicken simply because there's something amusing about poultry.

8:56pm Jack messages Chloe

There's an almighty row involving Donald, Mary, Trevor and Schmidt. Christian is refusing to deliver his lines up on scaffolding level 1 (he claims the location is too remote meaning the audience won't be close enough to witness his character's solemnity when he delivers his line 'Did I bollocks').

PS The incident presented me with an opportunity to escape from my line-learning with Tiny and I took it.

Tiny had particular difficulty saying the name of the colliery owner 'Barchester'. She couldn't get past the first syllable with the resulting sound effect being a cross between the Pearl & Dean riff and a sheep.

PPS Hang on, it's kicking off again…

9:00pm Chloe messages Jack

I can hear Gary McPeter sharpening his pencil as I type.

9:05pm Jack messages Chloe

Update. A compromise was reached over the GPS location Christian is to deliver his lines from. However, after five minutes of debate on how he should convey to the audience that he was waiting for 'Maisy' (Charlotte's character), Val entered the fray and likened Christian's approach to that of a rank amateur. Mary agreed with Val. Donald sat on the fence. Tiny offered something conciliatory that began in English but ended up sounding like an intro from a Showaddywaddy B-side 'Who Put the Bomp (in the bomp, bomp, bomp)'

I digress. Christian's approach to convey impatience while he waited for Maisy to enter was to look repeatedly at his watch. When I say repeatedly, I mean every couple of seconds. When Mary asked him what the hell he was doing, he told her that looking at your watch is what people do when they're impatiently waiting for someone. Mary replied with 'not every two seconds you twatwaffle!' Val chipped in with 'and is that the watch you intend wearing? It's digital you pecker head.'

That wasn't the end of it, Mary was on a roll… 'and while we're on the subject of shite acting, in Act 2 scene 5, the act of repeatedly tapping a pencil against your cheek does NOT effectively project to the audience that your character is thinking. It just shows them what they already know, that you're a bulbous wanghead.'

J

9:10pm Chloe messages Jack

Ooh excellent. Have things calmed down?

9:12pm Jack messages Chloe

Eventually they did. While Christian considered his response, I kid you not, he tapped his pencil against his cheek before stammering over an insult which seemed to be directed at everyone. The room fell silent, the stillness only broken when a scaffold clamp inexplicably clattered down onto the stage. Christian took that as his cue and strode purposefully to the exit doors, smouldering, chin pointed indignantly towards the ceiling, climbed into his car and reversed straight into a parking bollard.

Jack

PS When he stammered, Tiny snickered.

9:15pm Chloe messages Jack

The fact he tapped his pencil against his cheek while he considered his response, unfortunately lends his acting technique some credibility.

9:17pm Jack messages Chloe

You're right.

In a moment of genius, and as a nod to Schmidt's method acting, Val made a point of checking her watch (that she wasn't even wearing) when Christian laboured towards the exit doors.

9:20pm Chloe messages Jack

If only the end production was likely to be this entertaining.

C

9:25pm Jack messages Chloe

Yup.

The rehearsal's been abandoned. Donald tried to give a unifying speech as people were sidling out to maximise pub-time. By the time he had finished, I glanced back and only Trevor was left and he wasn't listening. He had his back to Donald and was gazing skywards to try and work out where the stricken scaffold clamp had come loose from.

Speak later.

J

9:28pm Chloe messages Jack

Maybe. I have homework. I've got to translate some German text into English. From first glance I'd say the gist of it is that ten people have been gunned down in a shopping centre and the assailant has stopped to ask directions to the pub (or it could be the church – I think they're similar)… or something like that.

Chloe

9:30pm Jack messages Chloe

Isn't it more likely your assailant is trying to get to the airport or railway station?

Jack

9:32pm Chloe messages Jack

Right. Have you studied German? No. No you haven't.

Chloe

9:33pm Jack messages Chloe

No, I haven't.

9:33pm Chloe messages Jack

No.

9:34pm Jack messages Chloe

It was just a hunch. Playing the percentages.

Catch you later Fraulein.

Jack

11:28pm Jack messages Chloe

Back in my room. The earlier rehearsal histrionics were the talk of the night. There were plenty of gags flying around. One person would say 'are you waiting for me?', the other would say 'do I look like I'm looking at my watch?' or 'does anyone have a pen because I need to think about that?' etc. etc.

11:33pm Chloe messages Jack

I take it Sekonda Schmidt didn't go to the pub.

11:34pm Jack messages Chloe

No. He'll be meeting with the car insurance loss adjuster. I feel a bit sorry for him. It's going to be tough to get past this and return to rehearsals.

Nervous Charlotte came along though, and I think she enjoyed it.

11:35pm Chloe messages Jack

Oh, I shouldn't worry about Schmidt. People like him always crawl back. Christian will make it clear that he's only returned because he's a professional and he owes it to his public.

11:37pm Jack messages Chloe

We're off to see an amateur production of 'Beauty and the Beast' tomorrow. There's a minibus laid on. Trevor's going so there's a great deal of seat-number anxiety. I'm not big on Disney but it should be a laugh. I think Mary has played Belle before so she's keen to run a critical eye over it.

11:38pm Chloe messages Jack

Belle? Mary? Bloody hell! When was that? 1962?

11:39pm Jack messages Chloe

How did your German translation go? Are there any townsfolk left alive? Did your assassin make it to the church in time for tea and scones with the vicar?

11:42pm Chloe messages Jack

I fathomed it out. Ten local primary school children visit a zoo, and a parrot subsequently escapes.

11:43pm Jack messages Chloe

Right. I take it the parrot went on to massacre half the village before settling down for a pint of shandy at the Red Lion (also an escapee).

11:44pm Chloe messages Jack

Night Jack.

11:44pm Jack messages Chloe

Night Chloe.

12.

Wednesday 23rd January

5 days 'til curtain up

7:29am Jack messages Connor

Hi Connor. How goes it?

You're a man with loads of tattoos. Give me an example of a tattoo that would be categorised as 'miscellaneous'.

Jack

7:31am Connor messages Jack

Alright mate. All good here.

I have four tattoos which compared to the number you have might seem loads, but in the grand scheme of things is probably well below the national average.

Connor

7:32am Jack messages Connor

Right. Thanks. I'll check that out later with The Office for National Statistics, but in the meantime, perhaps you could give me that example I asked for: (a miscellaneous tattoo?)

7:34am Connor messages Jack

Oh right, yeah.

A briefcase.

7:35am Jack messages Connor

What?! Who has that?

7:36am Connor messages Jack

I dunno. No one I know.

7:37am Jack messages Connor

Right. So... What, you've seen it in a book in a tattoo place?

7:38am Connor messages Jack

No.

7:40am Jack messages Connor

OK. I'm not sure you're getting the hang of this. How about we pretend it's a game, a game in which you give me examples of tattoos you've actually seen on a person or in a catalogue?

7:41am Connor messages Jack

OK. Sounds like a shit game though. Can't we play Words With Friends or something?

7:43am Jack messages Connor

No. Try again.

7:44am Connor messages Jack

A jar of pickled eggs.

7:46am Jack messages Connor

Okaaay. There are two things I find troubling about this example. Firstly, wouldn't this be classed as culinary? Secondly, I refuse to believe that this tattoo exists, except for in the mind of a very ill person.

7:48am Connor messages Jack

Sinead, our director of marketing has one tattooed on her back.

Connor

(It's not culinary because it's empty*)

*That's not strictly true. It's empty but for her Dad's ashes.

7:50am Jack messages Connor

Crikey! What's worse? Storing your father's ashes in an empty pickled egg jar or getting a tattoo to commemorate it!?

7:58am Connor messages Jack

Are we still playing the game? Do I need to answer?

Connor

7:59am Jack messages Connor

No. As always, you've been a great help.

Thanks.

Jack

8:05am Jo-Ann Pinchley-Cooke messages Jack

Hey snog-pants (did we kiss for a little too long the other night? I think we may have).

Today is all about seating – specifically the importance of seat selection. Under no circumstances do I want to be sat next to Trevor, Christian, Tim, Donald or Mary.

So, I need your help. Tiny holds the tickets. What are the chances of Tiny taking a bribe? Or blackmail? Do you have any dirt on her?

8:07am Jack messages Jo-Ann Pinchley-Cooke

I think Tiny has cornered the market on dirt. There's a curious item on the third tread of the staircase in the pub. It frightens the life out of me every time I pass it because it looks for all the world like a spider. I bent down to take a closer look at it the other day and thankfully it isn't a creature. My best attempt at categorising it would be five-year old scrapings from a shower drain. Incredibly, Tiny was dusting the banisters yesterday and completely ignored it. If there was more of it, I shouldn't doubt Christian would gather it up for the top of his head.

I'll make discreet enquiries about seating.

Jack

PS It would be helpful if scripts gave an indication of estimated time to be taken over each kiss (in seconds). Instead, we get 'with vigour', which could be anything from a peck, to a lingering puckering-up, to a prolonged nibble, right up to a seven-course tasting menu*.

Jack

* (you'd probably pass on the cheese course)

8:10am Jack messages Tiny

Hi Tiny.

Is there allocated seating for Beauty and The Beast?

I'd rather not sit by a 'Beast' (Mary/Trevor/Christian), so if you could arrange for a seat by a 'Beauty' (Mel/Jo-Ann) that would be grand.

Thanks.

Jack

PS You're a beauty too Tiny (obviously) but you'd be annoying in a theatre – too chatty.

PPS I enjoyed the pineapple ring served alongside the breakfast sausage yesterday, but if there's a choice of fruit on offer this morning, I'll go for crushed Kumquat atop my bacon. Thanks.

8:13am Chloe messages Jack

Morning old man.

Since your show is getting ever closer, I thought I'd give you a confidence boost by sending you a Gary McPeter review. A nice one.

Gary McPeter reviews The Attic Priory Players' production of Arthur Miller's 'All My Sons' 14ᵗʰ June 2010.

When is a tree not a tree? Easy. When it is a dead branch bearing virtually no leaves and being waved about in the wings. Waved about by a man who has dressed in black to make himself inconspicuous, but who has made no attempt whatsoever to ensure the audience can't see his hands clutching the end of the twig he's twirling.

If while reading this, your first thought is why is a man waving a dead branch from the wings? then you wouldn't be alone. The twenty-seven people in the audience were equally at a loss.

The twig-waving is presumably what the director thought would best represent a tree – a tree struggling to stay rooted against the most ferocious of storms. The fact that a preservative-treated bright orange fence panel from B&Q was able to withstand this veritable hurricane defied logic. One must conclude that when the time comes for the curtain to drop after the final performance, the fence panel will be winging its way back to the DIY store in exchange for a refund.

A more difficult refund to negotiate would be for the newspaper that ex-aircraft component manufacturer Joe Keller spent the entire production reading, which given the play's timeline stretched to three years, was quite a feat.

Away from these moments of farce, Jo-Ann Pinchley-Cooke turns in a half decent performance as the intelligent and beautiful Annie Deever, while Kate Keller played by Mary MacMary proves why she's the region's shining theatrical light.

It's difficult to imagine how someone could be more wooden than a dead branch or a fence panel, but somehow Christian Schmidt as the needy Chris Keller manages this, and is duly acted off-stage by both.

The rest of the cast, somehow contrived to be more anonymous than Larry Keller, a man declared 'missing in action' and an unseen character in the play.

Larry's Mother sees twig waving and horoscope readings as signs that her son Larry may still be alive and return home one day. The hapless audience were clinging to their own hope, the hope that the play was only two acts long. It was three.

No amount of carbon offsetting could ever repair the damage inflicted on humanity by the staging of this forgettable, nay pointless production.

'All My Sons' runs nightly until 19ᵗʰ June.

8:16am Jack messages Chloe

Thanks Miss Walker.

You're all heart.

Jack

PS I notice you haven't been quick to pass me any reviews of shows *you've* appeared in.

8:32am Chloe messages Jack

Tony A Ward reviews 'The Hammersmith Houselights' production of 'My Fair Lady' 18ᵗʰ August 2015.

In Hertford, Hereford and Hampshire, hurricanes hardly ever happen. That my friends is because there's a storm brewing elsewhere - in Hammersmith to be precise, with the eye of the storm being up-and-coming, multi-talented actress Chloe Walker.

And much like being caught in a storm, you couldn't help but be 'blown away' by the sheer energy and skill displayed by Ms Walker.

Yes, she was ably assisted by a supporting cast but there was only one star of this show, and I for one, could have watched her 'dance all night'. 'Wouldn't it be luverly' if this young, vivacious performer were plucked from the relative obscurity of this 200-seater theatre and thrust onto a larger stage due West where she unquestionably belongs. 'Just you wait', 'with a little bit of luck' that's exactly what will happen.

'I'm an ordinary man', but 'I've grown accustomed to her face', not to mention her perfect size 10 body and slender elbows.

'My Fair Lady' runs nightly until 22nd August.

8:45am Jack messages Chloe

I fear Tony spends his time standing 'on the street where you live' and looking in through your bathroom window.

Jack

PS Have you ever appeared in 'Beauty and the Beast'?

8:47am Chloe messages Jack

Yes. Once. The society in question cast a chap called Graham Platt as The Beast in order to save money on a mask.

C

9:15am Jack messages Chloe

I'm at breakfast. I was on high alert as I sat waiting for my fried breakfast to be brought out, mainly due to the burning smell and shouting emanating from the kitchen.

When my plate was slammed down in front of me, I glanced up at Tiny and was sorely tempted to ask if it had arrived via the crater of Krakatoa. She had a look on her face which suggested any sort of comment would be unwise. The underside of one grilled tomato was the only offering that wasn't charcoal in colour.

I really wanted to follow up on my earlier message to her regarding seating arrangements in the theatre (i.e. don't sit me next to x, y or z) but all I could manage was to ask if I could have some water. I calculated that if I was to eat what was in front of me, I would need approximately two pints of liquid to replenish the moisture snatched from me by the Chernobyl sausage alone.

Jack

9:19am Chloe messages Jack

I've always said there should be a 30-mile exclusion zone around your unfortunate sausage.

C

10:45am Jo-Ann Pinchley-Cooke messages Jack

OMG! Christian just knocked on my door. Last night he was rooting around in the props room for a pocket watch. I told him I had one (it was my Granddad's before you ask).

Anyway, he's only gone and got himself a spray tan. I could smell biscuits which is always a giveaway (well, that and the fact he's bright orange lol). I could be wrong, but I'm also fairly sure he's been 'botoxed' in his forehead.

I thought I'd let you know so you were prepared. It's hard not to laugh at first.

Jo-Ann xxx

10:48am Jack messages Jo-Ann Pinchley-Cooke

No problem. I've just learned a technique whereby if you don't want to laugh, you focus on the person's forehead... oh wait…

Jack

10:50am Jo-Ann Pinchley-Cooke messages Jack

Lmao! Tim Waddle does that all the time. It's disconcerting. I stand on tiptoe to make him look me in the eye. It's already comical because I'm about a foot taller than him (although he thinks any height difference is negated by him turning his shirt collar up).

J-A xxx

10:52am Jack messages Jo-Ann Pinchley-Cooke

Has Christian borrowed your pocket watch so he can study it while he's impatiently waiting for Maisy to enter? If so, I'm nominating you to explain to him that it wasn't the *type* of watch that was bothering Mary, rather the *frequency* with which he was looking at it.

Jack

PS I'm off to google whether Botox and spray tans were commonplace amongst miners in 1920s England.

10:55am Jo-Ann Pinchley-Cooke messages Jack

Hahaha lol

Did you have any joy bribing Tiny for favourable seats?

Jo-Ann xx

10:57am Jack messages Jo-Ann Pinchley-Cooke

Given the atrocity that was my breakfast this morning, I'm inclined to heed the advice that you should never negotiate with terrorists.

(I'll ask her on the minibus).

Jack

11:12am Jack messages Chloe

I'd like to report that I've now learned 101 lines. My favourite so far is:

274

'Eeh man, ahm gannin te tha booza! If ah find oot you've nicked me canary, I'll put yee in the meat wagon yee faffin' mustard plaster.'

J

11:15am Jack messages Chloe

My second favourite is:

'Tha' lass Chloe Walker's got summat wrang wi' hor. Thar wouldn't want tuh share the bath wator wi' tha' skanky pickle bagger.'

11:16am Chloe messages Jack

I see your playwright has taken great care to avoid regional stereotypes.

C

11:18am Jack messages Chloe

Indeed.

Word has it Christian's paid a visit to the tanning salon.

J

11:19am Chloe messages Jack

Isn't he playing the part of a miner? Forgive me, my history knowledge is best described as rudimentary, but didn't miners spend up to twelve hours a day below ground?

I'm going out on a limb here, but it could look a tad incongruous when David Dickinson pops up from the pit-head.

Chloe

11:21am Jack messages Chloe

Funnily enough, that's exactly how Christian makes his entrance.

The moment he emerges, we should all shout 'Bobby Dazzler!'

Jack

PS Right, I need to get ready, the minibus gets here at 12pm.

11:23am Chloe messages Jack

Have fun. Choice of outfit is always troublesome when it comes to a visiting an am-dram show. The auditorium will either be of sub-zero temperature in which case you'll need your gilet under a survival suit, or alternatively it'll be a blistering 35^0C with the relative humidity of Guatemala and you'll be too hot sat there in nothing but your crusty boxers.

11:25am Jack messages Chloe

I'm going to lawyer-up.

11:25am Jack messages Chloe

*layer-up.

11:26am Jack messages Chloe

My auto-correct is shot. In its defence, it's trying to refine its vocabulary using our conversations as a benchmark. It's all it's got to go on.

It's the same with those children who are raised by wolves. They aren't going to have the skills to land a job in IT, but they'll be well versed in stealth and how to isolate a lone deer before bringing it down and tearing it apart with their bare hands. Much like my phone, it's all they know, and they think it's normal.

Jack

11:28am Chloe messages Jack

Probably best if you avoid that analogy on a first date, I would have thought.

C

PS You haven't met 'Basement Stuart' from our IT department. He was definitely raised by wolves.

11:40am Val messages Jack

Heads-up Jackie – wear something warm otherwise you'll be freezing your tits off in that theatre later.

Val

11:41am Jack messages Val

Thanks Val. I've taken the precaution of wearing my jumper. I'm pairing it with my black combat trousers, so I'll have plenty of pockets if you need anything storing like sweets for the journey, Valium for the theatre etc.

Jack

12:02pm Jack messages Chloe

I'm on the minibus!

J

12:03pm Chloe messages Jack

Well done! Did you manage that all on your own or did you get an adult to help you?

C

12:04pm Jack messages Chloe

Tiny's just announced that we're waiting for two people. Not sure who.

Jack

12:05pm Chloe messages Jack

Did you get a good seat? At the back with the naughty boys?

C

12:05pm Jack messages Chloe

I'm next to Jo-Ann. She must be excited about this trip because she was on-time (oh, and she keeps telling me how excited she is).

I feel like I'm on a school trip but instead of going to the zoo, we're off to watch some likely dreadful theatre.

Jack

12:07pm Chloe messages Jack

Thigh-gap Pinchley-Cooke is probably thinking she's already at the zoo. Gorilla enclosure.

C

PS What's she wearing?

12:08pm Jack messages Chloe

Not a lot.

Look, I'd better pause our chat. The rest of the whoop are getting restless.

J

12:11pm Jack messages Chloe

FFS. Colin Inglis has just boarded.

J

12:12pm Chloe messages Jack

Who?

C

PS You lasted three minutes before messaging me. You didn't tell J-A the wolf analogy did you, with the result you're both now sitting in awkward silence?

12:13pm Jack messages Chloe

No.

Colin Inglis is the bloke I'm to work with at the office. Y'know 'comedy' tie, 'comedy' mug, 'comedy' socks, comedy everything except comedy person.

J

PS I don't know for sure that he was wearing comedy socks when I met him, but I don't think it's too much of a stretch to put it out there.

PPS He's taken a seat next to Val. She doesn't look impressed. Hahahaha

12:14pm Jack messages Chloe

THE

NUN

HAS

JUST

GOT

ON

!!!

12:15pm Chloe messages Jack

What?! Wait, is it the same one?

C

12:16pm Jack messages Chloe

I don't know. She's wearing the same outfit…

FOR CHRIST'S SAKE!! COURSE IT'S THE SAME ONE!!

12:16pm Chloe messages Jack

'Thou shall not take the name of the Lord thy God in vain.'

Chloe

PS Given who you're currently sitting next to, it's also worth being mindful of 'Thou shalt not commit adultery'.

12:17pm Jack messages Chloe

If we're being righteous, let Mike know that 'Thou shalt not covet they neighbour's goods!!!'.

Jack

12:17pm Chloe messages Jack

You've added unnecessary exclamation marks there. Moses didn't report seeing any. You've now upset the balance of things by making stealing look more of a crime than committing murder.

Chloe

12:18pm Jack messages Chloe

When I've worked out a strategy, I'm going to wander down the bus and ask her who she is.

J

12:19pm Chloe messages Jack

Strategy?! You don't need to write a procedure document!

I know, why don't you stand at the front of the coach and get the passengers to watch a risk assessment through the medium of a PowerPoint presentation?!!

Just go and ask her for Christ's sake!

12:20pm Jack messages Chloe

No need to be blasphemous.

Jack

PS The driver is called Ken. Coach drivers are only ever called Ken or Les (or Vince if you're going to London).

12:22pm Chloe messages Jack

Have I got this right? You don't know the identity of the nun, but you know the bus driver's name; a fact which, from where I'm standing, is completely irrelevant.

C

12:23pm Jack messages Chloe

Why are you standing? If all your colleagues are sitting, you're going to look weird. Sit down.

J

12:24pm Chloe messages Jack

It's quiz night tonight by the way. Frightening how quickly it comes round. You have a rehearsal I assume.

C

12:25pm Jack messages Chloe

It comes round once a week. You've become a pensioner. A twenty-nine-year-old pensioner. Next, you'll be saying 'where's the year gone, it only feels like yesterday it was Christmas'.

Jack

12:49pm Chloe messages Jack

Nun update?

12:51pm Jack messages Chloe

I haven't got around to it yet.

However, Mary reckons she's shaken Terry Nutkins' hand. I asked her if it felt odd, maybe a bit like a Masonic handshake? She said she didn't think so but couldn't be sure because it was over a year ago.

I think she's what the police would describe as an unreliable witness.

Jack

PS Colin Inglis is chatting away to Val who's looking like she could rip the 'comedy' tie from his neck and garrotte him with it at any second.

12:52pm Chloe messages Jack

Nun...

12:52pm Jack messages Chloe

Alright, alright.

J

12:58pm Jack messages Chloe

OK. That could have gone better.

I asked her why she was here. She replied that she, like everyone, was here to serve God. I laughed. She didn't.

She asked me what my name was. I told her. She informed me that Jack was of Old English and Hebrew origin with the meaning 'God is gracious; he who supplants'.

I didn't know how to respond, and it gets a bit hazy here, but I think I said 'cool'.

She added that even as far back as the 13th Century, Jack was such a common name that it is was used as a general term for a peasant. After she took a moment to smooth out her habit, she went on to tell me that despite the evolution of language, even jackass, the commonly used term for a donkey and the derogatory term for an idiot, retains its essence in the word Jack.

I got a bit flustered, thanked her for her time and re-took my seat.

1:02pm Chloe messages Jack

I didn't realise that your brief (the brief that took you half an hour to put together) was for the nun to find out everything about you, and you to come away knowing absolutely nothing about her.

Chloe

PS Jackass.

1:03pm Jack messages Chloe

The day is still young.

1:04pm Jack messages Val

I notice you have a new friend. How's your journey been?

Jack

1:05pm Val messages Jack

It's been fine ever since he asked me what I did for a living.

Val

1:05pm Jack messages Val

What *do* you do for a living?

J

1:05pm Val messages Jack

Contract killer.

1:06pm Jack messages Val

Do you enjoy your work?

What's the going rate for a single hit these days? Ballpark: for someone, for example, who's easy to spot due to their brightly coloured head?

1:08pm Val messages Jack

It varies. Today it's two double vodkas and a packet of salted peanuts.

Val

1:08pm Jack messages Val

Sounds reasonable.

I trust half now, half when the job's complete is OK with you?

1:09pm Val messages Jack

Yes. I'm also doing a special (today only) 3 for the price of 2.

1:09pm Jack messages Val

I'll leave instructions under your napkin at lunch. This message will self-destruct in 10 seconds.

J

1:11pm Jack messages Chloe

I think we've arrived at our destination. Tiny stood up and bellowed something into a microphone. She's been using it all trip. She thinks she's a tour guide; a tour guide who's forgotten that we're within a one-hour radius of everyone's homes.

Like her tour commentary, no one is quite sure what she's just said.

Oops, Colin Inglis took a chance and made to leave the bus. Tiny yelled 'SIT DOWN!' (there was no mistaking that). She's now handing out interval drinks slips. Everyone's terrified. Jo-Ann and me have put 4 gin and tonics, 3 pints of lager, a smiley face and 6 kisses.

1:12pm Chloe messages Jack

Don't you have a rehearsal tonight?

1:12pm Jack messages Chloe

Let's worry about that later.

Jack

PS Christian Schmidt has definitely had Botox.

1:45pm Jack messages Chloe

I'm in a good position in the restaurant.

I have the seat right at the end of the table, so I have a great vantage point.

'Mel's to the left of me, Joker Colin to the right.'

There was a row about whether people should have a starter or not, because it mightn't leave enough time for those who wanted a pudding. I didn't fancy a starter but ordered one purely because Christian Schmidt was in the dessert camp.

Colin introduced himself to Mel with 'I'm Colin Inglis but you can call me Cunny. My boss gave me that nickname. I don't know what it means or why he started calling me it, but I guess he's just being friendly'.

Mel spat out most of her vodka and coke and focused on my forehead for the next ten minutes.

1:47pm Jack messages Chloe

Oh, and there've been some classic moments at Christian's expense. Val kicked things off by ordering Duck à l'Orange despite it not appearing on the menu. This kickstarted a flurry of orange-themed requests including orange juice, orange Fanta, Tequila Sunrise, Tango and a Buck's Fizz. Not to be out-done, Tiny asked if they could knock up a Monkey Gland which she explained was an orange-coloured cocktail. You had to feel for the waiter.

Jack

PS A seemingly unaware Schmidt said, 'I'll have a Fanta too if you have it'.

1:50pm Chloe messages Jack

A bit surprised no one asked for Sunkist.

C

2:09pm Jack messages Chloe

We've just finished paying. I don't think I've ever felt more stressed. We were £48.50 short of the bill total after the first pass. Most of that was the bottle of wine The MacMarys had 'forgotten' to account for. I could see that Cunny had added his portion up wrong which is a worry given his job. Trevor asked if he could pay in Bitcoin, (we still aren't sure if that was an attempt at a joke or not) and clearly there wasn't much in the way of tipping happening. It got sorted in the end, mainly because Mel and me added tips that would wipe out the national debt of Burkina Faso.

Jack

PS It's showtime!

2:10pm Chloe messages Jack

Cunny!

hahahahahahahaha

2:25pm Jack messages Chloe

We're in our seats. Tiny put the uncool kids together in front of us. Our row, from the aisle in: Nun – Me – Mel – J-A P-C – Tiny – Cunny.

I told the nun that there's a great responsibility that comes with occupying the aisle seat and that it's incumbent on her to make a dash for the bar at half-time to locate our interval drinks. She quipped that that would make her a 'nun on the run' so I'm given to thinking she's warming up a little – talking of which it's bloody roasting in here! I'm struggling to breathe.

I'd best turn my phone off.

Jack

2:26pm Chloe messages Jack

It's called an interval, not half-time.

Chloe

PS Now you've broken the convent ice, bloody-well find out what her story is you moron.

3:45pm Jack messages Chloe

It's half time. WTF was that I just watched?!

I'm having to make notes. I don't want to ever forget.

I'll message later (probably after rehearsal).

Jack

5:35pm Jack messages Chloe

On the minibus heading home (if you can call a pub bedroom, 'home').

I've no idea how the rehearsal will pan out later. Everyone's hammered including the director and the sound/lighting guys.

I'm going to need a sleep.

Oh, further jokes were made at Christian's expense in the interval. Val was on top form again with some not-so-subtle ribbing about his Botox. I can't remember all of it but:

Val: 'Did you know that if you walked around the world, your head would have travelled a slightly longer distance than your feet? Christian, you look surprised.'

Val: 'A group of hippos is called a bloat and there tends to be 10-20 hippos in each bloat. Christian, you look surprised.'

Val: 'A jiffy is about one trillionth of a second. Christian, you look surprised.'

7:26pm Chloe messages Jack

I feel Val missed out by not using 'Did you know a ripe orange can be green?'

10:15pm Jack messages Chloe

I'm in bed. No one could face a post-rehearsal drink. The evening was a bit of a write-off. I tried one of my costumes on; the trousers were about 4 inches too long. Kitty looked me up and down and said, 'You'll do'.

J

PS Oh, how did you get on at the quiz?

10:52pm Chloe messages Jack

6th. It was a mightily strange quiz tonight. It felt like it had been compiled by someone who'd done too much LSD.

Our downfall was the round called 'Who said that?' We played our joker on it thinking it would be famous quotations. As it happened, it was ten questions on ventriloquists and their dummies. We did badly. 2/10. (Nina Conti and Bob Carolgees).

C

10:53pm Jack messages Chloe

I'm brilliant at ventriloquists. I know them all. What did you struggle with?

10:54pm Chloe messages Jack

Name a Keith Harris puppet other than Orville.

10:56pm Jack messages Chloe

Cuddles the monkey! 80's classic! How come none of you knew that? Everyone knows that! He had his own show 'The Keith Harris Show'. Bernie Clifton was on it – I mean, he was a bit of a one-trick-pony, (well one-trick-ostrich to be precise). He had one joke fewer than Norman Collier, but it was a belter!

Can't believe you didn't get 'Cuddles'.

J

PS Give me another!

10:56pm Chloe messages Jack

Oh God, alright. Who voiced the puppet Lenny the Lion?

10:57pm Jack messages Chloe

Terry Hall. Not to be confused with the lead singer of 'The Specials'.

How come none of you got that? What have you been doing with your lives?

10:58pm Chloe messages Jack

Er… having a life.

10:59pm Jack messages Chloe

I knew the team would struggle when I moved away.

11:00pm Chloe messages Jack

Yes. It's been a constant uphill-battle.

11:01pm Jack messages Chloe

You only appreciate things when they're gone.

J

PS I'll have to tell you about 'Beauty and The Beast' tomorrow. I'm too knackered now.

11:02pm Chloe messages Jack

I'll look forward to it.

Night Jack.

C

11:03pm Jack messages Chloe

Night Chloe.

J

2:17am Jack messages Chloe

Was there a question about Ray Alan and Lord Charles?

2:18am Jack messages Chloe

Roger De Courcey? (Nookie Bear)

13.

4 days 'til curtain up

9:04am Katie messages Jack

Mike, Connor and me are planning on coming up to see the show on your last night. To be honest we were all reluctant to give up a Saturday night, but Connor suggested it might be entertaining for all the wrong reasons. Mike liked the idea of cramping your style just by being there.

Katie xx

Btw, Mike wants to know if there'll be a VIP area with free drinks.

9:06am Jack messages Katie

Hi Katie. Good to hear from you.

Yeah, sorry but the show's sold out for the whole run. Never mind. Maybe next time.

Jack

PS I hear you did rubbish at the quiz last night.

9:07am Katie messages Jack

It wasn't our finest hour, but round five had questions that only a knuckle-dragging fuckstick who was dropped as a child, would ever have known the answers to.

I mean what sort of loser would know or care who worked Nookie Bear from behind?

Katie x

(Nice try but I've seen the ticket charts and as of last night, the most seats sold for any one night was 47).

9:08am Jack messages Katie

I'm sorry the questions didn't fall your way.

Jack

PS I have it on good authority that Mike was dropped as a child, which explains a lot.

9:09am Katie messages Jack

Chloe tells me you singularly failed to find us a suitable holiday, so I've found a villa in Portugal. It has four rooms and a private swimming pool. Plus, if we put Mike down as a child, it'll only cost £578.00 each for a week (including flight).

Sound OK?

x

9:10am Jack messages Katie

It's a little unadventurous but sounds like fun. Count me in. I've still got 'Wendy' the shark from when we went to Mallorca.

J

PS Does the villa come with the use of a car?

9:11am Katie messages Jack

After Mallorca, I rather think it's best to stay car-free.

9:12am Jack messages Katie

I still maintain there was an obligation on the part of the rental company to point out that the handbrake was foot operated.

9:13am Katie messages Jack

It was my name on the hire contract. Have you any idea how embarrassing it was explaining that we were unable to return the car, but that they might want to ask the coastguard to keep an eye out for it.

9:14am Jack messages Katie

My Walkman went down with that car. The insurance company refused to replace it. It was a 'new for old' policy too.

9:15am Katie messages Jack

Could it be they couldn't replace it was because they stopped making them ten years previously?

9:16am Jack messages Katie

We had tickets to Flamingo World which we couldn't use too. They didn't reimburse us for those either.

9:22am Katie messages Jack

It was a Tuesday if you remember. It was our second day. I took a taxi to the rental car company's headquarters in Palma. I was there for three hours. The woman I spoke to looked at me with something approaching pity, but still played hard-ball over contract clause 3a.ii which was allied to mental competency. There was talk of me being evaluated by a panel of experts. I remember your calls well because they arrived just as the police joined the interrogation to try to establish if any maritime laws had been broken by the potential blocking of shipping lanes. I ignored your first five calls, but then, wracked with worry that I might be unaware of a medical emergency or the like involving one or more of my friends, I apologised to the table of six officials, explaining that I needed to take your call. Try and imagine my state of mind, when at this point, you uttered the words 'don't forget to give them a nudge about Flamingo World'.

I nodded thoughtfully for the benefit of the six pairs of eyes that were trained on me from across the table as you explained that even though we'd bought Mike's ticket as a concession, there was no way the insurance company could know that, and that I should push for a refund for five full price tickets at €13.50 each.

I thanked you for your call and resolved to hold your head under the water in the villa's pool until your thrashing body lay lifeless in my hands.

9:26am Jack messages Katie

Is that what that was? I took it to be a moment of aquatic flirting.

J

9:27am Katie messages Jack

So, in answer to your earlier question, no we will not have the use of a car.

9:28am Jack messages Katie

I shall remember that holiday as the only time Connor has ever been funny.

9:29am Katie messages Jack

I must have missed that.

9:30am Jack messages Katie

I think it was unintentional.

I brought up the non-reimbursement of our 'Flamingo World' tickets and Connor said that in hindsight we hadn't got a leg to stand on.

9:32am Jack messages Chloe

I'm lying here, looking at a suspicious brown smudge on the bathroom door. I could swear it wasn't there yesterday. What in God's name could have caused that?

9:34am Chloe messages Jack

How the hell am I supposed to know? Have you been flinging your excrement around again?

9:35am Jack messages Chloe

Well, it's disconcerting.

9:35am Chloe messages Jack

So, tell me about 'Beauty and The Beast'.

9:36am Jack messages Chloe

Absolute classic! Wish you'd been there. It's hard to know whether the level of incompetency on show was normal or whether everything conspired against them in that particular performance. I'm thinking the former.

9:37am Chloe messages Jack

Give me the edited highlights.

9:39am Jack messages Chloe

First up, after everyone had taken their seats, an elderly couple came round selling tickets for the tombola. This theatre group perform six shows per year, I checked. You'd think this would mean the tombola procedure would be slick. It wasn't. Tickets were passed along rows with money going the other way. Change would then make its way back to those who needed it. Cunny plucked a twenty-pound note from his comedy wallet, passed it along the row and received just three tickets and four ten pence pieces in return! I bought one pound's worth which was two tickets and donated them to the nun (I'd seen the prizes). She passed some comment about how this gesture proved that I loved my neighbour. I pointed at Trevor and told her that currently he was my neighbour, thus proving that her theory was flawed.

9:42am Jack messages Chloe

There was a kerfuffle at the back when the old couple were alerted to the fact there were two pink tickets in circulation carrying the same number. In the end, the Chairman stepped in and called out every number from 1 to 236. We were asked to raise our hand if we had a ticket bearing the number being called out so it could be established if there were any further duplicates. Three people had the number 69 which prompted a fit of giggles in Mel, that frankly she never recovered from.

9:46am Jack messages Chloe

Anyway, the whole process took twenty minutes and elicited mutterings about buses being missed etc. Apart from anything else, there was no element of surprise when the tickets were eventually drawn. 'Pink 35? Yeah, that's Mary sat in C7. Next.'

9:48am Jack messages Chloe

The Chairman had one of those voices that sounds like a frog in a headlock; like his throat had a diameter half that of normal people's. On the boring scale, I'd put him somewhere between Michael Brains and Tim Henman.

As we approached the number 180, I was sweating with anticipation. How would he call it? It was a moment that would define him. Showmanship was called for. Two people's hands shot up on 179 risking a loss of momentum. When the moment came, there was no flourish, no change in pace, volume, or inflection. It was just Kermit reading out three digits.

9:51am Chloe messages Jack

Which part of 'edited highlights' are you struggling with?

9:54am Jack messages Chloe

Firstly, the overture was terrific. I'm told this is normal and is down to the fact that the musicians are the only paid

303

performers. I'm not convinced the conductor was entirely sober though. He entered the auditorium via a fire door, turned and bowed to the audience, then spectacularly failed to negotiate the four steps down into the orchestra pit. A brief dusting-down and we were underway. The overture reached its magnificent climax, everyone applauded, and things started to unravel…

9:57am Jack messages Chloe

… During the overture, a castle was revealed in all its chipboard grandeur. Whoever had designed it, obviously hadn't given much thought to its manoeuvrability. Two large men clothed entirely in black, tried to heave the structure off stage (the practise of dressing the stage crew in black has always intrigued me – I mean, do they think we can't see them? Black is slimming but I don't think it's ever claimed to make a person invisible). Invisibility was a super-power the two hapless individuals probably wished they were cloaked with, as they tried, under the full scrutiny of the audience, to muscle the stricken fortress off stage.

You could sense the audience were willing them on. A few were even making the noise a person makes when lifting a heavy box or trying to squeeze out a particularly solid stool, as if somehow the projected noise would give the struggling crew more impetus.

10:00am Jack messages Chloe

Meanwhile, the conductor had managed to get an instruction across to his orchestra to repeat a dozen or so bars of music on a loop.

After a minute or so of pushing and pulling, grunting, and sweating, the two unfortunate souls on stage did 'helicopter arms' to signal more people were needed to join the fight.

They were joined by a tiny person; so tiny I had to peer hard to rule out the possibility of them being a toddler. It was clear to everyone that the addition of Jimmy Krankie wasn't going to bear fruit. Fortunately, a burly chap raced on (lumbered on really) wearing ill-advised grey skinny jeans and a bright red T-shirt which bore the slogan 'I WORK WITH A BUNCH OF C*NTS'.

By this time, the conductor had thrown his hands in the air, thrown the towel into the ring, and sat down, leaving the four exhausted stagehands to grapple with the scenery in total silence. When the castle was finally persuaded to make its exit, the audience cheered, and Jimmy Krankie took a small bow.

10:02am Chloe messages Jack

Crikey. We're barely into scene one. This is gold.

10:03am Jack messages Chloe

I know! It was already too much for Jo-Ann. A message was passed along the row that she had laughed so hard, she'd done a small wee. I turned to my left to pass on this nugget to the nun, hesitated, and decided against it.

10:04am Chloe messages Jack

Go on…

10:06am Jack messages Chloe

So… I was thinking it couldn't get much worse, but this show was the gift that kept on giving. We'd just about composed ourselves when Mrs Potts, Lumiere and Cogsworth joined the fray. To disguise Mrs Potts as a teapot, some bellend had decided to bandage-up her right hand and lower forearm. The result was a housekeeper who looked more like an amputee than a teapot. With her right hand rendered useless, she only had the use of her left for essential stage directions like opening doors and gesticulating. She was so demonstrably right-handed that even the act of picking up a tray of teacups, threatened to turn into a Greek wedding.

10:09am Jack messages Chloe

In Lumiere's attempt to be debonair, he walked with an upright gait and stood with a posture that suggested the candelabra he was supposed to represent was, in fact, rammed up his arse.

In the same way that Brian Barrowman has his foot-stamp before delivering his lines, Lumiere had a tic which always materialised at the *end* of his. He'd say his line, then extravagantly snap his head round to face the audience, before pursing his lips together and raising both eyebrows. Think Larry Grayson after he's said, 'shut that door!' or 'look at the muck in here!'.

He'd mastered a look of camp surprise, that Christian Schmidt has also achieved but only after parting with a hundred quid.

Debate raged during the interval as to why Lumiere had adopted this eccentric technique. Various hypotheses were put forward with most agreeing it was probably because he was an attention-seeking twat.

10:12am Jack messages Chloe

Cogsworth spoke with a heavy Brummie accent amongst a cast all doing their best off-the-shelf American. His accent, together with his monotone voice and slouched demeanour, contrived to present a character that was so charisma-free, you'd rather agree to a meal-out with Alan Shearer, Paul Burrell and conscience-pricker Bob Geldof.

J

10:13am Chloe messages Jack

Ooh, please say they'd be joined by David Coulthard, Victoria Beckham and Roy Hodgson.

10:13am Jack messages Chloe

'Too much tedium will kill you' (Brian May).

10:14am Chloe messages Jack

I think I've just 'done a Jo-Ann'.

I can't read this in here. Carry on while I make my way outside.

10:16am Jack messages Chloe

At the interval I nudged the nun to make a dash for the bar. Credit to her, she leapt up and was taking the steps two at a time before it became clear it wasn't the interval. She skulked back to her seat and fixed me with a stare that Mary MacMary would have been proud of.

When the interval arrived at its second attempt, we found our drinks and began dissecting what we'd just witnessed. It was then that the company's chairman wafted over to talk bollocks with our Chairman Michael Brains; mano a mano, chairman to chairman. Here we were, a group of giggling adults, trying to suppress laughter in front of the figurehead responsible for the horror we'd just sat through.

10:19am Jack messages Chloe

The experience of suppressing laughter felt similar to that of being at a funeral when the scraping of a chair makes a sound a bit like a fart, except it doesn't really sound anything like a fart, it's just an abrupt noise that briefly pierces the oppressive silence. But in your head, it's a fart, because that's inappropriate at a funeral. My point is, you're either a person who hears the scraping of a chair and logs it as such, or you're a person who hears a fart, logs it as a fart and finds it amusing.

In the interval, when the society's chairman was telling us that most people who'd seen the production had said it was better than the West End version, Mary, Donald, Trevor, Christian, Tim and Cunny heard a metaphorical chair-scrape and nodded in solemn agreement, whereas Mel, J-A, Tiny, me and the nun heard a metaphorical fart. Mel did that thing where her drink went up her nose which was a godsend because it gave us a legitimate reason to resume laughing.

10:20am Chloe messages Jack

Oh God. Terry Bleasdale's funeral.

10:20am Jack messages Chloe

Exactly.

10:21am Chloe messages Jack

Except it was the organist's pedal. Not a chair.

10:22am Jack messages Chloe

Was it? I thought it was one of the castors on the trolley the coffin was perched on.

10:23am Chloe messages Jack

No. We agreed the castor was Joe Pasquale.

Pray continue.

10:28am Jack messages Chloe

A man with a sixty-a-day-voice told us via the tannoy system to retake our seats. The couple who had been sitting behind us must have had a rethink and opted to spend the next hour of their lives elsewhere, anywhere.

Instead of the orchestra piping up though, Hinge and Bracket reappeared to draw the Tombola. Do you '*draw*' a Tombola? Like you '*draw*' a raffle?

10:35am Chloe messages Jack

Are you waiting for me to answer that? Seriously?

10:37am Jack messages Chloe

Ja.

10:39am Chloe messages Jack

'Tombola blah blah blah... tickets drawn from a drum.'

Satisfied?

10:41am Jack messages Chloe

Hardly. That's not what I asked. You 'draw a raffle' but do you 'draw a Tombola?'

10:43am Chloe messages Jack

Unsurprisingly, and judging by the meagre number of search results, I don't think it's the burning issue of the day.

PS I did however find some advice on acquiring a license to run an official Tombola. That got me thinking about other things one needs a license for, like a TV and... I dunno...

A GUN*

C

*(an application for which is underway).

10:45am Jack messages Chloe

Alright. I'm just trying to paint a picture here.

10:46am Chloe messages Jack

And I'm waving a twelve-bore about. Get on with it.

10:49am Jack messages Chloe

Tickets were drawn from the unlicensed Tombola which took an inordinate amount of time, mainly due to successful ticket holders being invited to the front to collect their prizes. I say successful, it's debatable whether the winning of some Parma violets fudge could ever be declared a victory.

Fifteen minutes later, we waved goodbye to Hinge and Bracket. There was a further hold-up when two wheelchair users were choreographed back to the foyer to create a thoroughfare wide enough for the tombola to exit.

10:55am Chloe messages Jack

Who/what the hell is Hinge and Bracket?

11:06am Jack messages Chloe

Must I have these constant interruptions?!

So… the show was underway again. Mel and Jo-Ann were struggling to hold it together.

The opening scene of Act 2 was something 'The Guinness Book of Records' people would have been interested in. The category would be 'the greatest number of people on a theatre stage at any one time'.

Bodies kept piling on at the back of the stage, forcing those already present to shuffle forwards. It was like a giant coin-push machine; the ones with the sliding shelves you find in amusement arcades with ten pence pieces and the occasional cheap watch moving back and forth. We held our breath waiting for the first row of townsfolk to topple into the orchestra pit. And *still* more people joined at the back, until it was obvious to all that there were more people on stage than in the audience.

In the blink of an eye, the stage went from a town to a conurbation.

By the time everyone had been shoe-horned onto the stage, the musical number was winding down, and the stage needed to be cleared for the next scene. The actors who were last to join the crush only got a couple of seconds of stage time before being shepherded off with the others.

When a scenery cloth depicting a forest was lowered, three actors were caught downstage of it instead of behind it.

Hang on, Tiny's shouting something up.

11:09am Chloe messages Jack

What did she want?

11:12am Jack messages Chloe

Hard to say. I definitely heard the words 'Aled' and 'Jones'. And 'Fucking Snowman'.

Now I think of it, I don't think she was talking to me.

11:14am Chloe messages Jack

Aled didn't sing that. It's an urban legend.

11:16am Jack messages Chloe

Hold up.

An urban legend is sewer alligators.

An urban legend is that Paul McCartney as we know him now, is a body double who replaced McCartney when he died in 1966.

You can't have an urban legend surrounding Aled Jones. He has to be the least 'urban' person I know. 'Legend' is hugely debatable too.

11:18am Chloe messages Jack

Alright 'Mr Underground'.

You were saying… Three people on stage stranded the wrong side of the cloth...

11:20am Jack messages Chloe

Right, yes. So, the cloth was deliberately ripped into long shreds, to represent leaves and tree branches, I think.

Two of the stranded actors played the situation nicely by calmly turning to their left and nonchalantly walking from the stage (although an audible 'shit, bollocks!' was heard from one of them as they reached the safety of the wings).

The third cast member wasn't so lucky. He made to exit right but the spear he was carrying on his back, snagged on one of the ripped ribbons of the forest stage cloth. The unfortunate spear-carrier couldn't work out why his legs were pumping but his body was pinned. One of the men-in-black appeared, freed him and the band played on.

11:24am Jack messages Chloe

There was still one final treat. Belle's father, a crazy inventor called Maurice entered stage-right in a motorised vehicle. Post-show research has revealed that the likely nature of this vehicle was a ride-on wood-cutting machine. A wood-cutting machine this was not. What it was, was a shop-mobility scooter with a sheet of plywood nailed to each side in a futile attempt to disguise it. The small grey tyres, handlebars, shopping basket and maroon paintwork were some of the clues available to the trained eye, but even to the cataract-afflicted it was bleeding obvious what it was.

When the time came for Maurice to drive off stage, the turning circle was so large that a seven-point turn was initiated. The music ran out after turn two, after which time you could hear the whine of the electric motor, the squeaking of the rubber tyres, and a voice, which while whispered, was unmistakably Val's saying 'Attention! This vehicle is reversing!'.

Jo-Ann did another wee.

11:28am Jack messages Chloe

In the foyer after the production, the Chairman slithered over and asked us what we thought, adding 'It was spectacular wasn't it?'.

I assured him that it was certainly 'a spectacle'.

11:29am Chloe messages Jack

Are you still in bed? Oh, it seems we have a good holiday option courtesy of Katie. She found it online within ten minutes of searching.

11:29am Jack messages Chloe

Sounds under-researched.

11:32am Jack messages Derek Street

Hello Derek.

I was lucky enough to be in the audience yesterday to witness your group's interpretation of 'Beauty and The Beast'. We met briefly. I'm with The Attic Priory Players. I hope you don't mind me getting in touch (our group's secretary passed me your number. You might know her, she goes by the name of Tiny).

I just wanted to say I thought your stage was packed with talent. Literally packed. If I'm honest, I thought it was better than The West End version.

You must be a very proud Chairman.

Thanks again,

Jack White

PS Could you put me in touch with the stagehand who wore the red t-shirt?

11:45am Mel messages Jack

Hey gorgeous.

Are you doing the publicity thing at 2pm?

Also, are you in a team for the car treasure hunt on Saturday? Shall we team up?

Mel xx

Btw, I don't think the nun was too impressed with her Tombola prize.

11:49am Jack messages Mel

I think she was playing it down. Who wouldn't be thrilled to win a one-gallon catering-sized jar of salad cream?

J

PS Yes to a team on Saturday. My first choice would have been navigator for Christian, but you'll have to do. I can't remember if Jo-Ann mentioned it too.

PPS Publicity thing????

11:53am Mel messages Jack

Singing on the village green. To give the public a taster of what they can expect. I'm only there to meet the photographer.

11:55am Jack messages Mel

Whose idea was this? Two words spring to mind: 'counter' and 'productive'.

Our best chance of securing an audience for our three hours of mediocrity would have been to keep quiet and rely on the element of surprise.

No one in their right mind will buy a ticket once they've listened to 'It's The Pits'.

And those unfortunate bastards who've already bought a ticket will be demanding a refund if we give them even five minutes of 'Canary Blues'.

Jack

PS Village green singing sounds like fun.

PPS It also sounds like something that calls for drinks beforehand...?

J

11:57am Mel messages Jack

I think you're underestimating the marketing potential of 'Slag Heap Shuffle'.

Mel

(I'll be over at 1pm for drinks)

11:58am Jack messages Mel

Bring the out-of-date bottle of Cava you won yesterday. We can mix it with something potent and in-date. Something brain-numbing that'll make 'You've Got a Fissure In Your Shaft' sound less like a double entendre.

12:01pm Mel messages Jack

If it's going badly later, we can always resort to a public hanging. I'm thinking we could string Trevor up using the length of washing line that PINK 23 bagged him yesterday.

J

12:02pm Jack messages Mel

I'm making a note to never ask you out on a date. I'll be filing you under 'women scorned'.

Jack

PS Would it have been more, or less funny if the rape alarm had been won by the nun instead of the old guy in the wheelchair?

12:04pm Mel messages Jack

That's a tricky one. When that one was drawn, another few millilitres of wee escaped from Jo-Ann and I made a mental note to buy her a 'shewee' for her birthday. I'm thinking the 'flexi' model.

Mel

Btw, how bad does a prize have to be for the organisers to feel it doesn't stand up as a single offering, and so pair it up with something else? All that's achieved is that some poor sap ends up with two lots of shite instead of one.

Like that poor bastard who came away with a 'Brotherhood of Man' cassette and an organic dog biscuit.

12:06pm Jack messages Mel

That combined prize has massively short odds of reaching a grateful recipient. David Blunkett maybe. As it was, I heard the successful ticket holder explain to the person in the next seat, that he keeps fish.

12:08pm Jack messages Chloe

Chloe. What's the weirdest thing you've ever won in a raffle?

12:09pm Chloe messages Jack

A tin of artichokes and a frisbee.

That's not weird though. What's weird is you starting your message with my name. Why the formality?

Chloe

PS Our theatre group do a raffle. The done thing is for people to gather after the draw, and swap prizes until everyone ends up with something to their liking.

12:11pm Jack messages Chloe

That's a great idea. If yesterday's winners had played swapsies, wheelchair guy could have bagged the bike pump.

The frigid-looking woman on row O could have secured the rape alarm.

If Val had been canny, she could have walked away with the Brotherhood of Man cassette.

Tiny could have exchanged her inflatable referee for the one-gallon catering-sized jar of salad cream.

Mary could have had the organic dog biscuit.

That would just have left the second-hand foot spa.

12:12pm Chloe messages Jack

Awww. Does Mary have a dog?

12:13pm Jack messages Chloe

No.

12:18pm Derek Street messages Jack

Good afternoon.

I'm afraid it's theatre policy not to pass on staff's personal details.

I'm glad you enjoyed our production. You weren't the only one who said that ours compared favourably with The West End version.

I like to think we set a standard here that's unrivalled.

Kind regards,

Derek Street

12:20pm Jack messages Derek Street

I quite understand.

Let me say once again how terrific your production was. It was, quite frankly staggering. Unrivalled? Yes, almost definitely.

If I had to pick out a favourite moment, I think it would be when The Beast knocked the basket of flowers into the orchestra pit. It was a lovely touch on the part of the Director to show us the Beast's clumsiness juxtaposed with the delicate beauty of the flowers. I hope the bassoon player makes a full recovery.

Good luck with the rest of the run.

Jack

PS Is red t-shirt man a gynaecologist by any chance?

12:23pm Jack messages Chloe

A few of us are going to be promoting the show on the village green later. I hope we don't come in for any abuse.

J

12:24pm Chloe messages Jack

It's Attic Priory, not Croydon. You're unlikely to be abused/slashed/robbed/pimped/trafficked.

C

12:25pm Jack messages Chloe

Easy for you to say. You're not the one who'll be singing 'Mineral Deposits on the Seam (on the Seam)'.

J

12:27pm Chloe messages Jack

Is your show a comedy?

C

12:28pm Jack messages Chloe

It's not meant to be, no.

Although I'm worried people will misconstrue Act 2's opening number 'The Oldest Face-Drilling Swinger in Town'.

J

12:29pm Chloe messages Jack

I fear a public stoning.

C

12:32pm Jack messages Jo-Ann Pinchley-Cooke

Hey J-A

Did we talk about teaming up for Saturday's car treasure hunt? I have a vague memory of this which means I was probably drunk.

Jack

12:34pm Jo-Ann Pinchley-Cooke messages Jack

Hey J.W.

I see our relationship has moved to the next level - the one where you have a cutesy abbreviation for my name.

We did mention teaming-up yes. I'm very excited about it. Do you want to ask Val too?

J-A xxx

12:36pm Jack messages Jo-Ann Pinchley-Cooke

Hey Jungly-Ass Peachy-Carpet (better?)

Cool. Should be fun. Mel wants in too. I'll message Val. That should make four of us in one car.

Mr White

12:37pm Jack messages Val

Hi Val

Fancy making up a treasure hunt team with Jo-Ann, Mel and me on Saturday?

I don't mind driving.

Jack

12:38pm Val messages Jack

Bloody brilliant! I know this area like the palm of my hand.

I'll drive. Gives me a chance to give the old motor a run-out.

Val x

12:38pm Jack messages Val

Hi Val

I'd be more reassured if you were familiar with the *back* of your hand, but beggars can't be choosers!

I'll let the others know and we'll meet in The Hunter's car park!

Jack

12:39pm Jack messages Jo-Ann and Mel

Hi Jo-Ann & Mel

It's official. We're a team. Us three plus Val.

12:40pm Mel messages Jack and Jo-Ann

Excellent. Looking forward to it. Meet first for a swift one?

12:41pm Jack messages Jo-Ann and Mel

Definitely!

Oh yeah, I meant to say, Val's offered to drive.

12:42pm Mel messages Jack and Jo-Ann

Hmmm. Quick question: Have you ever been driven by Val before?

12:43pm Jo-Ann messages Jack and Mel

Val? Driving? Really?

Well, OK. I hope you've got a Sat-Nav*.

J-A

*and a crash helmet.

12:44pm Jack messages Jo-Ann and Mel

Listen to you two. She can't be that bad. Just have an extra drink before we set off.

3:29pm Chloe messages Jack

I hope you haven't been publicly humiliated or driven out of town by a seven-year-old on a tricycle.

3:32pm Jack messages Chloe

I kept a low profile.

Christian Schmidt came in for some mild abuse from one of the local farmers; bit of an eccentric chap called Bernard.

3:34pm Chloe messages Jack

Why? Was Christian singing a solo?

3:35pm Jack messages Chloe

Yes. It's a love song near the end of Act 1:

'Two Can Drain That Vein.'

3:36pm Jack messages Chloe

Oh, and the photographer from the local rag kept fiddling with the settings on his camera. He was moaning that the colour of Christian's face was affecting the white balance of his shots.

3:36pm Chloe messages Jack

Katie tells me you tried to dissuade those three from coming to see your show.

3:38pm Jack messages Chloe

Yes. It was a smart move, especially now I've witnessed Bernard the farmer, heckling us. Those three wouldn't need any encouragement to join in. I shall pray to The God of Theatre Benevolence that Bernard doesn't buy a ticket. He holds more fear for me than Gary McPeter.

J

PS Sadly, Katie knows that cack-all tickets have been sold and they're intending to watch on the last night.

3:42pm Chloe messages Jack

Let's hope they've booked accommodation. I can't cope with more bathroom tantrums if all three were to doss-down in your room.

3:45pm Jack messages Chloe

I take it you won't be coming up with them then?

3:48pm Chloe messages Jack

I can't. I have my Mum's 60th birthday on that Saturday. Dad's hired the function room at the golf club so not only will we be celebrating in the beigest room ever, but there are likely to be fat men wearing checks, claiming a level of athleticism, and maintaining that golf is a sport.

3:50pm Jack messages Chloe

Sounds ghastly.

J

PS Any sport which allows its 'athletes' to get about on an electric cart is quite clearly a pastime.

3:53pm Chloe messages Jack

I do feel guilty though because I can't get away during the week to see your show either. It's all hands to the pump at the office this week because of the conference. We've all been told we can't take leave. I'm so sorry. You need to make sure you remember the funny stuff and message me each night.

(a very apologetic) Chloe

4:37pm Chloe messages Jack

You there? Oh dear, I think I've upset you. Honestly, if there was any way I could get up there, I would. You've always sat through the shit I've been in. Aaaarrrrgggghhhh.

Chloe

5:02pm Chloe messages Jack

I'll make it up to you. I'll take you to the zoo, you'll like that.

C

5:03pm Chloe messages Jack

Scratch my last message, it made you sound a bit 'special'.

C

5:28pm Chloe messages Jack

OK you big twazock, your silence isn't making me feel guilty anymore. I've moved on. In fact, I might sack off my Mum's 60th, go out with the girls, and bring a stripper home for some no-strings sex. That's how little I care right now.

C

5:32pm Chloe messages Jack

Oh Lord, it's no good, I'm still feeling guilty, I'm not confident a stripper would come home with me, and I need strings with my sex.

Chloe

5:45pm Jack messages Chloe

Hi. Sorry, I fell asleep.

Christ, what was all that sentimental drivel you've been writing? Don't fret about it. This way I get to tell you how brilliant my performance was, and you'll have to take my word for it.

Wow, I feel better for that nap. I'm ready to face tonight's rehearsal head-on now.

Jack

PS What're your plans tonight? (aside from bagging yourself a stripper).

5:52pm Chloe messages Jack

There's a ceramics course I might register my interest in.

5:54pm Jack messages Chloe

What happened to your German course?

5:56pm Chloe messages Jack

Oh, I'm not doing that anymore. There was a creepy guy called Martin on it. I realised last week that I needed something more creative than sitting there saying 'mein Name ist Chloe. Ich bin funfundzwanzig Jahre alt'.

5:57pm Jack messages Chloe

You're not twenty-five.

5:58pm Chloe messages Jack

No, but Lorenzo from Milan didn't need to know that.

Chloe

PS Right, I'm going to brave the Underground. I was groped yesterday. My first thought was to take to Twitter to log my abhorrence on behalf of all women, everywhere, but it turned out I'd been violated by a suitcase handle. I'm not gonna lie, it's lean times and I'm taking what I can get.

6:02pm Jack messages Chloe

Wow. Where did it grope you?

J

6:03pm Chloe messages Jack

The District Line.

C

6:04pm Jack messages Chloe

I meant what part of your body.

6:04pm Chloe messages Jack

I know you did.

6:05pm Jack messages Chloe

My sympathy is waning. So?

6:06pm Chloe messages Jack

My butt. If I'd known it was about to happen, I'd have clenched, so it felt firmer.

C

6:07pm Jack messages Chloe

I'm not sure what's more concerning: taking pleasure from sitting on a suitcase handle or worrying about what an inanimate object might think of the firmness or otherwise of your arse.

6:08pm Chloe messages Jack

Sigh.

11:02pm Jack messages Chloe

It was good fun tonight (well, the pub was). Every time Jo-Ann returned from the toilet or the bar, someone would claim to be able to smell wee.

Since the chat was revolving around bodily functions, I thought I'd pitch in with the story of when I went to Evesham for that work training day. Do you remember? At the end of the day, I visited the toilet before heading home, and in the urinal next to mine was a turd. A large one at that. In a urinal! So anyway, I told the story and sat back satisfied that I'd recited it well. After a few beats, a confused-looking Tim Waddle said 'Evesham?'.

I wasn't the only one who was puzzled that Tim should think that Evesham was the pivotal part of the story.

11:04pm Chloe messages Jack

I think you need to mix with some new people. What was rehearsal like?

11:06pm Jack messages Chloe

Oh, overall, the rehearsal was a shambles.

We did the show in costume, and have the completed set now, so we attempted a full run-through (minus the orchestra).

Donald instructed us to treat it like a performance. We were told that the time for joking around was over and that we should ensure we were fully focused.

Five minutes in, we arrived at the scene where Christian's character is trying to raise money for the family's coffers. A gentleman agrees to buy Christian's pocket watch. The two men swap handshakes, and a bank note is passed in exchange for the timepiece.

Val took this as her cue to shout out 'Cheap as Chips!'

11:09pm Chloe messages Jack

Hahaha. How did that go down?

C

11:10pm Jack messages Chloe

Not well. Mary charged out of the theatre protesting about having to work with amateurs. Donald Sinden's name was mentioned but the context wasn't clear.

Mel had earlier overheard Donald telling Mary he thought he'd left a tap on in their bathroom, so it's likely Mary used the commotion to nip home.

11:13pm Chloe messages Jack

Excellent stuff.

11:14pm Jack messages Chloe

Yup. The trouble was, Tiny, being our prompt, was asked to read-in Mary's lines. She had nine goes at a line that read 'No, Mr Tapper'. By the time Mary returned, we'd only advanced two pages. Moments later, a stage light exploded, and we all took a break to calm our nerves.

11:19pm Chloe messages Jack

I was close to a stage light once when it exploded. Terrifying.

11:21pm Jack messages Chloe

Yes!

Val had palpitations. Dick Rump swept up.

11:23pm Chloe messages Jack

I'm surprised you had time to get through the rest of the show.

11:24pm Jack messages Chloe

Oh, we didn't. We made it all the way to the second scene in Act 2 and called it a night. There are three scenes in that act that I've never run since we blocked them.

We had some warm wine at the theatre while Donald gave us his notes before high tailing it to The Hunter's for some light relief.

11:27pm Chloe messages Jack

Are you nervous about the show?

11:33pm Jack messages Chloe

Very. I have way fewer rehearsals under my belt than the others, so I'm winging it a bit. We don't seem to be able to get through a page, let alone a scene, without the whole thing falling on its arse. Some people are a worry to be on stage with.

There are some people who spend more time reassuring you that they'll know their lines come opening night, than they spend trying to *learn* them!

But they're not the worst. The ones who don't know their lines but *think* they do, petrify me. To those people, an approximation of a line is one perfectly memorised. Cracked. Perfected. Down pat. Those people give no thought to the person opposite them. Me! The poor anxiety-riddled, bum-clenching, twastard who's shaking like a shitting dog while trying to decipher their meaningless paraphrasing, work out where the hell they are on the page (if they're even *on* the same page) and reply with a line of my own.

Don't you worry, I'll burn the midnight oil to make sure I know both of our lines.

I think I need another drink.

11:37pm Chloe messages Jack

I know these people. They're everywhere. They're breeding. They're multiplying. They'll bleed you dry.

Chloe

PS In my experience, they're also rubbish on stage.

PPS Don't let the bastards grind you down.

11:38pm Jack messages Chloe

Thanks.

11:39pm Chloe messages Jack

Now sleep my brave soldier.

Chloe

11:40pm Jack messages Chloe

Night.

J

11:40pm Chloe messages Jack

Night.

C

14.

3 days 'til curtain up

9:15am Mel messages Jack

Hey

The photo from yesterday's village green debacle is in today's newspaper. It's already up on their website so I've emailed the cast a link. It should be in your inbox.

Mel xx

9:19am Jack messages Mel

Oh priceless! Have you noticed they've accidentally spelled Christian's surname wrong?!

J

9:19am Mel messages Jack

Oh, that was no accident.

Xx

9:21am Jack messages Chloe

I've emailed you a link to our local newspaper's website which shows the photo taken on our village green yesterday. Notice anything? (other than me looking particularly beguiling).

J

9:24am Chloe messages Jack

Schitt!

9:24am Jack messages Chloe

Quite.

9:29am Jo-Ann messages Jack, Mel, Tiny and Val

Hi kids.

Anyone up for seeing the new Will Schitt movie. Dame Maggie Schitt is in it, and the music's by Sam Schitt.

Jo-Ann x

9:32am Val messages Jack, Mel, Tiny and Jo-Ann

Is that the one about the lockschitt who's actually a gunschitt supplying arms to some bad guys on FBI's most wanted list?

If so, I don't think the music is by Sam Schitt, but rather by The Schitts*.

Val xx

*(it might have been Morrissey as a solo artist – you'd have to look it up)

9:34am Jack messages Val, Mel, Tiny and Jo-Ann

Has he seen the article? If so, 'Heaven knows he's miserable now'.

Jack

9:34am Mel messages Jack, Val, Tiny and Jo-Ann

Has anyone heard from 'This Charming Man?'

Mel x

9:36am Jo-Ann messages Jack, Mel, Tiny and Val

Not yet. It'll be Tiny he complains to.

Then the schitt will really hit the fan.

Jo-Ann xx

9:47am Tiny messages Jo-Ann, Jack, Mel and Val

Christian has just messaged me. He's not happy. He's on his way over (I schitt you not).

Tiny xx

9:50am Jack messages Val

Hi Val. Charlotte told me last night she'd like to be involved in the treasure hunt. Will there be room in your car for her to join us?

Jack

9:50am Val messages Jack

Yeah, the more the merrier. Plenty of room.

Val x

(Who's Charlotte?)

9:50am Jack messages Val

The nervous girl. Doesn't say a lot. Smiley though.

Jack

9:52am Val messages Jack

Oh yes. Plays Maisy. Bless her, she only has a few lines but she's great. See you at rehearsal later my lovely.

Val x

9:54am Jack messages Val

The new eyeshadow looked good last night Val. Were you intending to wear it on stage (in front of an audience?).

Jack

9:56am Val messages Jack

Oh, that's nice of you. Thanks Jack. I followed your advice and got it from Boots yesterday morning.

Yes, I think it's perfect for my character.

Val

9:58am Jack messages Val

It is. Perfect. I just wonder if it might be best to tone it down a smidge (in colour and area). The red looked a bit menacing under the stage lights. It was a bit Nosferatu. Like I say, it's lovely. It suits you. It's just the stage lights doing weird things.

Jack

PS You make a great miner. The best.

10:01am Val messages Jack

I don't know what I'd do without you Jackie boy. I did wonder if it was too much. I'll make it more smoky and less crimson. Thanks, darl.

Val xx

10:48am Mel messages the cast & crew

Hi all. As per usual, I'll be running a book leading up to show-week on whose line the guy in the front row will fall asleep during. We'll have lots of eyes trained on him: Tiny and 'Norm the horn' in the orchestra pit ('Norm the horn' is a musician not a nymphomaniac), Dick and Trevor in the lighting box (they're rigging up a camera for monitoring purposes) and Cunny Inglis (our eagle-eyed stage manager) from the wings.

Odds have principally been calculated based on the timing of characters' lines and how they align with previous shows' sleep patterns. Additionally, an actor's tendency to deliver their lines in a lifeless, flat, self-harm-inducing, and more importantly *sleep*-inducing way will have the effect of their personal odds being shortened.

The odds:

- Charlotte Young – 17/1

- Jack White – 7/1

- Mary MacMary – 10/1

- Tim Waddle – 5/1

- Val Gordons – 5/1

- Christian Schitt – Evens (fav)

- Brian Barrowman – 11/1

- Bill Freynolds – 11/1

- Jo-Ann Pinchley-Cooke – 7/1

- Tiny – 3/1

A line can be spoken or sung. If sleepy head falls asleep during an instrumental piece of music or a gap between dialogue, the cast member whose line was closest to the point of sleep will be identified using the recording equipment installed by Dick and Trevor.

Players can place their bets (max £2) with me up until 7pm on the opening night. No correspondence will be entered into.

Thanks

Mel

10:53am Jack messages Mel

Hi Mel. I like it.

You've added Tiny to the list even though she's not in the show. Was that done in error?

Jack

10:55am Mel messages Jack

No. No mistake. Tiny won it twice in a row last year. As prompt she usually ends up with more lines than some of the cast. Bill Freynolds and Brian Barrowman both regularly stuff-up, resulting in interjections from Tiny. You'll see that Bill and Brian personally have longish odds here though, because they don't feature until scene 4. Tiny is second favourite at 3/1 and Christian is favourite, partly because he speaks first but mainly because it'll piss him off.

Mel xx

10:57am Jack messages Mel

You're a very thorough woman, so I'm probably insulting you by asking if you've considered that an entirely different member of the audience could choose to get some shut eye. Has this eventuality been accounted for? I only ask because unlike me, you haven't had the misfortune to witness our show at close quarters. As a piece of theatre, it would be too gracious to characterise it as uninspiring, characterless, and vanilla. It could be the natural-remedy anaesthetic the world has been waiting for.

Jack

10:58am Mel messages the cast & crew

Dear all,

As a footnote to my previous message, if one or more members of the audience slip into a coma (other than our regular Mr Snooze), they shall not be considered legitimate subjects for the purposes of betting.

11:02am Tiny messages Mel, cast & crew

I was just going to ask that, only because the clarinet player was seriously drowsy towards the end of scene two (and she sits next to the percussionist).

Thanks for clarifying.

Tiny x

11:03am Jack messages Mel, cast & crew

Hi everyone. What happens to the pot if Mr Forty Winks doesn't fall asleep at all? Is there a precedent?

Jack

11:04am Mel messages the cast & crew

There's more chance of hell freezing over or Gary McPeter writing something nice.

Don't you worry your pretty little head about it Jack. Ain't never gonna happen.

Mel xx

11:05am Val messages Mel, cast & crew

Aloha my beauties!

Could we have some guidance on the definition of sleep please? If Mr Slumber shuts his eyes, we currently have no way of knowing if he's technically asleep or not. Might I suggest we plant someone in an adjacent seat to be on the look-out for signs of snoring or dribbling?

Thanks

Val xx

11:09am Tiny messages Mel, cast & crew

I can confirm that Mr Zonk has booked seat A8 for the Tuesday night. I'll remove seat A9 from general sale. I propose that since neither Brian nor Bill appear until scene 4, one of those two could do the honours. Historically, Mr Catnap has never got past scene 2 so there should be plenty of time to get back to the dressing room, costume-up and get on stage.

Thanks

Tiny xx

11:12am Jack messages Mel

I think I may have started something.

Sorry!

Jack

11:12am Mel messages Jack

You owe me drinks*.

Mel xx

*note the use of the plural.

11:14am Mel messages cast & crew

There will be a sheet pinned up backstage for you to write your chosen actor and value of bet to be placed.

Mel x

11:25am Val messages Mel, cast & crew

Will we be betting on first mistake too? I love that. It's my favourite.

Val xx

11:28am Mel messages Val, cast & crew

I'm currently working out the odds for that particular competition and will be in touch shortly.

Mel x

11:45am Jen messages Jack

Hi Jack!

Guess what?! I've managed to get some time off work so I'm going to come up and see your show next Tuesday. I'll stay at least one night, so I'll call Tiny at The Hunter's and make sure I have a room (feel free to visit for nightcaps etc.*).

Maybe we could go to the beach again. I LOVED THAT!

Can't wait!

Jen xxxxxx

*I'll leave the 'etc.' up to you – use your imagination! Hee hee

11:48am Jack messages Jen

Hi Jen

Lovely to hear from you.

I'll look forward to your visit (although are you sure? It's an awfully long way to come and see a poxy show. We also had a tsunami here recently, it was devastating).

Oh, hang on, Tuesday you say. Would you like me to book you a ticket? I can see that seat A9 is free.

Jack

11:50am Jen messages Jack

Course I'm sure!

Yaaaaaaayyyy! Front row!

Jen xxxxxx

11:54am Jack messages Chloe

Dear Chloe

I can't go on. My life has spiralled out of control. It's nobody's fault. Where I used to see light, I now see only darkness. I long to move forward but my mind will only look back. Despair has become all-consuming. I'm sorry if I've let people down along the way and I'm especially sorry for not being a better friend to you Chloe. I'll miss our banter; I'll miss our heady, sun-drenched days on long holidays, and I'll miss your Atari. If I'm honest I probably won't miss your elbows or your slightly too curvy butt. Know that deep down I was always fond of you (in a cohabiting dog and cat sort of way). After my death I hope you'll find comfort in the little things, like my wallet, my unwashed boxers and the A0 sized framed photo of me I've arranged to be sent to your flat.

Kindest regards

Jack

PS If you could play 'Who Wants to Live Forever' by Queen at my funeral I'd be grateful. I know it's a cliché, but it'll induce a lot of crying and that's what I'm after.

11:55am Chloe messages Jack

Jen's planning to visit isn't she.

11:56am Jack messages Chloe

Yes.

11:57am Chloe messages Jack

I planned your funeral years ago when you caught headlice and convinced yourself you were going to die.

You're getting 'Shaddap You Face' by Joe Dolce and 'Mr Blobby'.

12:02pm Mel messages the cast & crew

Hello again.

As promised, below you'll find the betting odds for who among the cast will be the first to make a catastrophic mistake. It usually happens on the first night (let's face it, first scene).

Using a series of complex algorithms, odds have been calculated as to the likelihood of each actor making a *catastrophic mistake.* Factors considered include quantity of lines, history of reliability, proximity of lines to beginning of the show and general hopelessness.

As per the sleep-betting, it's a maximum £2 bet.

Odds have been calculated as follows:

- Charlotte Young – 200/1

- Jack White – 6/1

- Mary MacMary – 15/1

- Tim Waddle – 8/1

- Val Gordons – 7/1

- Christian Schitt – Evens (Bet 365 have stopped taking bets)

- Brian Barrowman – 2/1

- Bill Freynolds – 3/1

- Jo-Ann Pinchley-Cooke – 7/1

- Tiny – 3/1

Examples of a catastrophic mistake:

1. Missing out three or more lines of dialogue (yours or another actor's)

2. Any miner who forgets to wear his helmet in two or more below-ground scenes

3. Failure to enter a scene in time to deliver a line

4. F**king up a line so badly it renders your fellow actors speechless (Bill Freynolds: 'An Inspector Calls' 2003)

5. Failure to bring a crucial prop into the scene e.g. a shovel in the musical number 'Shovelling grit, Shovelling shit'

6. Falling into the pit-head (through the trapdoor)

7. Failure to get up after a death scene due to the actor having actually died (a death certificate may be required). Note - claiming that another

actor 'died' the moment they walked on stage, will not be permissible in this instance.

8.   Experiencing a bout of incontinence that results in a damp shaft

9.   Falling into the drum kit during a quiet bit (Tiny: 'Brigadoon' 1998)

10. Dramatically throwing yourself to the floor upon hearing the pit explosion, only to realise it was merely the sound of the Ladies' toilet door slamming shut (when is that going to get fixed by the way?)

11. The release of a small but audible fart during one of Christian's heart-wrenching monologues

12. Ditto if released just before Jack's ballad 'My Father's Helmet' (a bonus point will be awarded)

13. Being in the wrong place at the wrong time e.g. The Hunter's after Act 2 has started (Val: 'Gaslight' 2013)

14. When referring to Mr Tapper's maid, Fanny, accidentally preceding her name with the word 'bucket'

15. Any involuntary stage Tourette's (Val: 'Fuck-it, I've forgotten my binoculars', Ascot Gavotte, 'My Fair Lady' 2016)

12:12pm Jack messages Mel

Hi Mel

Being the new boy, I'm not exactly sure how this works. Do I have to pick a person AND a catastrophic mistake? If so, I think I'll plump for Bill Freynolds having helmet issues.

Jack

12:14pm Mel messages Jack

That's a fair question.

The answer is no. You pick an actor only (so no need to do as you did there and pick a catastrophic mistake too).

You'll probably want to reconsider your bet now you know the mistake made is irrelevant, especially given you accidentally picked an actor who isn't even a miner.

Mel

12:15pm Jack messages Mel

Oh, that was no accident.

12:15pm Mel messages Jack

Touché hahaha

xx

12:17pm Jack messages Mel

I notice that your list comprises 'Examples' only. If a mistake is made which doesn't comfortably fit one of your examples, how is it determined if the cock-up in question is to be classed as catastrophic?

Jack

12:19pm Mel messages Jack

Another good question Jack. My, you must have been not in the slightest bit irritating at school.

The answer is that I decide what constitutes a catastrophic mistake. As with the betting on sleeping guy, my decision is final, and no correspondence will be entered into.

Mel xx

12:21pm Jack messages Mel

My drinks bill is racking up, right?

Jack

12:21pm Mel messages Jack

Yes. You may want to consider a second income.

Mel xx

12:22pm Charlotte messages Mel, cast & crew

50p on Christian please.

Thank you

Charlotte

12:23pm Val messages Mel, cast & crew

I'm fully aware it's crap odds but it's hard to look past Christian here. £1.

Val x

12:24pm Tiny messages Mel, cast & crew

Will there be a pre-show parade ring? It's amazing what you can learn from watching the competitors walk round in a circle - are *they nervous, fit, hungover, sweating etc?*

If you need my bet now, I'll have an each-way bet on Christian (£2).

Tiny xx

12:25pm Mel messages the cast & crew

Right. For the avoidance of doubt, there will be no each-way betting permitted. This is strictly on a first past the post basis.

Mel

12:27pm Brian Barrowman messages Mel, cast & crew

I'd like £2 on Tim Waddle. Judging by what came out of his bottom on skittles night, the odds on him farting are very slender indeed.

All the best,

Brian Barrowman

12:28pm Tim Waddle messages Mel, cast & crew

I'm putting £1 on each of Brian and Bill. The last time either of them remembered three lines in a row, JFK was still alive.

Tim

12:28pm Val messages Mel, cast & crew

Objection!

Betting on two people is forbidden (isn't it?)

Val x

12:29pm Mel messages the cast & crew

The mediator reminds group members to adhere to the forum's guidelines and remain within the framework of what is considered acceptable behaviour.

Mel

PS No you can't bet on two people you fucking shit-stick (no offence Tim).

12:30pm Tim Waddle messages Mel, cast & crew

None taken.

Tim

12:31pm Jack messages Mel, cast & crew

I'm putting my life savings (which coincidentally is £2) on 'Beauty and The Beast' pant-wetter Jo-Ann Pinchley-Cooke.

Jack

'Show me the money'

12:35pm Donald messages Mel, cast & crew

Hi Jo-Ann.

I meant to say, I'll help you with your quick costume changes in the wings. Oh, and no need to be embarrassed if there's a bit of wee. I've always been good around that sort of thing. Truth be known, I quite like it.

Donald xxx

12:36pm Val messages Mel, cast & crew

Still on GROUP chat Donald!!!

FFS! And eugh!

I'm changing my bet to Donald. He'll either lose his helmet cos Mary MacBobbitt will have chopped it off, or he'll wind up dead in the middle of the stage: Death by shovel.

Val xxx

12:37pm Mel messages the cast & crew

Donald duly added to the list at odds of 7/1

12:39pm Jo-Ann messages Mel, cast & crew

I watched Christian reverse into that bollard the other day. He's an accident waiting to happen. £2

Jo-Ann xxx

12:40pm Dick Rump messages Mel, cast & crew

I used to know Christian's Mum quite well. Once, after an evening of drinking Dubonnet, she told me Christian had been a mistake.

£2 on Schmidt please Mel.

Cheers

Dick

12:42pm Bill Freynolds messages Mel, cast & crew

Good afternoon.

I will be placing my bet on myself. It's the pit explosion. I have a weak heart, you see.

Sincerely,

Bill

12:42pm Mary MacMary messages Mel, cast & crew

£2 on Bill.

Mary

12:42pm Val messages Mel, cast & crew

I'd like to change my bet please. £2 on Bill Freynolds.

Val xx

12:42pm Tiny messages Mel, cast & crew

Oh Bill, you never said. That's awful.

Tiny xx

(Mel, change mine to Bill too. Cheers.)

12:44pm Trevor messages Mel, cast & crew

I'll have two quid on Christian please.

Trevor

12:44pm Trevor messages Mel, cast & crew

Yeah, I'll have two quid on Christian too, please.

Douglas

12:45pm Trevor messages Mel, cast & crew

Two of my shiny new pounds says the gaff will be Christian's.

Ethel

12:45pm Trevor messages Mel, cast & crew

£2 on Christian for me too.

Arthur

12:45pm Trevor messages Mel, cast & crew

£2 on Christian. Cheers Mel.

Gertrude

12:47pm Mel messages the cast & crew

Thanks to everyone for the early flurry of betting. Just a couple of things:

1. I'm not putting in money for anyone. You'll need to
    hand over the cash to me.

2. Trevor. Placing multiple bets using aliases was never
    going to work, firstly because you've used names
    from the 1930s and secondly because your bets have
    all been sent from the same mobile; I know this
    because owing to the wonders of technology, my
    phone states that they're from 'Trevor' (which I've
    now changed to 'Twattor').

2:56pm Chloe messages Jack

Just back from lunch with Katie and scrutinising your group
photo from yesterday. Have your legs shrunk?

Chloe

2:58pm Jack messages Chloe

That's my costume (one of them). Kitty Cooper seemed to be
under the illusion the trousers looked fine.

Jack

2:59pm Chloe messages Jack

Yeah, they're fine, if you don't mind looking like Toulouse Lautrec!!

They look ridiculous (and given your personal wardrobe, that's saying something).

Chloe

PS I have a bad feeling that Katie is going to propose to Mike.

3:00pm Jack messages Chloe

Woah! Back up! You can't add that as a PS! A PS is for 'I'll pick you up at 7' or 'See you there (wear something slutty)'.

Expand please.

Jack

3:02pm Chloe messages Jack

Who, in the past have you typed 'wear something slutty' to? It wasn't me. You've not just made that up. You should have typed it to me, I've got slutty stuff - I just need an excuse to wear it.

3:03pm Jack messages Chloe

Connor typed it to Mike and me. It was when we went to see 'The Rocky Horror Picture Show' for Ticket Tony's stag do. You were at Meatball Sharon's hen party.

3:05pm Chloe messages Jack

Oh. Right. Yes. Didn't Afghan Jan get off with Johnny Two Dogs afterwards?

3:06pm Jack messages Chloe

No. Meatball Sharon did, which, I'm guessing, is why the wedding was called off!

3:06pm Chloe messages Jack

Oh yeah. That's right. Happy times.

3:07pm Jack messages Chloe

KATIE???!!

3:09pm Chloe messages Jack

Oh God, yes. We'd had a bit to drink, otherwise I don't think she'd have said anything.

Anyway, she's off to some hotel tomorrow to give it the once over, but she reckoned from the photos on their website and the brochure she'd received, it looked stunning. She said that as a wedding venue, it was pretty much top of the pile. Great function room, nice bedrooms for the guests and attractive staff (I did point out that those people probably didn't work there). She said she's going to book it for the second weekend in February to give it a trial. She winked when she said that! Winked!

3:09pm Jack messages Chloe

Right. Yeah. OK.

Right. Actually no. I don't follow.

3:09pm Chloe messages Jack

OH FFS. WHEN IS KATIE'S BIRTHDAY?!

3:10pm Jack messages Chloe

Shit! February 14th. I know that's a thing, but have you ever actually met a woman who's proposed on that date? I haven't.

3:10pm Chloe messages Jack

Jack. Two weeks ago, you only knew two women full stop (three if you count Claire from reception).

3:11pm Jack messages Chloe

That's not true. I know Heather the DPD driver, Helen Hunt and your Mum.

3:12pm Chloe messages Jack

Helen Hunt?! *You* know Helen Hunt? What??!!! From the film 'What Women Want?' co-starring Mel Gibson? What??!!! Why haven't you mentioned this before? And why have you put her second on your list behind Heather (whoever the hell that is)?

Chloe

PS My Mum? That was creepy.

PPS By the way no one is on first name terms with their delivery driver.

3:14pm Jack messages Chloe

- DPD is Heather

- Hermes is Ahmed

- Parcel Force is Barry

- UPS is Sandra (I forgot to add her to my list of women I know, but I only get UPS deliveries about twice a year)

- Asda is Colin

J

PS Helen Hunt: long story.

PPS Heather has a place in Spain. If Katie hadn't rushed in, I might have been able to get that for a week.

J

3:17pm Chloe messages Jack

My boss is giving me evils. I need to be quick. Concentrate on Katie. What are we going to do?

C

3:18pm Jack messages Chloe

Do you really think she intends proposing at this hotel? Just because she's earmarked it as a wedding venue, it doesn't necessary follow that she'll propose there. She might be waiting for Mike to propose to *her*.

J

3:19pm Chloe messages Jack

I don't know. No. Yes. Probably. Why would she go there on the 2nd weekend in February otherwise?

And Christ, she's not going to wait for Mike to ask. Mike took three years to build that brick BBQ, which by the way doesn't even have mortar between the bricks. A toddler with a basic grasp of Lego could have thrown it up in less than half an hour.

C

3:20pm Jack messages Chloe

Yeah, as BBQ's go, that's a shite one. He promised Connor at least five years ago that he'd bleed his radiators for him, on account of Connor having weak thumbs.

If you need me around for urgent message exchanges on the 14th, I'll need to check my diary. I have a feeling this coming Valentine's Day might be tricky.

3:21pm Chloe messages Jack

Why? Are you expecting a delivery from DPD?! Heather delivering herself and bursting out of a cake?

C

3:23pm Jack messages Chloe

Alright. Here's the plan. I'll follow them wherever they go; to the spa, the restaurant, the en-suite. Actually, yes, for nostalgia's sake she'll probably ask him while he's taking a dump. When I think she's about to pop the question, I'll leap out from behind the shower curtain and say 'NO! DON'T DO IT. THE MAN'S A CREEP, A CIRCUS FREAK, A BUTT FUNGUS, A PIFF POFF, A NUFF NUFF, AND A BLITHERING SILLY HEAD*. YOU CAN DO BETTER WOMAN. RUN…RUN!'

Jack

*I ran out of steam a bit there.

PS Or alternatively we could do what any normal people would do, which is NOTHING!

3:23pm Chloe messages Jack

What's a Nuff Nuff?

3:24pm Jack messages Chloe

A person with a very low IQ.

3:25pm Chloe messages Jack

I think it's a 5-star hotel so I doubt there will be a shower curtain. A hiding place re-think is required.

3:25pm Jack messages Chloe

Leave it with me.

4:45pm Christian Schmidt messages Michael Brains

Hello Michael,

I thought it only right to inform you about some unsavoury behaviour that's been taking place.

Name-calling is one thing, but encouraging gambling is quite another. I'm concerned that these pursuits will ultimately be detrimental to both the show and the society's reputation.

It's unprofessional and I request that this isn't merely passed off as a harmless prank. There's no such thing as a victimless crime.

Kind regards,

Christian Schmidt

5:52pm Michael Brains messages Christian Schmidt

Good afternoon Christian,

Thank you for bringing this matter to my attention. I shall conduct a thorough investigation and report my findings at the next committee meeting. If I feel the matter needs addressing in advance of next week's production, rest assured I shall act swiftly to bring this matter to a satisfactory resolution.

Sincerely,

Michael Brains

5:56pm Michael Brains messages Mel

Afternoon Mel,

I'm hearing noises about a gambling racket.

Sincerely,

Michael Brains

5:58pm Mel messages Michael Brains

Hello Michael

Yes, that's right. Pretty low-key stuff.

Mel

6:00pm Michael Brains messages Mel

Hmmm. What is it this time? Sleep, or mistake?

6:02pm Mel messages Michael Brains

Both, Michael. I know you don't like to be directly associated, which is why I left you off the list. I was going to message you personally.

Mel

6:04pm Michael Brains messages Mel

Good girl. Is Schitt the favourite again?

6:06pm Mel messages Michael Brains

Yes. For both.

Mel

6:07pm Michael Brains messages Mel

Excellent. Put me down for £2 on each.

Best wishes,

Michael

6:25pm Jack messages Tiny

Hi Tiny.

You're the ticket secretary, right?

Jack

6:27pm Tiny messages Jack

I wear many hats in this society Jack, but ticket secretary is one of them, yes.

Why?

Tiny xx

6:29pm Jack messages Tiny

Good.

Two things:

1. Keep seat A9 free for me.

2. Has Terry Nutkins bought his ticket yet?

Thanks

Jack

6:31pm Tiny messages Jack

Terry doesn't pay for his seat. It's a perk of being our patron.

I've looked and he's requested a ticket for the first night.

Tiny xx

6:33pm Jack messages Tiny

Thanks, Tiny.

PS Things I would happily class as a perk: a company car, a Christmas bonus, a complimentary Latvian hooker.

PPS Things I would NOT class as a perk: a free ticket to our production.

6:45pm Jack messages Christian Schmidt

Hi Christian

Do you think you could get to the theatre 15 minutes early tonight? Just wanted a quick chat. Let me know.

Thanks

Jack

6:47pm Christian Schmidt messages Jack

I suppose so. Why?

6:48pm Jack messages Christian Schmidt

Good. Don't worry, it's nothing heavy.

8:38pm Mel messages Jack

Hi Jack

I'm holding the fort at the pub tonight. It's deathly quiet. Tiny messaged me to ask if I knew why you'd had a clandestine meeting with Christian before the rehearsal tonight?

Mel xx

PS How's it going?

PPS You coming back for drinks after? I feel like getting squiffy and being irresponsible.

8:42pm Jack messages Mel

Hi Mel

You just caught me. We have to go back in in a minute. *'How's it going?'* It's not. It stalled and has been kangarooing ever since. Donald's in a state, Mary's in a tizzy and Dick nearly choked to death on a dry roasted peanut.

Seeing as Christian sees some of us as grossly unprofessional, I was worried he might be a flight risk, which is why I met with him. If truth be told, I also felt just a teeny bit sorry for him. All I did was suggest that sometimes he might find it easier to deflect our nonsense if he weren't quite so defensive. I hinted that, while we might not be completely his cup of tea, he should try embracing us (and generally chill out a bit). I did encourage him to follow his instinct though and sing the song that isn't scripted, but which he wants to add at the end of the show. I told him not to clear it with Donald first, but to surprise him with it instead.

Jack

PS How irresponsible? Borrowing a colleague's stapler and not returning it irresponsible? Or having a fifth pint when you know your cut-off is four irresponsible?

8:44pm Mel messages Jack

I was thinking more… hiring a bucking bronco, donning a pair of assless chaps, and buying a couple of litres of baby oil irresponsible.

Mel xx

8:47pm Jack messages Mel

I think we're edging into 6-pint territory for me there.

Jack

PS Good thinking with the baby oil. Very practical. Those bucking broncos sound like a chafing hazard.

8:48pm Jack messages Chloe

What's the kinkiest thing you've ever done?

J

8:48pm Chloe messages Jack

I went skinny dipping once.

You?

C

8:49pm Jack messages Chloe

I ran to the toilet naked one night when we went camping in Devon. It was 4am, you lot were all asleep and I was busting for a pee; in those days I was a crazy kid and slept in the raw.

J

PS Who were you skinny dipping with?

8:49pm Chloe messages Jack

I was on my own.

Chloe

8:50pm Jack messages Chloe

Thank God. I thought you were going to say Matt from Halfords.

8:52pm Chloe messages Jack

Oh God, I'd forgotten about him. His neck was weirdly thin. Horrible.

Chloe

PS It doesn't say a lot for our respective sex lives when the kinkiest things we've done have been solo ventures.

PPS We all saw you run to the toilet. Katie still has the video.

PPPS Why do you want to know about kinky stuff?

8:53pm Jack messages Chloe

No reason.

9:50pm Mel messages Jack

Hey.

Gonna have to take a rain-check on being irresponsible. I've had my head down the toilet for the last half an hour. God, I feel rough. Could you ask Tiny to get over here as quick as she can to take over?

Thanks (and sorry).

(I'll keep the baby oil and chaps and get a refund on the bull).

Mel xxxx

10:02pm Jack messages Mel

Hi Mel. Only just seen this. Tiny's on her way. You poor thing.

You didn't touch the door from the bar to the kitchen, did you? I always use my elbow for that one. The other thing I always avoid touching at The Hunter's is… oh yes… everything.

Take care Mel

Jack

PS I'll keep the Stepson handy.

10:02pm Jack messages Mel

*Stetson

11:12pm Jack messages Chloe

So… at the risk of sounding like a broken record, I don't think that rehearsal went too well. We did get to within half an hour of the finale though so it's important to look for the positives.

11:16pm Jack messages Chloe

Oh, and as if things couldn't get any worse, I was told that alcohol isn't allowed backstage. Fortunately, the people who matter, told me that they hide their booze in the scenery store. There's even a fridge in there, hidden behind a Welsh dresser. Val installed it five years ago apparently and no one has ever found it. We have to keep it secret from the likes of Tim Waddle and Christian etc. I've noticed that Brian Barrowman likes a drink. In fact, I've decided that I'm somewhat in awe of the man. He has a unique talent. He sits in the scenery store drinking his whisky, and he can somehow sense when his lines are approaching, so he finishes his drink, eases himself out of his chair, saunters out of the scenery store, through the green room, up the steps into the wings and straight onto the stage, without breaking stride. It's all done calmly. No part of it is rushed and he arrives on stage at exactly the point he's required to. I mean when he's on stage he's useless; can't remember his lines. Probably because he's pissed.

I've taken to following him. I've witnessed him make the same journey three times now and every time he's walked straight onto the stage without so much as a pause. Incredible.

Jack

11:18pm Chloe messages Jack

It's nice you've found a role model.

I watched this week's University Challenge. One of the contestants called Paxman a Kant.

Chloe

11:20pm Jack messages Chloe

Oh, I forgot to say, Dick Rump (who didn't come for a drink) was the talk of the pub and the butt of everyone's jokes over his earlier peanut-choking incident: 'Contagion', George Bush and his pretzel (which morphed rapidly into merely choking on a bush), 'Tecwen Whittock' etc. Much hysterical laughter, during which Tim Waddle leaned into Mel and said 'Awww, poor bloke, I love Dick'. The trouble was, somehow our laughter had stopped abruptly. I'd pinpoint the moment the room fell silent as precisely after the word 'bloke'.

Bernard and the other dyed-in-the-wool farmers, who've long eyed us with suspicion looked like they would like nothing better than to leave, before returning with their pitchforks.

Jack

11:30pm Jack messages Chloe

I think you may have fallen asleep. A sure sign I need to work on my material.

Goodnight my chocolate ring.

Jack

15.

2 days 'til curtain up

8:42am Katie messages Chloe, Jack & Connor

Right, this is important. Keep these dates free: Provisionally, Saturday 27th April and Saturday 18th May (if by some miracle, any of you have become popular since I last saw you and have a commitment on either of those dates, please cancel).

Katie xx

8:44am Chloe messages Jack

Bloody well told you! WTF?!

Chloe

8:46am Jack messages Chloe

Yeah, and Mike isn't part of the circulation! My copper's nose was twitching immediately! What's she thinking of? Mike's alright but he's a bit of a dickhead. I could ask Katie to marry me instead. I've always liked her hair and ears. She's 'the gir

382

next door' type but the sort that could handle an axe if needs be. It takes the pressure off if there's an intruder.

Jack

8:48am Chloe messages Jack

You're obsessed with intruders. Just get a decent lock on your door and I'll lend you my gun.

C

PS You've never mentioned you fancy Katie. What does she have that I don't?!

8:49am Jack messages Chloe

Apart from a PlayStation and a nicer flat?

Jack

PS You have a better collar bone.

8:52am Connor messages Katie, Chloe & Jack

I'm good for either date.

Cheers

Connor

8:55am Chloe messages Jack

You tell her you can't make the April date and I'll tell her I can't make the May one.

C

8:56am Jack messages Chloe

Alright. I'll go first. Leave a decent gap between mine and your message though.

J

9:01am Chloe messages Jack

What are you doing? Get on with it!

C

9:02am Jack messages Chloe

Tiny's hoovering (unbelievable I know). It's hard to concentrate.

9:03am Chloe messages Jack

Concentrate on what?! You're sending a one-line message for fuck's sake!

9:04am Jack messages Katie, Chloe & Connor

Hi Katie.

Listen I'm very sorry, but I can't make that date in April. It's something I can't rearrange. I can make the one in May though.

Jack

9:04am Chloe messages Katie, Jack and Connor

Hi girlfriend. I can't do that date in May. Soz.

Chloe

9:05am Jack messages Chloe

You must have left all of a two-second gap there!

9:05am Katie messages Chloe, Jack & Connor

Jack. Don't piss about. What are you doing that's so important?

Katie x

9:06am Jack messages Katie, Chloe & Connor

Hi Katie. It's complicated. I'll leave it to Chloe to explain. I've gotta dash.

Jack

9:12am Chloe messages Katie, Jack & Connor

Hi Katie. We've booked each other activity days (belated Christmas presents). Jack's going potholing and I'm doing a wing-walk.

Chloe x

9:13am Jack messages Chloe

Katie's never going to believe that. She knows I'm claustrophobic.

J

9:14am Katie messages Chloe, Jack & Connor

Aren't you claustrophobic Jack?

Katie x

9:14am Chloe messages Katie, Jack & Connor

It's part of Jack's on-going aversion therapy treatment. His specialist says he's been making great strides.

Chloe xx

9:15am Connor messages Katie, Chloe & Jack

Which airport are we flying from? Is it Heathrow (for both dates?). Any thoughts on how we'll get from the airport to the villa. Taxi presumably?

9:16am Chloe messages Katie, Jack & Connor

I've just scrutinised the small-print and it seems we can both reschedule without penalty. I'm good for both dates. How exciting!

Chloe x

9:16am Jack messages Katie, Chloe & Connor

Yeah, I'm good too.

Jack (also very excited).

PS Chloe, can I leave it with you to ring 'Adventures R Us'?

9:17am Chloe messages Jack

Idiot.

9:20am Katie messages Jack

Hey

I know you're dashing out so there's no immediate rush, but can you have another think about what we can get Chloe for her 30th. Despite being generally hopeless, you know her better than the rest of us. Plus, I'm pretty busy over the next few weekends so my chances of finding time to buy a gift are slim.

Thanks

Katie xx

Btw, I'm ~~really~~ looking forward to seeing your show next weekend! Try not to fuck it up. X

9:50am Jack messages Katie

Hi Katie

Yeah, sure.

So… what are you filling your weekends with? Anything nice? (apart from next weekend which won't be nice for you).

Jack

9:55am Katie messages Jack

Oh, this and that. Nothing special.

Katie x

10:22am Jack messages Katie

I do have an idea as it happens. Chloe mentioned that she'd love to go on one of those paranormal nights. I've done a bit of research and there's one scheduled in a desolate old place in Warwick. It prides itself on being one of the most haunted places in Britain. I was thinking we'd all do it as a group and pay for Chloe's ticket and accommodation. The night starts at 10pm (*no alcohol to be consumed either before or during the evening's activities* – yeah right) and finishes at 4am. The idea is that the group is taken to the rooms thought to be the most haunted and see if any spirits are in the mood for a natter. What do you think? I'll email you a link.

10:25am Katie messages Jack

Oh, that sounds perfect. We can train-it up to Warwick There's a slow train from Marylebone. I'll look at possible accommodation.

Good work.

Katie xx

Oh, I'll bring the booze bra. It holds the equivalent of a bottle of wine so that should keep us going for a while.

10:27am Jack messages Katie

A bottle of wine in each breast?

Jack

10:29am Katie messages Jack

No! Half a bottle in each. I'll put something worthwhile in like vodka. They won't smell that. Plus, if I wear long sleeves, I can hide the drinking tube too.

Katie xx

10:31am Jack messages Katie

Ever stop to think you might have a problem?

Jack

10:32am Katie messages Jack

You'll be grateful on the night to have a suck*.

K

*Scratch that. It sounded weird.

10:32am Jack messages Katie

I'll be keeping my distance. I find overly large breasts intimidating.

10:34am Katie messages Jack

Are you getting Chloe anything personal that's from just you?

10:36am Jack messages Katie

Yes. I'm getting her some Luminol spray and a voodoo doll in the image of Mike.

10:38am Katie messages Jack

Right. Okaaay. Please don't feel you have to get me anything for my birthday. A card will do.

Katie

(I wouldn't say no to a Mike voodoo doll)

10:42am Jack messages Katie

It's not long 'til *your* birthday. Planning on doing anything 'special'?

Jack

10:43am Katie messages Jack

Okaaay. Strange use of speech marks there, but since you ask, I have a cheeky weekend away booked. Somewhere swanky, so I'll be pestering Mike to buy himself some new clothes. I was telling Chloe about it the other day. We had lunch (liquid).

K xx

10:45am Jack messages Katie

Oh, that's nice. Chloe didn't mention anything. How special/swanky/cheeky?

10:47am Katie messages Jack

Oh, proper posh. It's maxed out on its star rating. I have my eye on the place for something big later in the year and I wasn't going to look a gift horse in the mouth when they encouraged me to try it out for a couple of days. So… I booked it for my birthday weekend. It'll be populated by loved-up nauseating couples poring over what's bound to be an overpriced, limited Valentine menu, but hey, it's free!

10:48am Jack messages Katie

That's great. How many people will it have to accommodate for your function later in the year?

10:49am Katie messages Jack

Just shy of 150. As venues go in Reading, it's pretty much the only one that can cope with that many people and be posh enough to keep everyone happy. The bedrooms are lush too.

10:49am Jack messages Katie

Reading?

10:51am Katie messages Jack

Er, yes. Reading. Berkshire? You may have heard of it!! South of you, North of here? WTF? Anyway, I've got to get it right. There'll be some pretty important people from the world of real estate marketing in attendance. I'll bore you more about it next weekend (after I've taken the piss out of your show).

Katie xx

10:53am Jack messages Katie

I'll look forward to it.

Jack

10:55am Jack messages Chloe

Exactly how much did you drink when you met Katie for lunch?

11:21am Chloe messages Jack

Two glasses of sauvignon. Why?

C

PS (large)

PPS (it might have been three)

PPPS It was four.

11:21am Jack messages Chloe

Reading, Berkshire.

As in:

READING VENUE

11:21am Jack messages Chloe

NOT

11:21am Jack messages Chloe

WEDDING VENUE

11:22am Jack messages Chloe

It's a bloody conference she's organising! I'm guessing the wink she shot at you was because she's getting a free weekend out of it!!!

Jack

11:22am Chloe messages Jack

Oh!! Thank God I didn't buy a hat.

C x

12:00pm Tiny messages the cast & crew

Hi all,

Just a reminder about today's car treasure hunt. Sort yourselves into teams/cars and meet in the car park ready for the off at 3pm. I'll be doing some nosh for when you get back!

Tiny

1:20pm Jack messages Chloe

We've got this car treasure hunt this afternoon. No idea what to expect. I don't think I've ever done one before.

1:35pm Chloe messages Jack

Yes, you have. We did one that was organised as a fundraiser when the library burned down. Connor borrowed his Gran's car. The sat-nav was about ten years out of date and we sat there for fifteen minutes waiting for it to find a GPS signal.

1:40pm Jack messages Chloe

Oh yeah. I think we still won, despite Katie insisting we stop so she could return a bra to M&S.

J

1:42pm Chloe messages Jack

Yep, that's the one.

1:44pm Jack messages Chloe

Are you around for the rest of the day?

1:45pm Chloe messages Jack

Yep, I'm not long back from my first ceramics class.

C x

1:46pm Jack messages Chloe

How did you get on? Did you make anything?

1:47pm Chloe messages Jack

We had about 40 minutes of health and safety nonsense, after which some dickhead called Simon burned his hand on the kiln. There wasn't much time left but I made a pot.

1:49pm Jack messages Chloe

Isn't it called *throwing* a pot? What's it like?

J

1:51pm Chloe messages Jack

Bloody hell, stand down Clarice Cliff, we've an expert in the house.

If you must know, my pot is brown and misshapen. It's like something that might be dug out of a hole on Time Team by some cider-swilling, Che Guevara lookalike, and held aloft with an "ere Tony!'.

C

1:52pm Jack messages Chloe

Maybe it'll benefit from some paint.

J

1:53pm Chloe messages Jack

What colour do you want? You're getting it for your birthday.

1:54pm Jack messages Chloe

Thanks. I'll put it next to the wooden toast rack Connor made.

1:54pm Chloe messages Jack

I don't ever remember seeing that.

1:56pm Jack messages Chloe

You wouldn't have. I keep it in the communal store. It was from when Connor signed up to that basic carpentry course, remember? He must have got his measurements wrong (unless he buys exceptionally thickly sliced bread). In fact, the only way you could tell it was a toast rack was the presence of the word 'Toast' that Connor had burned into it. It was beautifully finished though and, as good fortune would have it, it made a very acceptable bike rack.

1:57pm Chloe messages Jack

Connor made me a cube.

1:57pm Jack messages Chloe

What was its purpose?

1:57pm Chloe messages Jack

I was never entirely sure. He'd only sanded it on 5 sides.

1:58pm Jack messages Chloe

I wonder if it was supposed to be a paperweight. Did it have felt on one side?

1:58pm Chloe messages Jack

No.

1:59pm Jack messages Chloe

So essentially, he cut a piece of wood (possibly only once). Send me a picture. Have you still got it?

2:01pm Chloe messages Jack

Christ, no! I used it to cover a piece of vinyl flooring in the bathroom that was peeling away, but Mike splashed it while taking a drunken piss, so I donated it to a charity shop.

2:51pm Jack messages Chloe

I've come down to the car park to wait for my team to arrive. We'd planned to have a drink first but Jo-Ann was running late.

Christian and his team are here early. They're standing around a people carrier with a vanity plate. I'm guessing SCM 1T means it's Christian's ride. Looks like they're having some sort of a team talk headed up by Christian. Their team comprises Christian, Donald, Mary, Brian, Bill, Kitty & Howard Cobham. Our team is Val, Mel, Jo-Ann, Charlotte & me.

J

2:53pm Chloe messages Jack

No Cunny?

C x

2:54pm Jack messages Chloe

No. He's doing practical stuff with Dick and Trevor back at the theatre.

Oh, here's my lot! Dear God.

2:54pm Chloe messages Jack

?

2:55pm Jack messages Chloe

Think World War 2 jeep.

Forget that, it IS a World War 2 jeep. Open top! It's so old it has one of those black and silver square number plates on it.

Val's behind the wheel and appears to be wearing goggles.

There's a spaniel looking at me from the back seat. I don't know who that belongs to.

2:58pm Chloe messages Jack

Wow. It sounds sorta cool.

2:58pm Jack messages Chloe

t is actually. Really quirky.

Hang on, I'm dashing back up to get a coat. The others have hats. I don't own a hat.

J

2:59pm Chloe messages Jack

Shouldn't everyone be learning their lines? This seems a weird thing to do so close to opening night.

3:03pm Jack messages Chloe

You'd think so, yes.

Right, I'm in; in between Mel and the spaniel.

3:04pm Jack messages Chloe

The spaniel belongs to Charlotte. She didn't want to leave him at home because he'll be on his own tonight while we're rehearsing.

J

PS the spaniel's name is 'Fibonacci' (I'm told he'll answer to 'Fib')

PPS We're being pressed for a team name. Christian's lot have put their collective heads together and settled on the imaginatively titled 'The Attic Priory Players'.

3:06pm Chloe messages Jack

'Jeepers Creepers.'

'Chirpy Chirpy Jeep Jeep.'

3:07pm Chloe messages Jack

Oh, hang on, what about:

'Four cocksuckers, a cocker and a cock.'

3:08pm Jack messages Chloe

All good suggestions. Thank you. I think we'll go with 'Jeepers Creepers'.

PS Christian's lot have gone haring out of the car park. Maybe they know something we don't. We're still trying to find seatbelts and check life insurance policies.

3:09pm Chloe messages Jack

COME ON!!! What's your first clue?!

C

3:09pm Jack messages Chloe

I'm not sure many of these will mean much to you, on account of you living in Hammersmith an' all.

First Clue:

'Artemis is very majestic but how many windows does he preside over?'

3:10pm Chloe messages Jack

What? What the hell does that mean?

C

3:11pm Jack messages Chloe

I dunno but Charlotte leapt out and told us to wait for her. Val's telling us about the bloke she bought the jeep from. Reckons he was a right weirdo.

3:13pm Jack messages Chloe

Charlotte's back. Apparently, Artemis is a mythological hunter. He's on the sign above the pub. She went to count the windows. Haha. Kerr-ching.

J

3:15pm Jack messages Chloe

On our way to Val's house.

Second Clue:

'Comedy and Tragedy are knocking on the door. How many colourful pots can you count?'

Val reckons she has 87 pots in her front garden but we're insisting we take the time to go and count them.

3:16pm Chloe messages Jack

Excellent! Any sign of Christian's lot?

3:16pm Jack messages Chloe

Nope!

3:17pm Chloe messages Jack

I'll leave you to it for a bit. I fancy dying my hair. I don't want to be one of those people who gets stuck in a rut. Like you.

C x

3:26pm Jack messages Chloe

We're on our way to Alnwick. It's a good 45 minutes away. It's the town where I reluctantly helped Mel out of one dress and into a more sensible one.

J

3:52pm Chloe messages Jack

It was about three days ago. I have a memory you know. Sounds like you've burned the image into *yours*.

You've distracted me now, I was going to ask you something.

3:54pm Jack messages Chloe

I'm saying nothing…

3:56pm Chloe messages Jack

Oh, I know what it was. My birthday. Will probably just go for drinks. It falls on a Saturday this year. I'm sure it's always landed midweek for the whole of the rest of my life. Will you be able to get down for that? I mean, I know I'm not coming up to see your show but frankly we both know my birthday will be more entertaining.

3:57pm Jack messages Chloe

What date is it?

3:57pm Chloe messages Jack

You'd better be joking Jack White.

3:58pm Jack messages Chloe

It's just I've been asked to do backing vocals for 'Scooch's' next tour. That night could be one of the stadium gigs. I'll have to check.

4:00pm Chloe messages Jack

God yeah, I remember them.

4:00pm Jack messages Chloe

A staple of Magic Chilled FM. The Eurovision voters tossed them aside like a used nappy.

4:01pm Chloe messages Jack

I take it I'll be seeing you on my birthday then.

4:03pm Jack messages Chloe

Turns out, that isn't a stadium gig night but rather a working men's club in Toxteth. Consider my contract ripped up. I'll book a Travel Lodge.

4:03pm Chloe messages Jack

You can stay at mine. I've cleaned and had a remodel.

4:06pm Jack messages Chloe

Last time you had a remodel you claimed to have moved from rustic to shabby chic. The only discernible difference was the addition of four (badly) painted coasters depicting different types of hens. From memory, the retailer described them as 'timeless pieces', but someone, somewhere was punching the air having palmed their junk off onto someone else.

4:07pm Chloe messages Jack

I've fused Vintage with a Beach/Nautical style. You'd think you were by the ocean. White and blue walls frame feature such as jute ropes and rowing oars.

4:08pm Jack messages Chloe

Where does the 'vintage' element fit in?

4:08pm Chloe messages Jack

That's all my old rustic and shabby chic stuff.

4:09pm Jack messages Chloe

Am I to be greeted by shells in the bathroom?

4:09pm Chloe messages Jack

Yes. They've been donated by Jen.

4:10pm Jack messages Chloe

We're stopping to buy me a hat. I can't feel my forehead.

4:10pm Chloe messages Jack

Nor can Christian, but for different reasons.

4:14pm Jack messages Katie

Hi Katie

Have you been to Chloe's flat recently?

4:15pm Katie messages Jack

Yesterday. She's done a makeover.

Katie xx

4:15pm Jack messages Katie

Has much changed?

J

4:16pm Katie messages Jack

Other than the small piece of driftwood on the coffee table which on closer inspection proved to be part of an old pallet?

4:18pm Jack messages Katie

Right. Is it habitable?

4:19pm Katie messages Jack

Last I heard, she'd eradicated the deadly spores from behind the kitchen kick rails. You can stay at mine if you like?

K

4:19pm Jack messages Katie

1. Will Mike be there?

2. Have you added a lock to your bathroom door?

4:20pm Katie messages Jack

1. Um…yes.

2. Um…no.

4:21pm Katie messages Jack

Oh! I see!

4:22pm Jack messages Katie

Yeah, I'll give it a miss. Thanks anyway. I'll do a risk assessment on Chloe's place. If that raises red flags, I'll see if Lenny Henry can fit me in at The Premier Inn.

5:31pm Jack messages Chloe

Hi. We're back at the pub. Tiny did some hot dogs which I have to say were amazing. There's ice cream on the way. No sign of Team Attic Priory. Tiny's going to ring one of them to see where the hell they've got to.

5:33pm Chloe messages Jack

Is Tiny catering for a children's party later?

5:34pm Jack messages Chloe

What culinary wizardry will *you* be creating tonight Nigella?

5:35pm Chloe messages Jack

Pot noodle and oven chips. Katie's coming over and bringing her chocolate Guinness cake. We're going to watch something mindless on Netflix and then head out to sample the sights of London… vomit, graffiti, knife crime etc. etc.

5:36pm Jack messages Chloe

If you're very lucky, you might see a body in The Thames.

J

PS You are aware of the nutritional content* of your proposed meal? (*lack of).

5:38pm Chloe messages Jack

I hardly think someone who's just shoved a processed willy and ice cream down his throat is morally placed to pass judgement on the merits of a balanced diet.

Chloe

PS What time does your rehearsal start? (I'm not trying to get rid of you*).

PPS *I am.

5:40pm Jack messages Chloe

In twenty minutes. We've handed our answer paper in.

Tiny is going to wait here for the Flintstones to pedal back, tot up the results and announce the winners later.

Right, we're off to the theatre. Proper dress rehearsal.

Wish me luck.

J

5:48pm Jack messages Chloe

Me again. I'm pretending I have an urgent matter to deal with concerning my sister (that's you, remember?). We've been asked to bring the planters in from outside. I should explain: There's a garden as part of the set, but for the plants not to be starved of daylight and water, they are moved outside when we aren't rehearsing. This means someone must bring them back in each night to complete the set. I'm keen that the *someone* isn't me - they're a spider risk. There were two on one planter last night. Huge ones.

J

PS What colour did you dye your hair?

5:55pm Chloe messages Jack

'The Herbal Bed'. Tooting. Same thing: planters brought in from outside for each performance. Act 1 saw The Bishop's puritanical assistant Barnabus Goche (an exceptional performance by a decent actor), give an impassioned and intimidating speech. The expression to have an audience 'eating out the palm of your hand' was made for this actor. He was brilliant. The audience hung on his every word. Every single pair of eyes were trained on him – well they were until a frog hopped out of one of the planter troughs, paused, presumably to make sure it had everyone's attention, and then bounced its way across the stage. It seemed hell-bent on getting its full 15 minutes of fame (nearer 3 minutes), then with perfect timing to coincide with Barnabus' final line, leapt into another planter. The spotlight that was trained on the unfortunate actor meant he couldn't see the amphibious action unfold. He would have heard the gasps, laughs and the crescendoing oooooooooooooooohhhhhhhhhhhs though (that's the noise people make as they build up to the climax of an event, like the popping of a champagne cork, or a person walking while trying to balance a pint of beer on their head, or in this case, the frog shaping-up to hop into the second planter).

Chloe

5:57pm Jack messages Chloe

see you struggled to come up with examples that didn't involve alcohol there.

411

5:58pm Chloe messages Jack

You've become an alcohol wanker. Those people who frown if you order a large instead of a medium.

C x

PS You'll have to wait for my birthday to see my hair. It's elegant yet playful, aristocratic yet frisky, comely yet coquettish, classic yet blithe.

6:00pm Jack messages Chloe

Comely? Sounds like you're on the cusp of a size 14.

Gotta go. Don't wait up.

J

PS I've asked Tiny if she'll add my 'sister' to the group messages when she reveals the treasure hunt results. Saves me giving you the highlights.

6:17pm Jack messages Chloe

The other team have just burst through the theatre doors. 15 minutes late. Val had got hold of Christian's pocket watch, positioned herself centre stage and swung it back and forth as they entered the auditorium (one eyebrow was raised for effect).

She placed one hand on a hip and explained that this was a far better method for demonstrating impatience than the shite 'pencil-tapping method'.

Donald apologised for his tardiness, while his 'Wacky Races' team scurried off to get into their costumes.

J

9:03pm Tiny messages the cast, crew & Jack's sister

Hi my lovelies.

A big thank you to everyone who took part today and to 'Know-it-all-Nigel' for compiling this year's clues.

Here are the results of the Hunter's jury. In the interests of message size, I shall message the clues/answers one-by-one.

Clue 1:

Artemis is very majestic but how many windows does he preside over?

'Jeepers Creepers' successfully deciphered this clue, working out that Artemis, the mythological hunter presides over 8 windows at the front of our pub. The Attic Priory Players who henceforth shall be referred to as 'TAPP' appear to have driven North for 45 minutes to Bar Artemis. For anyone who doesn't know this venue, it's an avant-garde, progressive drinkery which boasts an eclectic clientele. Perhaps a more relevant fact about Artemis is that it's a cellar bar with no windows.

Tiny xx

9:08pm Chloe messages Tiny, the cast & crew

Oh, that's so funny!

Chloe xx

9:12pm Kitty messages Tiny, the cast & crew & Jack's sister

Sorry, who's Chloe?

Kitty x

9:14pm Chloe messages Tiny, the cast & crew

Hi Kitty! (hi everyone!)

I'm Jack's cute baby sister. I'm kind of surprised he hasn't mentioned me.

Chloe

9:15pm Kitty messages Tiny, the cast & crew & Jack's sister

Oh, hey there Chloe!

Oh wait... Jack mentioned a Chloe when I was sizing him up (for his costume lol). When it came to inside-leg-time, he was in a big hurry to tell me all about you. I assumed you were his girlfriend. Between me and you I think I was a bit much for him. I had to buy him a drink to calm his nerves. Poor Jackie! lol

Kitty x

Hahaha. How funny.

Girlfriend? Jack's? Hahahaha!

I don't think my brother has ever had a girlfriend. His scoring drought has now eclipsed that of Fernando Torres' during his ill-fated move to Chelsea, 2011/12 season (I had to look that up). It was one barren year after the other through his teens and twenties until as a family, we concluded that Jack was almost certainly gay.

I'm surprised you were taken in, although I suppose he hasn't been there long enough for you to see the signs a sister - with 29 years and 11 months of sibling rivalry under her belt - would.

It's the small things you notice, like him taking me clothes shopping, and having the knack for picking out things that were so perfect, you'd think he was getting advice through an earpiece from Gok Wan. In hindsight, there were earlier signs we could have picked up on; he was always quick to help his Aunt with the dishes after dinner and he's always been a quick walker. More ambiguous were the rolling up of his t-shirt sleeves and ham-fisted attempts at undoing bras. Screamingly obvious were the Mariah Carey CD and Yentl Blu-ray with bonus material.

Chloe x

PS Try not to ply Jack with booze too often. His therapist has made it very clear that his current medication and alcohol are not a good mix.

9:22pm Val messages Tiny, the cast & crew & Jack's sister

I knew it! No straight man would be that comfortable bringing me sanitary towels!

Poor Jackie. I know all too well what it's like to be trapped in a body that doesn't feel like it's your own.

He's lucky to have you, Chloe.

Hugs to both of you.

Val xx

Shit a brick, I just missed my entrance.

9:25pm Tiny messages the cast, crew & Jack's sister

… ahem… and so on to our Treasure Hunt's next clue:

Clue 2:

Comedy and Tragedy are knocking on the door. How many colourful pots can you count?

The location for clue 2 was only a quarter of a mile from clue 1. (20 miles for TAPP)

Unfortunately for TAPP, they high-tailed it to the wrong location - our lovely theatre - where they counted up the number of paint pots. Given the numerous crossings-out on their answer sheet, this was apparently an exercise that TAPP struggled to reach a consensus on before finally settling on six.

Jeepers Creepers correctly identified the location as Val's front garden (comedy and tragedy masks adorn Val's front door) and gave the number of coloured plant pots as 87. (I would have accepted 88 in consideration of the presence of a weed growing out of a gnome's watering can).

Tiny xx

9:32pm Mel messages Jack

Hey

I'm not sure what would have been more irresponsible; me plugging in an electric cow, or you not telling me you didn't fancy me in my assless chaps and continuing with your elaborate charade!!

I was convinced you fancied me. I know I was well into *you*. I'm floored.

Sigh.

Mel x

9:38pm Howard Cobham messages Jack

Hi Jack

Sometimes it's good to talk about these things. I'm free for breakfast, lunch or dinner (every day).

Howard xxxx

PS I'm also available for dinner followed by breakfast (if you catch my drift).

9:40pm Donald MacMary messages Tiny, the cast, crew & Jack's sister

WILL PEOPLE PLEASE SET THEIR PHONES TO SILENT!!!

9:42pm Tiny messages the cast, crew & Jack's sister

Treasure Hunt's next clue:

Clue 3:

Christian might like this main street in Alnwick. But don't let it slip! How many chimneys can you count?

TAPP punched another hole in the ozone layer and after putting their thinking caps on, decided to count the chimneys on an icy Smith Street. Given that the clue contained the words '*main street*', it seems unfathomable that they should start looking for answers in an entirely different road. I can only speculate that TAPP headed for Smith Street by virtue of it containing Christian's surname (except it doesn't, unless our hunt had taken us to Cologne – which it didn't)

Jeepers Creepers puzzled it out and headed to 'The Tilted Wig' pub, on top of which sits three chimneys.

Tiny xx

418

9:46pm Jo-Ann messages Jack

Hey

I don't know what to say.

Jo-Ann xx

PS Is that why you wanted to know if I had a boyfriend?

PPS If so, I'm giving you the green light (get it?). lol

9:48pm Jack messages Chloe

YOU

NEED

TO

RIGHT

THIS

WRONG

NOW!!!!!!!

PS I MEAN IT!

9:50pm Chloe messages Tiny, the cast & crew

Hi everyone. Me again!

I think I may have misled you earlier.

It was Ariana Grande not Mariah Carey (or was it Cher?).

Chloe xx

9:52pm Jack messages Chloe

!!!!!!!!!!!!

9:54pm Chloe messages Tiny, the cast & crew

Chloe here (again)!

I take it back about Jack being gay.

HE. DEFINITELY. ISN'T. (GAY.)

I was just joshing, that's what sisters do.

Jack's had girlfriends. They've never lasted long but that's more down to Jack being a dickwad than anything else.

He likes women. He likes my butt* and my collar bone – he told me.

He's never picked out clothes for me, which I'm mercifully grateful for (has anyone seen his new jumper/gilet? what's that all about?).

He *has* however watched 'A Star is Born', but then who hasn't.

Chloe xx

*it's also worth mentioning that I'm not his sister.

9:56pm Chloe messages Tiny, the cast & crew

PS To my knowledge Jack is neither taking medication nor seeing a therapist (although you could make a case for him needing to do both those things).

9:58pm Mel messages Chloe

'A Star is Born'. Worth watching?

10:00pm Chloe messages Mel

Oh yeah, definitely!

(I'm not mad about the abusive-relationship-bits, so I always jettison after 'Shallow' and make up my own ending).

Chloe

10:00pm Tiny messages the cast, crew & Jack's *'FRIEND'*

Treasure Hunt's next clue:

Clue 4:

Deposit yourself on Church Street. If you wanted to get on the ladder, how much would you spend on bottom right.

You could make a case for TAPP being somewhat unlucky here. Having sought out a hardware store, I'm prepared to believe that there was some 120-grit sandpaper (pack of 5) available to purchase for £1.79.

The ladder in question within clue 4 is a metaphorical one; one you climb onto when making your first house purchase (after finding a 'deposit').

Congratulations to Jeepers Creepers who were spot-on by writing £225K, the asking price for the two-bed starter home (complete with Jack and Jill bathroom) whose details were placed in the bottom right corner of the agent's window.

Tiny xx

10:03pm Jack messages Tiny, the cast & crew & Jack's 'FRIEND'

Hi everyone.

While I'm thrilled that the early indications point towards a landslide victory for our treasure hunt team, I'm keen that everyone who hasn't read every post on this thread, should take the time to scroll back and acquaint themselves with some of the more recent offerings.

I'm particularly eager for the group to focus on the retraction made by my 'sister'* following her earlier post which questioned my sexual leanings.

In short, please direct your attention to Chloe's post delivered at 9:54pm in which she asserts that her brother** is NOT GAY***.

Jack (who isn't gay).

*Chloe is not, nor has ever been, my sister.

** I am not Chloe's brother (I make no apologies for driving this point home).

*** I AM NOT GAY.

10:06pm Kitty messages Tiny, the cast & crew & Jack's 'FRIEND'

Me thinks the boy doth protest too much.

Kitty xx

10:08pm Jack messages Tiny

Hi Tiny.

Might I suggest you remove the member *Jack's 'FRIEND'* *(formerly referred to as Jack's sister)* from the group to ward-off any further bogus revelations.

Thanks

Jack

10:10pm Mel messages Jack

Consider the bucking bronco re-hired.

Mel Xxxx

PS I knew you weren't gay.

10:12pm Jo-Ann messages Jack

This is exactly why I only have sex with women.

J-A xx

10:13pm Jo-Ann messages Jack

(that was a joke)

J-A xx

10:16pm Trevor messages Tiny, the cast & crew & Jack's 'FRIEND'

What? Who's gay?

Trevor

10:18pm Tiny messages the cast & crew

Treasure Hunt's next clue:

Clue 5:

At the end of the same street, you might find a bridge and a crown here. When was it established?

When TAPP found a bridge but no crown, alarm bells might have been ringing for some. Not TAPP, who I'm told assumed the bridge must have had its crown nicked, so ploughed on and wrote 1875.

1985 was the correct answer since that was when 'Tooth for Teeth & Teeth for Tooth' dental practice was established. Well done Jeepers Creepers.

10:20pm Tiny messages the cast & crew

Treasure Hunt's next clue:

Clue 6:

People who are trigger happy and like firing canons can often be seen here. But how many canons can you see?

TAPP used their initiative and headed for Alnwick Castle. Great thinking too, to send Howard to investigate, seeing as he was eligible for a concession ticket at £15 (a saving of £3.50 on full price).

Jeepers Creepers sniffed out photography shop 'Camaraderie' where a total of 7 Canon cameras were sat waiting to be counted. Well done Jeepers Creepers.

10:22pm Trevor messages Tiny, the cast & crew

That's a shite name for a camera shop. It doesn't work on any level.

Trevor

10:23pm Tiny messages the cast &, crew

You're quite correct Trevor. I'm awarding your team a bonus point for a rare moment of perception.

Tiny

10:25pm Mel messages Tiny, the cast & crew

I wonder if they ever have a flash sale.

10:27pm Val messages Tiny, the cast & crew

It was shuttered up last time I was there.

10:30pm Tiny messages the cast & crew

Thank you for your valuable input.

Treasure Hunt's next clue:

Clue 7:

Page 19 line 5 is Maisy's. For recreation, you might go here and count the elephants.

An informant (who wishes to remain anonymous) has disclosed that Howard's entry fee to the zoo was half-price due to the late arrival time.

Instead of feeding the sea-lions, TAPP's team would have been better placed if they had adopted the time-honoured mantra from their schooldays: 'always *read* the question'.

Elliot Park (the park referred to on page 19 of your scripts) has 9 elephant statues. A pat on the back goes to Jeepers Creepers for giving the correct answer.

10:34pm Val messages Tiny, the cast & crew

You could just call these out from behind the bar now we're here. Just a suggestion…

Val

10:37pm Tiny messages the cast & crew

Thank you, Val, but there's only one clue remaining:

Clue 8:

You must head towards Pillerton Priory. How many flagpoles where the young'uns use calculators where once they used abacuses?

TAPP failed to return an answer here.

Jeepers Creepers have excelled themselves by drawing the five flagpoles, complete with three sheep and a pterodactyl.

10:38pm Howard messages Tiny, the cast & crew

I object. That question meant that we, as a team, were discriminated against.

10:40pm Tiny messages the cast & crew

I disagree Howard. It's a one-mile exclusion zone. One of your team could have walked it.

Jeepers Creepers are this year's winners!

Thanks to everyone who took part.

Tiny

11:00pm Jack messages Chloe

Tiny rang for time twice.

Once, 15 minutes earlier than normal for those who were late to the theatre and once just now for the rest of us. Hahaha

I'm heading up to bed in a bit.

J

11:05pm Chloe messages Jack

When you're tucked in with your cuddly toys, you can tell me how the dress rehearsal went.

C x

11:20pm Jack messages Chloe

I'm in! One thing you're going to miss out on by not seeing the show, is the announcement to the audience just before curtain-up (the *no mobile phones* announcement). Ours is a recording by Bill Freynolds. It's a cracker.

'h'Ladies and h'Gentlemen. h'We would like to h'remind h'patrons that the use of h'mobile phones and other h'communcation devices is h'prohibited during this h'production. h'Thank-you.

As Dick played it over the PA system, I looked across at Bill who was bursting with pride.

J

11:21pm Chloe messages Jack

What a h'knob.

C

PS How did your bits go?

11:24pm Jack messages Chloe

Not good. Not good at all. Tonight's run-through went badly for me. My nerves are shot. I completely lost my way. It started going wrong when I made my way on to stage way too soon – a whole scene too soon! I sauntered over to Brian Barrowman and delivered my line 'Am I late?', to which he ad-libbed 'No. You're VERY, VERY early!'.

I never recovered. I was all over the place after that. I couldn't remember my lines, where I was supposed to be, what props I was supposed to bring on.

Mel is running a book on who will be first to make a mistake come opening night. I must have made three faux pas that would have paid out if tonight had been in front of a paying audience. I fear my odds will be shortened for the purposes of our betting scam.

1:27pm Chloe messages Jack

Oh dear. It'll all come back to you tomorrow, I promise.

C x

11:30pm Jack messages Chloe

I thought for one horrible second there you were going to tell me that no one would have noticed! Even Donald noticed, and he was busy studying J-A's tits all night.

On the plus side, there are headshots of us actors in the foyer. Presumably so the audience can work out who to throw their lighters/bottles/faeces at. Christian must have supplied his own photo because it's all soft-focus and dreamy. I'd put money on him having drawn in a lower hairline too. He's been captured looking wistful; wistful and constipated. I'll try and remember to send you a photo of it.

11:35pm Chloe messages Jack

You sound sad.

It was my fault, wasn't it? My bad. Sending those messages to your cast. It wasn't funny. I'm sorry it distracted you.

C x

PS It *was* funny, it was just the wrong demographic.

11:38pm Jack messages Chloe

It wasn't your fault. I hadn't even seen your messages when made my first cock-up, so don't beat yourself up.

J

PS Your demographic is the same as Norman Collier's.

PPS My brisk walking style has evolved because of my loathing of dawdlers (of which you are one).

PPPS You never liked Yentl. You always said it was too Jewish.

11:41pm Chloe messages Jack

Thanks.

(for not blaming me)

Chloe x

PS My primary beef with Yentl was that it looked as if it had mislaid a letter.

11:43pm Jack messages Chloe

You're welcome.

Oh, I knew there was something else!

Mary threw a dressing room strop. Charlotte had made the mistake of hanging her costumes where Mary would normally hang hers. Instead of negotiating, Mary just chucked Charlotte's costumes from the rail and onto the nearest chair. Mary has also commandeered the only mirror in the room (and the only surface). Charlotte needed consoling so I dug-out my best kind words.

PS I may have reserved some not-so-kind words for Mary when I suggested that a *Pittsburgh cumberbund* would be too good for her.

11:44pm Chloe messages Jack

I'm going to google that and then get some *zzzzzzs*.

Chloe x

11:45pm Jack messages Chloe

I shouldn't (unless you last ate a good while ago).

Night.

Jack

11:46pm Chloe messages Jack

Night.

Chloe x

16.

1 day 'til curtain up

7:25am Mike messages Jack

Hi mate.

Any idea what I can get Katie for her birthday?

Mike

PS Looking forward to seeing your bag of shite show next weekend.

7:28am Jack messages Mike

Hi Mike.

Yes.

A new boyfriend. One who doesn't have to ask another bloke what his girlfriend is likely to want for a birthday gift?

Jack

PS If that isn't possible to source in the time left available to you, I know she was after a Huckoo clock (it's like a cuckoo clock but instead of a cuckoo, you get Mick Hucknell popping out on the hour giving you 30 seconds of 'Something got me Started').

Jack

7:32am Mike messages Jack

Nice one.

I'll see if I can find one on Amazon.

7:33am Jack messages Mike

I hope Katie realises how lucky she is. She's really landed on her feet.

7:35am Jack messages Chloe

Long day today. Get this, we're in the theatre from 12pm until 10pm! Donald wants to do two runs today and 'brush up' any bits during whatever time is left. A brush won't be man enough for the job. I think we need to be looking at a road sweeper.

10:03am Chloe messages Jack

You're up early for a Sunday. Is there something special going on at church today?

The Sunday before opening night is always a bitch of a long day. The Director will be lurching from one technical crisis to another and becoming more and more of a monster as the day wears on. By four o'clock he'll be on the horns of a mental meltdown.

My advice is to avoid saying any of the following:

1. *Do you think it'd be possible to grab some food? I haven't eaten for eleven hours?*

2. *Are the orchestra going to be that loud on opening night?*

3. *I'm thinking of making my entrance from stage right instead of stage left. Is that OK?*

4. *Will I have time to nip home between run-throughs to take a bath?*

5. *Is that chair in the right place? I'm pretty sure it's not quite where we've had it during rehearsals.*

6. *My Mum wants to come on the Tuesday night. You don't happen to know if there are any tickets left on row O do you?*

7. *Will I have my own radio microphone?*

8. *Why haven't we started yet?*

9. *Just chill.*

10:07am Jack messages Chloe

Thanks for the advice, but Donald reached mental hysteria three nights ago, although he'd argue he was provoked by Val quizzing him about his height (lack of):

- *'Would you say you were taller or shorter than a decorating table?'*

- *'Is being diagnosed with vertigo something you can only dream about?'*

- *'If you stood back-to-back with 'zippy' from Rainbow, who'd be taller.'*

- *'If you weren't Sleazy, which of the other six dwarves would you like to be?'*

- *'Do you get fed up with always being put on a pedestal?'*

- *'Do you feel like lashing-out when Gabrielle sings 'Out of reach'?'*

J

PS What are you up to today?

10:13am Chloe messages Jack

I'm meeting my parents for lunch. They want to chat about giving me power of attorney. They'll bring it up somewhere between pretending to be appalled by the wine list and leaving a tip that's so insignificant it'd make Connor's stick insect seem noteworthy.

C

10:17am Jack messages Chloe

If you have power of attorney, you can pay your parents to leave you alone - out of their own money.

J

PS when did you clap eyes on Connor's stick insect?

10:19am Chloe messages Jack

2011. The royal wedding. Kate and thingy. A wasp found its way into Connor's shorts, and he panicked. He needn't have worried; that wasp could have been trapped in there for days and still not found its target.

10:22am Tiny messages the cast & crew

Hi everyone.

Sorry for the late notice but could any cast member who dances in 'Slag Heap Shuffle' please arrive at the theatre an hour earlier than planned today (11am). Robin wants to tidy that number up.

Thanks

Tiny

10:23am Jack messages Tiny, the cast & crew

I was supposed to be flying a kite with Benjamin Franklin, but I'll stand him down.

Jack

10:24am Jack messages Chloe

My day just got even longer. Some of us have been told to get to the theatre an hour early. FFS.

I'd best get ready.

I'll message you later

Jack

10:25am Chloe messages Jack

Crikey. Well, good luck!

Chloe

PS I take it you've already bought cards and presents.

10:29am Jack messages Chloe

What? No! It's still weeks until yours and Katie's birthdays. Talk about needy! No need to worry, I have ideas locked away and I'll turn my attention to present buying when this show's done and dusted. I take it Screwfix vouchers will suffice (again)?

J

10:31am Chloe messages Jack

Not birthday presents you twatwaffle, good luck cards and gifts for the CAST! Gifts aren't strictly necessary, though sometimes you might buy a small gift for your leading lady.

C

10:33am Jack messages Chloe

YOU TELL ME THIS NOW?!

J

FFS!

11:10am Jack messages Chloe

At the theatre. Nothing's happening! We're just sitting around while Robin is chatting to Donald. This isn't on. Someone should say something.

J

11:12am Chloe messages Jack

A quick recap: *'Why haven't we started yet?'* was on my list of things you're best not to say, so whatever you do, don't say it.

Hanging around is normal. It's infuriating but it's normal. Today is all about containing rage.

11:13am Jack messages Chloe

Fear not, I'm completely unruffled*

J

*you couldn't say the same about Christian's hair. He must have forgotten to brush it before mounting it on the mannequin head last night.

11:14am Chloe messages Jack

Oops! Haha

11:14am Jack messages Chloe

Gotta go, we're being summoned!

12:02pm Jack messages Chloe

Well, that's the dancing tidied up. It still looks like a pitch invasion, one where the crowd hold hands.

J

1:12pm Jack messages Chloe

Donald just asked Jo-Ann if she'd like to practise her quick change in private. It would appear that Jo-Ann hasn't had the benefit of your advice about keeping shtum, although in her defence, I don't think you specifically put 'I'd rather go dingleberry rimming with Jedward' on your list of things not to say.

1:18pm Chloe messages Jack

It's usually around now that cast members who are required to sing, start to get their excuses in about having sore throats, colds, laryngitis, throat cancer etc. It's an age-old trick, one that's mainly adopted by people who are shite.

C

1:22pm Jack messages Chloe

Very perceptive of you. Christian has a collection of throat sweets that my old local pharmacy would be proud of. He also has a throat spray that the International Olympic Committee should be adding to their list of banned substances. He's off his tits on it.

PS Where are you by the way?

1:24pm Chloe messages Jack

Oh, I'm stretched out on the sofa, enjoying reading all about your dress rehearsal without having to go through the personal anguish myself. Keep going (although I'll be heading out in a bit to fleece my parents out of their life savings).

1:50pm Jack messages Chloe

Good luck.

I've just seen Dick Rump. He's wearing a 'Blinded by the Light' Bruce Springsteen T-shirt. Ironic considering he hasn't successfully landed his spotlight on a single cast member thus far. I think he may be hung over.

1:52pm Chloe messages Jack

Tell him to sober-up unless he wants you all 'Dancing in the Dark'.

C

PS I've excused myself and made my way to the toilet. We're in the middle of the inevitable lecture about me only spending my parents' money if it's essential. I made all the right noises while quietly mulling over whether an all-inclusive holiday to Cancun qualifies as essential.

1:54pm Jack messages Chloe

Oh, it definitely does. Spending someone else's money can be exhausting. You deserve that break.

J

PS I'll buy you a pot noodle multi-pack if you can successfully weave ALL the following words into what remains of your financial discussions:

1. *Bacon*

2. *Bread*

3. *Dough*

4. *Lolly*

5. *Zloty (or Dong)*

4:24pm Jack messages Chloe

That's one run out of the way. Not too bad.

It's snowing outside and we've sprung a small leak above the dressing room. It's not the sort of thing that'll get any worse, so we've just stuck a bucket underneath it, but the sporadic dripping noises are making Jo-Ann dash for the toilet every ten minutes.

Have you managed to engineer an escape from lunch yet?

J

4:26pm Chloe messages Jack

Yes, and I'm now enjoying reading your messages poolside with a Margarita in my hand, but I'm concerned you might be incurring hefty charges from your network provider. My bartender assures me that you don't get many pesos to the pound these days.

Chloe xx

6:14pm Jack messages Chloe

You didn't tell me about the speeches! Everyone seems hell-bent on giving one. Michael Brains kicked things off with some nonsense about him being sure we'll do the theatre proud over the coming week. There was also some bollocks about us bearing the weight of responsibility that comes with performing for a theatre with over a hundred years of high-quality productions behind it. And some more bollocks about us being the next generation of flag-bearers, (all this was hard to take seriously with Cunny stood next to him wearing a t-shirt that read 'I Pee in Pools').

6:17pm Jack messages Chloe

Brains passed the speeches baton to comedy Cunny, who proceeded to bore us with health and safety guff. He told us that if there was a fire alarm, we should calmly leave the theatre via the nearest exit. I vowed to leave by the least combustible exit, even if meant calmly strolling a few paces more.

By the time Donald was ready to wow us with his speech about how proud he was, and how we'd got a fabulous show on our hands, and how there weren't many seats left for any performance, Val had decided that enough was enough and disappeared to the scenery store where she prepared five gin & tonics complete with sliced lime and sprigs of thyme. While Val, Jo-Ann, Tiny, me and Charlotte (she's now one of the gang) sat sipping our pre-final dress rehearsal drinks, we decided that despite what Donald had said, we were in fact part of something that was completely shite, but it had been an enjoyable shite and it was our shite.

J

PS So Val made five more.

PPS And now we're shite-faced.

6:20pm Chloe messages Jack

Katie say hellloo and sauys thast shell martyr you if yu buy het a new kttchen blind

6:21pm Jack messages Chloe

Does Katie want to martyr me or marry me? It's just the two are quite different, although what they do have in common is that with both, your life is over.

7:09pm Jack messages Chloe

The cast toilet has frozen again so it won't flush. There's a turd floating in it. There's lots of speculation as to who it belongs to. The presence of a single hair embedded into it has led Val to believe it's Christian's but he's denying it.

J

7:10pm Chloe messages Jack

Is it right in the middle?

C

7:11pm Jack messages Chloe

Well looky here, coherent Chloe is back!

The turd or the hair?

7:11pm Chloe messages Jack

The turd.

7:11pm Jack messages Chloe

Er… yes it's right in the middle of the bowl. Why?

7:12pm Chloe messages Jack

It'll be Mary's. It has her DNA so it was always going to move centre-stage.

C x

7:12pm Jack messages Chloe

I dunno, it's pretty large.

Tiny reckons she can see some sweetcorn in it which points the finger of suspicion at those who indulged in last night's special at The Hunter's. Namely Trevor and Bill.

7:13pm Chloe messages Jack

What colour is it? Does it have a hue?

7:14pm Jack messages Chloe

It's quite dark coloured actually.

7:14pm Chloe messages Jack

Do Trevor or Bill drink Guinness?

7:15pm Jack messages Chloe

Yes! Trevor does.

7:15pm Chloe messages Jack

I think we have a winner.

7:16pm Jack messages Val, Tiny, Mel & Charlotte

It's Trevor's. Sweetcorn, Guinness and scaffold-shaped.

Jack

PS Mel (we'll explain later). Must be quiet in the pub?

7:17pm Mel messages Jack, Val, Tiny & Charlotte

Deathly. I thought about starting a chip-pan fire, just for something to do.

Mel xx

7:18pm Jack messages Chloe

I was just on the receiving end of an almighty bollocking!!!!

Jack

7:18pm Chloe messages Jack

Why? You haven't been caught hiding Donald's Cuban heels again?

7:23pm Jack messages Chloe

No. I went to the toilet in the foyer. This woman (who I now know is the front-of-house manager, Mrs Tanner), yelled at me for coming front-of-house during a performance while wearing my costume! After she'd finished her ridiculous rant, I explained that while we were treating the dress rehearsal as a performance, it wasn't since it was minus an audience; a fact she may have noticed since she hadn't relieved anyone of their tickets.

I added that I was wearing my costume because I wouldn't have had time to change out of it into my civvies (yes I used that word – I was flustered), pop to the toilet, make my way back to the dressing room and costume-up again. I explained (with the air of someone who had vast knowledge on the subject) that holstering up a radio microphone was a lengthy process, the complexities of which, a front-of-house operative wouldn't be familiar with.

While I was on a roll, I apprised her of the presence of the bloody great frozen turd that was grinning at everyone from the murky waters of the cast toilet bowl.

I took my leave after asking her where the accident book was kept. I was met with a blank look, so was forced to explain that the act of cordoning off the only working toilet, would almost certainly result in a record number of accident book entries, from a cast that was metaphorically and literally shitting itself, and that this might not be something she'd want on her watch.

I excused myself from our tete a tete, but not before asking if she had drunk stout the night before, purely so we could eliminate her from our enquiries.

J

10:04pm Chloe messages Jack

Wow. I snoozed. Where are you? How did it go? God I'm hungry.

C x

10:25pm Jack messages Chloe

Went fine. We've just had our notes from Donald and getting ready to head to The Hunter's. We were going to stay in the theatre bar, but Mrs Tanner, the toilet monitor was still loitering .

10:26pm Chloe messages Jack

Did you remember your lines/props/entrances etc.

C

10:45pm Jack messages Chloe

Yeah mostly. Christian seems buoyed up by the success of the rehearsal. He's very chirpy, and even tried cracking a joke about using Tiny's warm beer to thaw the toilet out. He was immediately trumped (no pun intended) by Tiny who suggested that we'd be better off borrowing his hair to insulate the cistern.

10:46pm Chloe messages Jack

Hahahahahahaha

10:56pm Jack messages Chloe

Trevor and Bill have just checked with Tiny whether the pub will be open for food before our opening night tomorrow. She assured them that it will be.

I saw her chalking up tomorrow night's special. She scrubbed out cauliflower and added beetroot. Presumably this is her way of amassing evidence.

Right, well it's been a long day, so I'm off to bed.

10:58pm Chloe messages Jack

Sweet dreams.

10:59pm Jack messages Chloe

Venetian or roman?

11:02pm Chloe messages Jack

?

11:02pm Jack messages Chloe

Katie's blind. If I'm to marry her, I'll need more information.

11:02pm Chloe messages Jack

It's in a kitchen so venetian I'd have thought.

11:03pm Jack messages Chloe

For which window? The big one at the far end, or the small one near the fridge?

11:04pm Chloe messages Jack

The big one.

11:04pm Jack messages Chloe

Thought as much. Yeah, I'll give it a miss.

Night

11:05pm Chloe messages Jack

Night x

11:15pm Tiny messages Jack

Hey Jack

Try not to worry about earlier. You just had a bad night. It happens to everyone at some point. Just remember, it was a long day, and others were dropping lines too.

You've made that part your own and you really are ace. A very talented boy indeed!!

Tiny xxx

11:35pm Jo-Ann Pinchley-Cooke messages Jack

Hey babe

Just checking you're OK?

The audience would never have noticed.

Jo-Ann xxxxxx

17.

Monday 28th January

Opening Night

5:02pm Tiny messages Jack

Hey Jack

Hope you're OK. We'd normally have had at least half a dozen sarcastic messages from you by now (usually at the expense of one of us hahaha!).

Tiny xx

6:22pm Tiny messages Jo-Ann

Hi Jo-Ann

Have you heard from Jack today?

Tiny xx

6:23pm Tiny messages Mel

Mel. Has Jack been in touch since yesterday?

453

5:25pm Jo-Ann messages Tiny

No. Everything OK?

Jo-Ann xxx

5:26pm Mel messages Tiny

I haven't seen him since last night when he moved that chair all the way from one side of the pub to the other and made us guess what it was. Haha

5:27pm Tiny messages Mel

Oh yeah, and no one said, 'a chair'.

5:45pm Tiny messages Chloe

Hi Chloe darling,

You don't happen to have spoken to Jack today by any chance?

Tiny xx

5:46pm Chloe messages Tiny

Hi Tiny,

He hasn't messaged me today. I was going to message him to wish him luck in a minute so I'm sure he'll get back to me. Is anything wrong?

Chloe x

5:47pm Tiny messages Chloe

No darling, everything's fine. He probably told you he didn't have the best night last night and I think it was playing on his mind that's all. Everyone knows he's great. Christ, he's the best we've got but I think it's probably only just dawned on him that he'll be in front of an audience soon.

Let me know if you hear from him, will you?

Thanks

Tiny x

5:50pm Tiny messages the cast & crew

Hi everyone. I'm sending messages this year rather than ringing you all, and I'm giving you an earlier shout than normal with it being the first night. Let's all get to the theatre by 6:45pm please. If anyone has any inkling at all that they might be running late, please let me know!

Oh, and GOOD LUCK!!!!!!!! You're all FABULOUS!

Tiny xx

5:50pm Chloe messages Jack

Hey

You've been quiet today!

I just wanted to say Good Luck! You'll smash it!

Chloe xxx

6:05pm Chloe messages Jack

OK Jack. You're worrying me now.

Please let me know you're OK?

Chloe xxx

6:06pm Jack messages Chloe

Hi. Course I'm OK. How's things? Bloody hell it's snowing again!

Jack

6:08pm Chloe messages Jack

FFS. A few people have been trying to get in touch with you.

I think you'd better let them know you're OK.

6:09pm Jack messages Chloe

Yeah, I can see a few messages. My phone ran out of charge while I was out getting good luck cards. It's got a shit battery life. I probably need a new one. Right, I'll respond to these other messages and then get myself ready.

6:10pm Jack messages Tiny, Mel & Jo-Ann

Hi, Mums one, two & three. All good here. Chloe said you were worried. Dunno why? Phone ran out of charge, that's all

Everyone excited for tonight? I am! That pint in the theatre bar after is going to taste sweet!

Right, see you in a bit!

Jack

6:11pm Mel messages Jack

Not sure I'm entirely happy about being your Mum. It conjures up visions of the adult baby scene; those fellas who like to wear nappies and be bathed. They're usually called Bob or Toby.

It's the sort of thing Trevor would have requested. Ewww. Shudder.

Mel xx

6:15pm Connor messages Jack

Alright mate

Have a good one tonight.

Ravi and me are looking forward to seeing it next weekend.*

Connor

*we're not.

6:45pm Tiny messages Chloe

Hi Chloe

Jack's been in touch. Seems we were worrying about nothing!

Oh, I have a copy of the programme in front of me. I thought you'd like to know what Jack wrote for his biography. It's somewhat of a departure from the norm and I'm told Howard Cobham isn't at all happy about it! hahahahahahaha

Jack has enjoyed being a part of this show and its welcoming cast. He hopes you, the audience, enjoy the production as much as he has enjoyed rehearsing for it.

Jack White - Frederick

Jack's vital statistics:

Age: 32

Theatrical Experience: None

Occupation: Fashion Consultant

Hobbies: Ten-pin bowling, Entomology

Would love to meet: A dinosaur

Dislikes: Pol Pot, Andy Murray

Likes: Pork pies, Chloe (sometimes)

Notes: Jack would like to remind theatre critic and all-round great guy Gary McPeter of Jack's lack of theatrical experience, and, on a completely unrelated note, Jack points out that he maintains a friendship with a contract killer. A character assassin if you will.

(PS: Despite all of the above appearing to have been written by someone else, Jack can confirm that he wrote it all by himself)

6:47pm Chloe messages Tiny

Hahaha. I must be special to be ranked alongside a pork pie.

Thanks so much for sending.

Chloe x

6:55pm Jack messages Chloe

There's been a bit of a development here! Howard Cobham can't do the show (no reason given). He only plays the medium in the séance scene, but he has twenty or so lines. Tiny has agreed to go on with a script. They're trying to find her a costume that looks medium-esque and so far Kitty has produced a caftan and a head scarf!

Bets are already flying around on how long the scene will overrun by, given Tiny's now involved!

6:58pm Jack messages Chloe

I risked the wrath of Mrs Tanner earlier and poked my head in the foyer to see if 'Terry Nutkins' had showed up. I think it was still a bit early. I did spot Donald slithering about wearing a trilby and a heavy, long coat draped over one shoulder. I suppose he wants to leave the audience in no doubt as to who the director is, and frankly he's being a smidge transparent in his efforts to out-do Tim Waddle.

I must go and hand my cards out.

Jack

7:05pm Chloe messages Jack

I take it you ran out of time to buy gifts.

7:07pm Jack messages Chloe

Nope. I've bought everyone a toilet roll and a pair of woollen gloves to make toilet trips more bearable. I've written 'good luck' in brown pen on the first sheet of everyone's roll.

7:09pm Chloe messages Jack

I love the toilet roll idea. INSPIRED!

I take it the toilet's been defrosted then?

C x

7:13pm Jack messages Chloe

Yup. Val spotted a plumber with a blowtorch. The dressing room leak has-been plugged too, much to Jo-Ann's relief.

The planets must be aligning for us.

7:15pm Katie messages Jack

Hey!

LOADS OF LUCK FOR TONIGHT!!!!!!

YOU'LL BE ACE!!!!*

Katie xxxx

*you won't be (obviously) but good luck anyway.

7:16pm Jack messages Katie

Thanks Katie.

You always know just what to say.

See you next weekend.

Jack

7:17pm Mike messages Jack

Alright you big tosser.

Katie's told me to wish you good luck.

Mike

PS Try not to be too shit.

7:21pm Jack messages Chloe

Card and present update:

I've had a pack of tarot cards from Val, together with a good luck card containing part of Churchill's speech about fighting on beaches and never surrendering etc.

Tiny sent a card to everyone encouraging us to fuck up our lines so she didn't get bored.

Mel sent me a card about bucking (that's not a typo).

461

Charlotte's cards were hand-made and referenced the German philosopher Schopenhauer. We're sure there's a clever joke in there somewhere, but as yet, no one has managed to locate it.

Bill and Brian handed out a jointly signed postcard (even though they aren't a couple), which featured an ancient photograph of The Blackpool Tower. There doesn't seem to be a relevant connection to our show.

Neither Christian nor Mary gave cards.

Jo-Ann Pinchley-Cooke gave me a card too; on its cover was a black cat riding a unicorn. It is the single most glitter-covered card I've ever received in my life. At least half of it has now transferred itself to my face and costume. J-A also gave me a framed photograph of our treasure hunt team, all sat in Val's jeep (how she managed to organise the printing and framing of that in the time, I'll never know).

Cunny didn't send any cards, but he did give each of the female cast members a small bag of Haribo.

Donald sent a card to Jo-Ann telling her how brilliant she was and that she was the best actress he'd ever had the pleasure of working with. I moved it to Mary's make-up table and we're waiting for the fall-out.

7:22pm Chloe messages Jack

This is probably my last chance to say:

GOOD LUCK JACK!!!!!!!!

Xxx

7:24pm Jack messages Chloe

THANKS! I'm nervous but excited.

Brian Barrowman took the time to wish me good luck earlier. He said something that seemed curious at the time: 'See you on the ice!'

After he assured me that it wasn't an unsavoury offer to meet me by the outside toilet, he explained that an old actor had once said it to him when he was a much younger man.

It makes sense now. It's the perfect expression isn't it!? Brian felt it summed up the feeling of setting foot on stage; perilous and unpredictable but always thrilling.

7:25pm Jack messages Chloe

Right. Here goes!

You'll need to wait up later! I'll want to tell you how it went!

Jack

7:26pm Chloe messages Jack

Or…How about I tell *you* how it went.

Seat D8. Cute red-head, nice butt, freezing her tits off, but so proud of her 'friend' (and praying there isn't a raffle).

Xxx

.

EPILOGUE

The Review

Gary McPeter reviews The Attic Priory Players'
production of 'One Night in Barcombe' 28th January 2019.

As a regular reviewer of The Attic Priory Players'
productions, I always take my seat while wearing my halo of
hope; the hope that the evening that's stretched out in front
of me will turn out to be an enlightening one, or an
inspirational one, or even simply an enjoyable one. In most
cases, this hope is swiftly crushed by the shoe of
averageness, leaving on stage, a squished mess of misery for
all to see. The timing of this extinguishing of optimism can
vary from mid-overture in the most tiresome of offerings to
mid-way through Act One in more palatable productions.

This show was very different; the reason being because
the theatre decided to re-record its message to the audience
in which it requests the switching off of mobile phones.
They've re-recorded it with the addition of four words:

'... and other communication devices'.

In the past, I've always clung onto the small comfort
that if I needed to signal to be rescued, I could use a pager,
a fax machine, morse code, or two plastic cups joined by a

465

length of string. In this show, I lost count of the number of times I reached for my carrier pigeon only to realise it was no longer permissible.

I certainly would have counted on sending up a smoke signal when the pithead scene began, as we were treated to the limpest set of miners surely ever witnessed on a stage. The only credible pitman was Val Gordons who at least looked like he could handle himself. The other three were a comical camp turn, a hodge-podge of nothingness; three cardboard cut-outs could have been used to more convincing effect.

Only am-dram could allow its actors to roll around in the dirt outside the theatre five minutes before curtain-up, presumably to give the effect of ingrained coal dust on skin. If Tim Waddle thought rubbing dog excrement on his person was a valid exercise in method acting, he was sorely mistaken. In reality, I suspect that he simply rolled in the wrong patch. The smell the audience were treated to was a fitting metaphor for a show that was already in dire need of a poop bag. I wanted to set off a flare, a distress signal, at the very least light a scented candle, but alas I was prohibited.

There were highlights: Jack White in his first production for the group, showed much promise and delivered his songs with punch and tenderness when required, in equal measure. His use of glitter to resemble sweat from his toils, was a masterstroke. He was ably supported by Jo-Ann Pinchley-Cooke, who while not quite achieving the same lyrical qualities as her stage partner, treated us to a superb performance of great subtlety. Her rendition of 'When Your Borehole Runs Dry' was as stirring a piece of theatre as I've seen in a long time.

As always though, it was left to the minor principals and the company members to dismantle anything that was good about the script and musical score (which wasn't much).

Were this performance being held on a desert island, I would have carved a huge SOS in the sand in the hope that a passing aircraft would come to my aid and prevent me from enduring the séance scene. The actor due to play the medium was unavailable to perform and so a brave soul, a lady by the name of Theodora Imogen Nefertiti Young, was sent on in their place. I am nothing if not forgiving, and Miss Young played her role excellently (albeit with the help of a script), and she even lent an eccentricity through the skilful addition of a stammer. Sadly, she was let down by the sheer incompetence of the technical team led by Colin Inglis. Surely it shouldn't be beyond the wit of man to realise that an actor reading a script might struggle if the seance's near pitch black lighting wasn't lifted a little. Souls no longer of this world were asked by our medium if they were present, but by the time the stage lights had lifted to allow the scene to progress, I fear the spirits had grown tired of waiting and buggered off back to the afterlife.

Most of the other performances were laid bare for what they were – inept. A radioactive-looking Christian Schmidt carried a tune as effectively as a colander carries water (probably the colander Tim Waddle appeared to be *wearing on his head). Brian Barrowman had his moments, but half his lines were missed by either the actor himself skipping them, by Bill Freynolds talking over them, or by the pair of them masking each other's dialogue with their unrelenting, ludicrous foot stamping.*

If you have absolutely nothing better to do between now and Saturday night, and have ruled out self-harm, go along to The Attic Priory Theatre. But go with your eyes open and in the knowledge that no one will be coming to rescue you.

'One Night in Barcombe' runs nightly until 2nd February.

Acknowledgements

If you've ever dipped your toe into the world of amateur theatre, you'll know that the people who inhabit it are a curious mix. It's a unique universe that exists purely as a stomping ground for the odd, the introspective, the extrovert, the needy, the talented and the talentless, but mainly for people who can't play sport.

It's for this reason that I felt the urge to bring together a collection of such personalities, to celebrate their diversity, and to soak up their energy, fragility, humour, skill, and downright ridiculousness.

Writing a book consisting entirely of instant messaging was a challenge, especially given that I, myself, am a hopeless texter. While others summarise their posts using an effective couple of lines, I need at least six convoluted paragraphs to make the same point.

A drum roll of thanks to two people who aren't strangers to amateur theatre themselves. Both reluctantly agreed to read this book and to offer feedback. Jo (a person who I've come to realise is virtually impossible to offend) read it suspiciously quickly, while Raffi pointed out all the bits that Jo should have been offended by, but wasn't. Both women seemed convinced that Jack was an extension of me. He isn't. Jack is talented, funny and has no problem attracting beautiful women.*

I quickly realised that I needed to gauge reaction from people detached from theatre, and my sincere thanks go to Pete Sanders and John Friel for their generous and detailed feedback.

Finally, my utmost thanks to my wife and part-time leading lady, Sue. If it wasn't for her and her meticulous approach to proof-reading, Jack would have needed to be a clairvoyant or time traveller in order to compose some of his messages.

My intention in writing this book was to bring a smile to the lips of those who read it. I hope that applies to you. Thank you for taking the time to buy and read.

M. D. RANDALL
(played Jesus on stage four times - but only once at the right age)
*Sue - you're beautiful too (obviously)

Printed in Great Britain
by Amazon